BLUE SUN ARMADA

SCOTT MOON

CONTENTS

STAY UP TO DATE

Sign-up for my newsletter for notification of new releases and other stuff I'm doing.

Get Cool Stuff from the Moon by heading to *https://www.sub-scribepage.com/Fromthemoon*

BOOK ORDER

THEY CAME FOR BLOOD

Invasion Day

Resistance Day

Victory Day

Departure Day

A MECH WARRIOR'S TALE

(SHORTYVERSE)

Shorty

Kill Me Now

Ground Pounder

Shorty and the Brits

Fight for Doomsday (A Novel)… coming soon.

CHRONICLES OF KIN ROLAND

Enemy of Man

Son of Orlan

Weapons of Earth

DARKLANDING

Assignment Darklanding

Ike Shot the Sheriff

Outlaws

Runaway

An Unglok Murder

SAGCON

Race to the Finish

Boom Town

A Warrior's Home

Hunter

Diver Down

Empire

FALL OF PROMISEDALE

Death by Werewolf

GRENDEL UPRISING

Proof of Death

Blood Royal

Grendel

SMC MARAUDERS

Bayonet Dawn

Burning Sun

The Forever Siren

SON OF A DRAGONSLAYER

Dragon Badge

Dragon Attack

Dragon Land

TERRAN STRIKE MARINES

The Dotari Salvation

Rage of Winter

Valdar's Hammer

The Beast of Eridu

THE LAST REAPER

The Last Reaper

Fear the Reaper

Blade of the Reaper

Wings of the Reaper

Flight of the Reaper

Wrath of the Reaper

Will of the Reaper

Descent of the Reaper

Hunt of the Reaper

Bastion of the Reaper

ORPHAN WARS

Orphan Wars

Song of War

BLUE SUN ARMADA

Blue Sun Armada

Crisis…coming soon.

SHORT STORIES

Boss

Fire Prince

Ice Field

Sgt. Orlan: Hero of Man

The Darklady

ASSASSIN PRIME

The Hand of Empyrean

Spiderfall

BOOK DESCRIPTION

War is coming.

Duke Uron Marlboro led his mighty house to victory in the Zezner War. The last thing he expected was for his allies to turn on him. With a new civil war brewing, the duke and his family have one option to survive the king's wrath—

They must flee.

Will they survive the political games of their past? Can they escape their doomed planet and find a new place to thrive before their once great house is destroyed... forever?

Blue Sun Armada is the first in a new epic space opera set in the far-flung future. Legendary mech battles, intense fleet engagements, and deadly politics all make Blue Sun Armada a magnificent read. Pick your side and buy now to start the fight for survival!

CHAPTER ONE

RON FOUGHT to keep his eyes open as his mech tipped sideways.

A dream woman whispered in his head. *Send them out to make the universe fit for expansion.*

WHANG!

And then what do we do with them? A second stranger laughed through the chaos of his nightmare.

Ron blinked away his confusion.

WHANG!

Alarms blared. His mech plowed visor first into the ground. "When I find who's hitting me—!"

WHANG! WHANG!

He twisted the controls to spread his mech hands and feet, then rocked back and forth, struggling to get turned around. "I hate this part of kicking ass."

"Then stop going unconscious," a more familiar woman crooned in his ear. "And show me what kind of man you are."

"You sound sexy. Do I know you?" His body clenched in pain, muting his clever flirtations for several seconds. When he tried again, each word was strained. "Any chance I can buy you a drink when this is all over?"

SCOTT MOON

"Sure thing, big guy. But I'm married to Duke Uron of House Marlboro."

"Hey, that's me. How'd I get so lucky?" Ron had tried to ban Patricia Wilson-Marlboro from combat, but that had worked about as well as a parachute made of bricks. "Why is my mech all cattywampus?"

"Ron! Stop being an ass and get up!" she shouted, her voice distorting in his helmet speaker. "There's still fighting to be done. Don't embarrass me by dying."

He wanted to search for her but didn't have the energy. His mech was still on a hill or something with his feet above him. His short-term memory was fuzzy. An enemy pounded his armor with a hammer. *I feel like the inside of a gong.*

WHANG! WHANG! WHANG!

Ron turned on his side, swung his power-sword and missed, digging its oscillating blades into rocky soil. Grit and metal shavings peppered his visor. Sparks flew like a chimera's wings.

Another hammer blow to his mech's control center, the vehicle head that held most of his body, stunned him. This crazy Zezner was getting to be a problem. As distracting as the attack was, it didn't push the dream out of his head.

Who was the stranger and why did she visit him every night?

Send them out to make the universe fit for expansion.

The phrase was a sacred maxim as old as time. What right did this woman have to the words? And what did the rest of it mean?

And then what do we do with them?

Static scrambled the image. Blackness filled the inside of his mech's noisy cockpit.

"I really feel like I should be doing something," he said to himself.

"You. Should be. Fighting! Oh, I hate it when you get concussed!" Patricia cursed like a foot soldier for several

2

seconds, her voice modulated by the rhythm of her mech stomping over uneven ground.

Ron took a deep breath, held it, and exhaled slowly as many senseis had taught him. His mind quieted and his body relaxed. The violent insults to his mech armor seemed less important. His power-sword came out of the dirt. The warm dopamine feel of paradise beckoned him back to the dream.

"Just. Let. Me. Sleep."

"You can't sleep, Ron! You're getting smashed by a Zezner four-leg mech. Do I have to come over there and save you?"

"Stop nagging me, woman!"

"Ron!"

A new klaxon blared inside of his mech. "Alert! Alert! Alert!"

Duke Uron "Ron" Marlboro, lord and battle commander of his house, realized he was going to die right now if he didn't do something. And that seriously annoyed him.

The Zezner shouted, a rare thing for his kind. "Aha, the human makes a final desperate plea for mercy!"

Ron jammed his hand controls forward and thrust out his legs. His mechanized armor responded. Servos whined. Heat exhaust ports flared, illuminating his suddenly wary enemy. The Zezner had painted his four-legged mech bright red—probably matching his skin. Ron would find out when he pried the son-of-a-bitch from the carbo-fiber shell.

The four-legged mech slipped. Seconds later, they slid unchecked toward the edge of a cliff.

"Can you swim, near-human?" With a flick of his wrist, he extended a spike from his right arm and jammed it through Ron's faceplate.

"I'm human, you Zezner dog. What is it with this near-human crap?" Ron grunted, digging the wedge-shaped toes of his machine and the fingers of his free hand into the crumbling terrain.

"You will drown when we embrace the White Ocean," the

3

Zezner said. "My glorious emperor will lead my people to victory."

Ron scrambled over the four-legged machine, stepping on every surface of his enemy that would hold the weight of his battle mech.

"My face is not a step ladder," the alien said with classic Zezner stoicism.

"Hey, whatever works." Ron sliced off one of the alien's legs with his power-sword. The harder he tried to climb against the avalanche, the farther and faster he fell. Before long, he could see nothing through the upturned dust and debris. He grunted curses and was vaguely aware of his wife shouting at him again. The Zezner rattled strange words across the challenge channel.

Beyond the edge of the cliff was a six-hundred-meter drop to the White Ocean. The glacial flow into it was unforgiving. His inertial dampers wouldn't save him from the impact, and he had a hole in his faceplate. Glacial melt would carry his corpse to the oceanic trench and the darkness that waited at its bottom.

The Zezner four-leg went over.

Ron snatched hold of the ledge with one powered gauntlet.

"Patricia! What's the record for holding onto a cliff with one hand?" He wished he could see her one last time. His heads-up display was smeared with grime. For all he knew, she was on the other side of the fight.

"Are you holding a weapon?"

"Of course I'm holding a weapon!"

"Then drop it and use both hands. I'm sending Victor and his friends," Patricia said. "One second... no you don't you son-of-a—! Get some! Get some! You like that? Yeah? Eat this! Sorry, sweetie, I'm back now."

Ron heard the sound of micro-rockets being fired. She was from House Wilson and they loved their enhanced weaponry. He powered down his chainsaw and methodically sheathed it. Then, with two hands, he held on and waited. Physical strength mattered in a Mechanized Electro-Nuclear Combat Hulk. Everything was an enhancement. Otherwise mechs would just be robots better handled by remote control than pilots.

Time passed. The battle raged on without him. Victor seemed to be taking his ever-loving sweet time.

"Anyone up there? I'm growing alarmed."

"Father? What the hell are you doing?" Victor said from the top of Ron's inglorious descent.

"I was considering a swim in the White Ocean."

"I don't know. The ice is pretty thick this time of year. How're your impact dampers?"

"Less than optimal."

Victor laughed. "Mother says you're in time-out."

"I can't be in time-out! I'm the duke! Get me off this ledge!"

"Kilo and Marsten will pull you up. They're two of my best."

Victor's distinct squadron-leader unit backed away. Marsten and Kilo's flamboyantly painted mechs took his place and lowered cables. Ron attached them, nearly falling each time he switched hands. For all their polish and shine, Victor's friends fought as well as any in the service of House Marlboro.

As for his youngest son, the man was giving the Zezners grief—accelerator guns, rockets, and slashes with his power-sword, one after another.

"That's my boy. Go out there and get some!" Ron struggled over the edge, shooing away Victor's warriors with one of his giant hands. "Go watch his back. On the double, Marlboros."

Taking a deep breath, and readying a witty response to anything his wife might say when he limped into the fray, he stomped up the slope and gazed over an epic battle. All the houses of Gildain were arrayed against the Zezner invaders.

"This is my victory," he said quietly. His head throbbed and his arms felt like he'd removed them and had a cheap surgeon sew them back together with fire. Dead men, women, and destroyed mechs littered the wide field of destruction and chaos.

But the Zezners were nearly defeated. Ten years after their most recent invasion. After decades of struggle, humanity had finally emerged victorious. Once this battle was over. Which it wasn't. Not yet.

Send them out to make the universe fit for expansion.

Ron shook his head.

And then what do we do with them?

Who was the dream voice talking about? The people of Gildain, the Zezner, someone else? Ron, in his heart, knew the answer and didn't like it. His dreams were all about the people of Gildain. *And the narrator doesn't consider us human.*

Ron marched down the hill toward a Zezner giving his best warriors a hard time. Drawing his power-sword, he sliced off the alien machine's fourth leg, then split its head when it turned toward his attack. Unlike the hind leg, this part of the armor protected flesh and bone. The heat of the blade cauterized some of the blood and gore leaving his victim's skull.

He didn't look at it for long.

"Duke! Thank you! How goes the battle?" the warrior asked.

"Nothing the nanites and a malt whiskey can't fix. Get back on-line. We need to clean up this battlefield."

––––––––

ATMOSPHERE-VOID FIGHTERS, more often called AT-VO by the pilots who flew them, streaked across the sky, waggling their wings in salute, then strafing the enemy four-legs.

Ron took stock of the Gildain mech warriors. His colors, red and gold, dominated this area and were driving the Zezners toward the center. The sector on his right was held by blue and silver mechs belonging to House Spirit. They preferred lighter machines that were fast and operated by highly skilled pilots who were masters of personal combat outside of their armored machines. Ron had gone to boarding school with Stephani Spirit, their current duchess. He liked her more than his wife liked her.

To his left were the black and gray behemoths of House Bronc. The leader of that house was neither friend nor foe. Politically speaking. They respected each other, and that was enough. Today, all houses were united against the Zezner.

Human-piloted mechs steadily drove the alien invaders toward the center and forced them to dismount and kneel.

Ron's wife, Patricia, and two of his children stood by his side. Victor was all a son could be and his eldest daughter, Fortune, made him so proud he didn't feel like the day was real. Gregory, his eldest son, was otherwise engaged but deserved to be here as much as anyone.

Ron climbed down from his mech and took his wife's hand. "I am the luckiest man alive." He swept his eyes over her gymnast's body and thick blonde hair. Black with red and gold accents, her mech suit clung to every curve of her torso. She seemed to like the way he loomed over her.

"Who will have two black eyes and hundreds of stitches by morning," she said.

He laughed. "Nothing can stop us now, wife."

"Are you talking about all of Gildain or only House Marlboro?"

"Both. Either. You pick."

She reached one arm around his waist and hugged him as they walked to the victory ceremony. "We're together. That's all I ever wanted."

"Victor will get his own house, I think. No need for him to wait on an inheritance. There is enough glory for all of us. Fortune, as well. She did good work today. Proved her detractors fools."

"Or the kids can stay part of Marlboro-Wilson," she said, watching his reaction carefully. "As Gregory has chosen."

"Bah. Small thinking leads to small victories. Heroes of the

Zezner War should be rewarded properly. There isn't room in Marlboro for Gregory, Victor, Fortune, and Peps. The Legislature will approve Victor's war chest, and we will have two Marlboro armies."

Ron and Patricia separated to walk with a bit more dignity and joined the other war leaders of Gildain, where the Zezner emperor knelt in pools of oil and blood.

———

KING GERARD of House Gerard drove his gold-plated mech to stand over their defeated enemy. He climbed down, ignoring his warlords. Tall and gaunt, the widowed king had never been one for pleasantries.

"Someone needs to turn that frown upside down," Patricia muttered almost loud enough for others to hear.

Gerard took his time, fussing with the ritualistic tabard of his office, a gold tunic fringed with diamonds. Energetic and painfully diffident aides slipped the garment over him and adjusted it. He looked around.

"There's no promise he will call us to stand by his side for this. All of the great houses are here today," Ron said.

Patricia squeezed his hand and kept her eyes respectfully on the king.

Gerard stepped toward the defeated Zezner emperor and stared down at the red-skinned alien. For a moment, Ron believed Gerard would do this alone, against all tradition and every expectation of the Legislature and the Assembly of Nobles.

Gerard motioned someone forward. But not Duke Marlboro.

Stephani of House Spirit took her place at his side, resplendent in blue and silver gear. A moment later, he summoned another of his dukes. Duke Adams of House Atana moved forward, wearing his deep green tabard.

Disappointed, Ron didn't let it show. He'd done much for

the king, and they had taken part in many private conversations that had promised him a place at the victory circle—but this was a master class in politics.

"He could've chosen worse," Patricia said quietly.

"I have no alliances with either of them. Long-term, it'll be fine. But it's like starting over."

"We stand high in the king's favor, husband. That will have to be enough."

Ron returned the squeeze and watched the ceremony unfold. Declarations were made. The many invasions of the Zezner were described. Everyone understood the king would kill the alien emperor.

"What say you?" Gerard said, his diamond-edged power-sword held in one hand.

The emperor looked up with his black eyes, body trembling with rage and humiliation. "You're not the first to hold this planet. Your kind were never meant to be here. Those who sent you have abandoned this sector of the galaxy."

"Humans belong here," King Gerard said.

"You are nearly human, perhaps. Yet the machines in your bloodstream are an abomination. Without them, you would be short-lived and weak."

"I will show mercy on your people, but for you, no quarter will be given," Gerard said.

The Zezner emperor bowed his head. Gerard raised the power-sword, then swiped down without mercy.

CHAPTER TWO

RON WANTED to stride across his massive, marble-floored bedroom to reach the balcony where his wife stood with her arms crossed, staring into the night. She'd chosen a sheer dress just opaque enough to be worn in public if needed.

That was for Doctor Stacks, who had Ron on the examining table near the hot tub.

Had he been alone with his wife, she might have worn something more transparent. Soft music played from the sound system on the other side of the room and firelight gave the place an ambiance more fit for time spent with his beloved than his post-combat checkup.

"You have stress fractures to both forearms, and three lacerations I can't explain. Are you sure you were wearing your armor for the entire battle?" Stacks asked. "You are a master mech pilot. It would be best if you remained inside the machine. I told you, no more dueling for honor or fist fighting… not that I understand at all why you feel compelled to do those things."

"Yes, of course, Doctor. Are we about finished?"

"Tsk, tsk. Someone's in a hurry." The man double-checked his work with his usual attention to detail.

Ron tilted his head toward his wife, who looked far too gorgeous for words. "She's not gonna wait on me all night."

"She will," Stacks disagreed. "I can glue these lacerations. I'd also like to take a look at all your scars. But I'll be quick. Since you've so clearly stated your impatience."

"Then why continue, Doctor?"

"I would be remiss in my duty if I didn't give you a full examination after such a battle."

"You're a credit to your profession," Ron said to the doctor while using his eyes to flirt with his wife as she teased him from the moonlit balcony.

"A little surgical glue goes a long way."

"So you're finished?"

Doctor Stacks rubbed his chin. "I need to plug into your cybernetic enhancements. The nanites have created quite a support infrastructure; it's like nothing I've seen. It's one reason you are a master pilot, but the variation is also quite unexplainable."

"I have good nanites. And decent genetics. Gifts from my father."

"Of course," Doctor Stacks said, then examined the metal bands that merged flawlessly with the skin around his torso, giving him extra support to handle heavy loads and preventing dangerous gut wounds. Metal and flesh had grown together around his spine after a childhood incident where he was nearly broken backward by the overpressure of an explosion. Other cybernetics were under the skin and invisible, as they were for most people of Gildain.

Stacks looked contemplative. "Someday I will be able to make nanites from concept to completion. I'll make sure your children benefit first."

Ron laughed. The examination now complete, he stood and gripped the doctor's shoulder. "That's what I like about you, Stacks. You're more ambitious than I am, but not in a position where I'd have to kill you on the field of battle because of it."

He didn't wait for further conversation but went to his wife. Draping his arm over her shoulder, he enjoyed the feeling of her arm encircling his waist. They walked together to the edge of the balcony and watched the mechs of House Marlboro being repaired.

Ron's mech was already done and stood like a statue among the others. It was fourteen feet tall, red and gold, and scraped from many hard battles. His people polished the worst of the surface damage out, but there was no way it would ever be parade ground worthy in the traditional sense. While other houses saw parades as validation of status, as proof they were loved by the people and friends with the king, Ron saw them as silly, ostentatious displays of material wealth. He'd rather be useful to the king, and if that meant his armor got a little ugly, then so be it.

Truth be told, he liked that it looked well used. His unit was also the same size and contained the same armaments as the ones his loyal men and women used. This wasn't the case in most houses—another reason why the other battle lords didn't trust him.

"They don't understand me, wife," he said.

Patricia leaned in, hugging him again, burying her face against his right side. "They don't. Most of them are too weak."

He could have asked her for clarification, dug deeper into her statement. But he didn't. Sometimes it felt like they were sharing the same mind and talking wasn't necessary. "In a perfect world, I'd only ally our houses with like-minded people —only the strongest, most intelligent, most compassionate and dutiful citizens of Gildain should stand with us."

"Not all of the people you're talking about have money," she said. "And I think that's more dangerous than power-swords and plasma guns sometimes."

They watched the parade ground where Marlboro mechanics worked late into the night. Very few of the other houses were putting such effort into repairs, and maybe they were right. The Zezner were defeated. The planet was safe. So long as the king and all of the royal houses agreed upon the honors to be bestowed, and the rewards, there would be peace. Hopefully for a very long time.

"If I could get the doctor to leave, I would take you to bed, wife," Ron said.

Patricia turned away from him, but didn't let her arm slide too far from his body. With one hand still on his ass, she raised her voice and politely said, "Doctor Stacks, I believe we won't be requiring your services anymore this night. Perhaps you should check on our daughter-in-law. Young mothers-to-be can be anxious as their time approaches."

"Of course, my lady," he said, bowing and leaving his work analyzing their biometrics unfinished.

A silver moon rose higher on the horizon. Ron searched for all of his favorite places and gazed at them as though he might never see them again. It was a hard lesson his father had inadvertently taught him. Beyond the city were rich farmlands, and beyond that, foothills and mountains. Civilian vehicles were on the trafficways at night, something that hadn't been possible for over ten years.

Now that Stacks was gone, they clung to each other like young lovers despite all the years they'd been together. But they didn't rush to bed as Ron had hinted. Beauty was in the moment, and they were together. No reward was worth more than this to Ron.

"Are we going to talk about it?" she asked, her voice barely audible.

"The Blue Sun expedition doesn't need us. And it isn't ready. And why would I take our house to the stars when we worked so hard for everything we have here?" he asked.

"This world is more dangerous without the Zezner to keep the factions busy," she said, kissing him before pulling back to look up into his face. "You know that better than anyone."

14

CHAPTER THREE

CARTER DANESTAR MOVED to the front of his squad. "Where is he?"

Sven Morten, captain of the Danestar Guards, was hard-faced and unpleasant as ever.

"Well?"

"Well, you need to be patient," Morten said.

The man was easily the most seasoned veteran in House Danestar's militia. He'd trained with several of the best military units on Gildain, including the Marlboro Elites. Which made him perfect for this mission, Carter hoped.

"Were you friends with the little asshole during your internship?"

"I liked his father well enough. He wouldn't remember me, but we sparred. Take my advice, don't fight Ron one-on-one. Ever," Morten said, still watching the rolling hills and well-trimmed forests of the central park. "The advice holds for Victor as well. He'll grow into his father's mech-boots sooner rather than later."

"Yeah, you've mentioned how great they are more than once. Makes me question your loyalty."

"My loyalty is to House Danestar. Always. To death," Morten said.

A chill went up Carter's spine. He slapped the sergeant on the shoulder and went to check the rest of his assault team.

"Captain," Morten said.

Carter stopped. "What?"

"Be patient. He has to come this way. The punk lordling needs a wife if he's to have his own house."

Carter smiled. "Very good, Sergeant. I'm anxious to let slip the dogs of war. But I can wait half an hour. Once he is busy serenading my sister, we'll make our move at best speed."

He edged away from the observation post to the glade where two dozen stealth mechs were hidden in shadow. Each unit was the best money could buy—powered by state-of-the-art batteries with no nuclear power plant. That restricted how long they could operate but made them harder to detect. Danestar hadn't mishandled its fortunes like some, and his forebearers had done their part in defense of Gildain. Danestar children were born with good nanites, at least as strong as those common in the warrior houses—Marlboro, Spirit, Atana, and Bronc.

Wanting to pace, but knowing it wouldn't reassure his men, he decided on a walk through the park instead.

———

VICTOR CONSIDERED himself the soberest man in Lorne, Gildain's capital, despite the glorious victory of the previous day and the daunting courtship he was about to initiate. Penelope Danestar was the most beautiful woman alive and had not turned away his attentions.

On his back was a nine-stringed guitar crafted from bloodwood by a master luthier. His early education on the instrument had been adequate. Since learning Penelope's interests, he'd practiced several hours each day—virtually every spare moment that wasn't spent training or fighting for his father's house.

My father's house, he thought. Not standing with King Gerard at the end of the battle had upset his parents but probably wouldn't change Victor's own prospects. It was rare for a house to split, essentially to double in size and influence, but such was the rising power of House Marlboro.

And much of that is due to my own effort. Thinking of what he had accomplished made him feel small and humble when he supposed it should make him an arrogant jerk. Remaining the second son of House Marlboro would definitely be easier and safer than running his own. Going solo was a risk. Even though he would forever be an ally of his Marlboro father and Wilson mother.

When King Gerard made him a duke, he would choose a wife, and he hoped that wife would be Penelope. Danestar was weak militarily, but wealthy. She would bring corporate expertise and her own war chest. From what he had seen, her family was even more ruthless than those of the warrior elite.

And she was so beautiful, it made his chest hurt. When she looked at him, he was done.

He smiled as he strode through the one-thousand-acre park connecting all the great houses. Her light was on, hopefully for him. Other lords and lordlings moved about the gardens. Citizens not attached to a house or corporation celebrated. Some were drunk, others weren't. Everyone greeted him with cheerful smiles and respect.

He moved beyond the commons area and saw a squad of House Danestar men loitering near a footbridge. The park was well known to him, as he had explored the area with his brothers and sisters and their cousins for many years. Beyond the bridge was a secluded glade popular for nighttime ghost stories and truth or dare marathons.

It wasn't a great place to celebrate, being shaded by ancient

17

SCOTT MOON

trees native to the planet that didn't always tolerate humans. His youngest sister, Peps, called it the witch's tangle.

The Danestar men eyed him moodily. Victor wondered why they weren't drinking. He walked on, pretending not to notice them.

But he did notice. One of the men slipped into the shadows, moving with a sense of purpose.

He's a messenger, Victor thought. Probably headed to report Victor's presence.

A bad feeling grew in his chest. Aching to continue his journey to Penelope's balcony, he turned off the path and considered the ramifications of inaction. Moments later, he unslung the guitar and placed it next to a tree.

Creeping toward the glade was easy. He knew every tree in the place. The night quest felt vaguely childish, but he realized there would be killing before the sun came up. These men should be drunk, or with their families, or quietly burying the ghosts of the Zezner war. They wouldn't be here without orders—and what possible utility did a band of warriors have here?

Twigs snapped under his feet. He froze and crouched low. Nothing happened. He continued. When he neared the hidden place, he crawled on his stomach until he could see exactly what he expected.

A platoon of Danestar stealth mechs assembled in starlit shadows. Their units were Mechanized Electric Combat Hulks —short ranged compared to nuclear-powered versions, less powerful, and very quiet. Camouflage algorithms in the paint made them hard to detect even with radar and infrared sensors.

He recognized the opening gambit of a house war. It wasn't unexpected. Many political forces would be looking to move quickly now that the Zezner were defeated. He only wished it didn't involve Penelope's family.

Watching the stealth mechs in standby mode was boring. His guitar was probably warping horribly where he'd left it by the tree, collecting moisture in the cold damp. Penelope was probably being serenaded by some other young man.

His diligence finally paid off when he spotted Carter Danestar tromping across the bridge. Victor intercepted him on a secluded twist of the trail between the bridge and the clearing.

"Good evening, Carter Danestar," Victor said as he stepped into view, intending to discourage the man from starting trouble. How could he serenade Penelope with rockets going off in the park?

"You!"

Victor's world changed in an instant. He understood without a doubt who House Danestar would attack, and it broke his heart.

Carter stared at him, mouth curling into a snarl. Victor struggled for words. He needed to curse the man, threaten him, make him stop his sneak attack on House Marlboro.

Carter headed for the stealth mechs, shouting for his men. Victor raced home, doubting he could beat the Danestar stealth mechs once they were powered up.

Branches tugged at his best tunic and ripped his trousers—scuffing his boots every time he clambered over a fallen tree limb. He took trails and shortcuts wherever he found them. Several minutes after his horrible discovery in the clearing, he burst into a large family picnic that was going all night. The smell of good food and the sounds of happiness flooded over him.

He charged through the middle of the festivities, yelling for people to get out of the way.

"Was that Victor Marlboro?" someone asked.

Leaving confusion and questions in his wake, he ran across a narrow footbridge that swayed on its rope supports. He cut across the plaza near the main fountain and saw what he needed.

"You there, in the uniwheel—surrender it in the name of House Marlboro. I'll buy you a brace of them in the morning!"

He shoved the driver from the inside of the vertical hub, ignored the safety belt, and pushed forward with both feet and both hand controls. The rubberized outer wheel spun around him, grabbing the paving stones and propelling the vehicle forward. He shot across the plaza and onto the next series of sidewalks.

The walls of Marlboro palace came into view. He activated his communicator but only got hissing feedback. The Danestar stealth mechs raced toward the open postern gate, which by tradition, had been left unbarred for him as he'd gone to court the Lady Penelope.

Accelerating, he wove between the units, leaning right, then left, then back to center, still hoping there had been some mistake. Each maneuver threatened to dump him on his side like a plate wobbling until it was flat. Only one of his enemies bothered to aim—then hold fire. Their need for stealth saved him. The stealth mechs had silenced weapons, but the rate of fire was slow. At his current speed, they needed to strafe him to expect a hit—which they wouldn't, not yet.

Large shapes charged along a parallel trail. He spotted the leader glancing his way over and over again, glaring at him through the trees. Racing down an elegant walkway, he reached the bottom and took a hard turn—driving the uniwheel up a set of stairs. Children jumped out of his way, squealing with delight. They cheered like he was the hero of their favorite action drama. For about a heartbeat, he wondered if someone had given them alcohol or if they were just naturally exuberant.

One of the houses launched fireworks above the park, normally an extravagance to be frowned upon but something expected during the weeks of celebration to come. Other houses answered with their own multicolored starbursts. Some of the booming explosions were much lower to the ground than normal—*not fireworks, then.*

There was one section of the park both he and his adversaries needed to traverse. If he didn't get there first, Carter

Danestar could leave a single mech to block him from going farther.

And he wouldn't have to stall for long. Victor couldn't make contact with anyone from House Marlboro. House Danestar didn't have jamming technology, but had obviously paid someone for the service.

Victor mashed the accelerator and hoped he didn't tip the thing on its side. They were safe and stable as long as their limitations were respected, not something anyone from his family was good at.

The two main paths through the park converged. Closer and closer he came to his adversaries. Their stealth mechs made noise, but not much.

A grand finale of fireworks flashed in the distance, but from his vantage point as he raced up the stairs to Marlboro House, the display seemed to fill the entire sky. An airship emerged from the middle of the colors, and he knew who it was. Only one person would fly through bursting red and green canopies of light and the air traffic control restrictions that came with such a celebration.

Fortune Marlboro, his sister—the only person more foolish than he was right now. Blue, white, and copper colors bloomed in the night sky. Most of them grew behind the sleek, agile airship his sister favored. She'd be just in time for the fight.

But I won't, if I don't focus.

Victor raced along the path, and before he knew it, the uniwheel burst through the postern gate to sound the alarm.

CHAPTER FOUR

RON HAD NEVER SLEPT SO DEEPLY as he did with Patricia lying across his chest, her golden hair spread over him. Moonlight cut through the window, casting the ducal suite in silver tones. The crack of fireworks was so constant that it had lulled them both to sleep after their lovemaking.

But now he was awake. There were voices outside, most of them far away and consistent with celebration. High-pitched laughter, shared arguments between friends over who had the better polo team, and exclamations of appreciation at each multicolored explosion in the sky. Ron wasn't normally impressed by fireworks, preferring the quiet mystery of the stars when he looked up at night.

Everything was different now that the Zezner were defeated and people were finally able to enjoy generations of hard work and sacrifice.

Patricia stirred, her hands moving across his left arm, down to his hip, and back up his torso. "We have to get up soon, don't we?" she asked.

"Do you feel it?"

She laughed softly. "I told you I did."

"Not that. Something's wrong."

"I know." She rolled into a sitting position, the silk sheets dropping away from her shoulders. "I was hoping we could go one night without strife."

"I think I hear a uniwheel tearing through the park toward our gate," Ron said.

They stood in unison, then walked with purpose to stands supporting augmented battle armor (ABA)—small units that were insurance against assassins rather than something they would use in combat. His was larger, as it conformed to his physical stature, and red with gold highlights. The colors of her ABA were red, gold, and black—the colors of both House Marlboro and House Wilson.

"Check me, husband," Patricia said.

Ron moved nimbly across the marble floor, something not every mech pilot could do even in a unit like this. He thought about what Doctor Stacks had said about his nanites and his skill. It had bothered him as he fell asleep because he'd been taught skill came from hard training rather than being born lucky.

He ran his gaze over her entire unit, then physically checked her helmet—pressing several latches and buttons to be certain of their integrity. "You have a good seal. Looks like your power is maxed out. Now check mine."

She went through the pre-combat inspection rapidly. "It's time to fight."

"It is." He shifted to get comfortable in the armor. ABAs were a lot less comfortable without a pilot suit to protect him from chafing.

"Do you always pilot naked?"

He patted her fondly on top of her helmet. "Let's make sure not to take damage. I don't want you giving the man who has to pry you out of the wreckage a show."

Patricia reached toward her back, searching for something she couldn't quite reach.

Ron, knowing her martial habits, loosened the sheath to the

light power-sword she kept there in this unit. "You're too dangerous by half, wife."

"That's why you try to keep me out of battles."

He laughed. "Not tonight. This time, let the assholes have it."

"Maybe they're not that bad," she said as they walked together. "It could be a misunderstanding."

"Anyone attacking so soon after humanity's victory over the Zezner must have been planning a house war before the invaders were beaten. Nothing has changed," Ron said. "Damned opportunists."

"Did you think peace would end jealousy and ambition?"

"You think I'm a fool for hoping," he said.

"Oh, you are, my love! But you're *my* noble, stubborn, loyal fool."

A rocket streaked through the open window, slamming into the ceiling hard enough to send a shockwave through the room. The overpressure from the explosion would have killed them had they not donned their gear.

Neither of them ducked, preferring to move toward the balcony, scanning right and left. An attack could come from anywhere. A military strike didn't mean there weren't assassins stalking them, as well.

Patricia was faster and jumped first. Ron followed, landing two strides to her left, aiming his right fist toward the enemies that swarmed through the postern gate. For a moment, he was angry it had been left open until he remembered why. Victor had been courting Penelope Danestar. *Tradition…*

The mechs initiating this house war were, of course, Danestar mercenaries.

"This is a mess, my duke," Patricia said as she picked up speed, sprinting toward a Danestar mercenary in a medium mech. Jumping, she kicked him in the chest with both feet, knocking him backward.

The other medium war machines in the squad hesitated,

25

probably not believing their eyes. They had the element of surprise and a weight advantage—heavier armor and guns—yet one of their rank was on his back, struggling to right himself.

Getting up wasn't a simple thing in mech armor.

Patricia went down, as well.

Ron closed distance on his nearest enemy and shot the man's central servo cluster while the intruder raised a giant foot to smash his wife. This close, he easily sent rounds where gears converted power to work. That's where this type of mechanized unit was always the most vulnerable.

He didn't want to stand and slug it out, so he dove and rolled at a forty-five-degree angle, grabbed his wife by the back of her ABA, and heaved her to her feet.

Together, they ran into the smoke.

"Where's Victor?" Ron grunted through their encrypted radios. Not even their children could listen to them if they weren't invited.

"He's your son, you tell me," Patricia said, searching a downed Danestar mech without a pilot.

"He's your son, too."

"He's more your son right now."

Ron moved ahead of her, searching for a fight, or his son, or anything that would lead his house to victory. Marlboro fighters poured into the smoke-filled courtyard. Some were prepared, some were barely dressed, but they all fought the best they could.

"Mother, Father!" shouted their eldest daughter, Fortune, via a tactical comm. She was old enough to marry but just barely. Her childhood had been plagued by nanite malfunctions and autoimmune diseases even Doctor Stacks didn't understand. Despite all that, or because of it, she was an asset to their house and made Ron proud. The way she flew airships was like art in motion. Someday, she might do the same in the void.

"We're near the postern gate," Ron said, glad to hear she was in some type of vehicle.

"Get the hell out of there!" Fortune said. "That is where the Danestars are massing. I'm using my jets to blow out this smoke."

"She's in her jump ship," Patricia said with obvious pride. "How did you get in the air so quickly?"

"Sorry, Mother, I was heading out for a bit of a joy ride when Victor sent up a flare," Fortune said.

"Don't be sorry, girl." Patricia rushed toward a Danestar facing the other direction, jumping on the back of his mech.

Ron burst forward, slamming into the war machine's knees, hoping his wife knew what she was doing. Attacking the upper torso of a mech was risky because the head and cockpit were always the most heavily armored components.

The enemy unit tripped but caught its balance, turning in a tight circle to aim its heavy guns at Ron who fired back with his light, semi-automatic arm gun as he dodged sideways.

Patricia seized the edges of the mech's cockpit visor and pulled. She was small but strong and the ABA added to her power. "Open up and let me in, Danestar!" When the latch wouldn't break, she pulled the light, almost slender power-sword from the back of her unit—something meant as a nasty surprise for an assassin attacking her and her husband in their bedchambers. The women of House Wilson loved their enhanced weaponry, and were well known for their... enthusiasm when using it.

Ron jumped, lashing out with a kick. The bigger mech punched him backward with one hand and reached for Patricia on its back with the other.

Ron struggled to his feet and inventoried his meager supply of small-caliber ammunition—barely dangerous against an unarmored assassin, much less able to fend off a full-scale assault. "This is no way to fight a house war."

Jump jet engines blew smoke from the battlefield to reveal a

27

half dozen Danestars swarming after Victor in a uniwheel. Fortune flew over the scene to help her parents, auto cannons on the nose of the ship blowing apart the mech terrorizing Ron and Patricia. She pivoted expertly to assist her brother, but the scene in that direction was too confused.

"Hold your position, Fortune. We're on the way to bail out your romantically challenged sibling," Ron said.

"What the hell is your son doing now?" Patricia asked as she pressed into the melee. Ricochets and bits of shrapnel pelted them both. She slammed her light power-sword into the face of an enemy helmet, cracking the glass-steel and sending him backward in surprise.

Smaller mechs weren't supposed to rush larger mechs on the battlefield, everyone knew that—until they fought beside or against House Marlboro or Wilson.

"*Our* son," Ron insisted, and gave his wife's recent victim a hard kick. He headed toward a squad of his men, two of them in regular mechs and the others in augmented infantry suits.

Patricia cheerfully ignored him. "Overall, husband, I'm well pleased with the energetic and timely response of our security force," she said.

"We have Victor to thank for that, despite his many faults," Ron said, pointing toward the outer baily where Victor fought to defend the postern gate. "Danestar counted on surprise."

"Well... I suppose we'll keep him."

"Marlboro!" Victor shouted to acknowledge them both. "The alarm is sounded. We are betrayed!"

Patricia waved him nearer. "Fight beside us, son."

Ron flanked Victor opposite his wife. "Head for the armory. We all need an upgrade."

A medium-weight Danestar mech, shorter and less robust than a fourteen-foot Marlboro mech, appeared before them in the smoke, then hesitated to pick the most valuable target.

All three Marlboros rushed forward—Victor dashing between its legs, firing at vulnerable components under the hips and pelvic girdle; Patricia on their enemy's right, slicing off one of its firing mechanisms; and Ron on its left, shooting into its knee as he passed—a risky tactic with Victor, unarmored, moving in that direction.

But Ron didn't miss.

The Danestar machine went down on its face and struggled to turn over.

Marlboros rallied to them, creating a fast-moving, ever-growing force of armored and unarmored warriors focused on a single goal: victory for House Marlboro.

And that started with getting everyone into their best mechs.

A company of enemy troops raced to stop them.

Fortune shifted her airship sideways to make way for a drop ship, and Gregory Marlboro leapt down from an open hatch of the larger vehicle. His heavy mech smashed paving stones into the air and hurled Danestars back by the sheer force of his landing.

He opened fire with double chain guns and the slaughter began in earnest.

"Wait for us, son!" Patricia shouted.

"Hurry up! There will be a few alive when you get here," Gregory shouted back.

"Come with me. We're going to take the high ground and do some damage." Ron charged through the Marlboro gardens, up a twisting path to the House hanger where he had his heaviest mechs and airships.

"I'll rally the others and put out a call for allies," Patricia said. Redwine, Thunder, and Longwatch would respond with whatever they had ready to fight. As minor houses, that wouldn't be much, but they were reliable.

"Good," Ron acknowledged.

"Run from me, Danestars!" Gregory shouted through his external speakers and on all challenge channels.

"That one is fierce," Ron said.

29

Victor sprinted ahead of them to find his mech waiting for him, his mechanics anxious to see him locked inside.

Patricia's mechanics were all women, part of a bet she'd made with Ron years before. They were the best on Gildain, better even than King Gerard's, and everyone knew it. They competed constantly, not just with how fast or well they could fix things, but in fighting, dancing, reading—anything that could be measured.

A lot of Marlboro's people were like that.

Ron leapt into his seat, augmented battle armor and all, then closed the cockpit, double-checking the seals. House infantry scrambled away; moving slowly was to risk getting stepped on when the duke was in a mood.

Ron saw and heard all these things but didn't take time to analyze the images or sounds.

This is who I am!

He raced into Gregory's wake, determined to overtake his eldest son while there was still glory to be had.

———

"WE'RE WITH YOU, MY DUKE," said a lean, scarred bull of an older man.

"Thank you, Master Sergeant Neen."

"Captain Echo is looking for Peps now," Neen said, striding beside Ron, face shield transparent as was his way.

"The young ones are always the hardest to gather up during a surprise attack," Patricia said, then climbed into her battle mech. "Give me an update the moment he has the child. What about Hannah?"

"Sir Gregory left most of his personal guard in protection of the house hospital," Neen advised.

"Understandable," Patricia said, then bullied her way around Gregory to run beside Ron again.

Ron looked around for Victor and saw him on a parallel

course, a faster way but far more dangerous because he lacked the support of the main Marlboro force now. Only a few of his friends ran with him, probably operating on an additional channel.

"What are you doing, Victor?" Ron asked privately, a privilege of his rank.

"Gregory has enough glory," Victor said, panting as he pushed his mech harder. "After tonight, I will need all I can secure if I am to snatch Penelope from the Danestar traitors."

Ron fought hard, but watched his son, aware of what a broken heart felt like and how fatalistic it could make a young man in battle.

"Wife," Ron said on another channel.

"Husband."

"Victor is heartsick over the Danestar girl."

Patricia fought past a row of armored cars, jamming her foot through one of them in frustration. "I hope she's worth it."

———

PEPS PEEKED INTO THE HALLWAY, squinting to see through the smoke that seemed to be everywhere.

It wasn't supposed to do that. Nothing could overwhelm the ventilation system of her family's dwelling, or the redundant air scrubbers. That's what the house engineer claimed.

She pulled her backpack higher on her shoulder. The drill was easy—grab what she needed and find a house guard.

Maybe it would be Mark, the captain of her father's security force. Not that she would call him Mark. He was a handsome young man well liked by the household troops. And young, very young, for his station.

But too old to notice a twelve-year-old girl, even if she was a Marlboro. And she wasn't sure if he was a dream from a storybook or gross like every other boy in the world. Her opinions on the matter seemed to be in flux, which Fortune laughed about whenever they discussed the issue.

"Oh, you'll know soon enough, little sister..."

A squad of men hurried from room to room, listening to their helmet radios but also calling out short bits of information and using hand signals. The soldiers aimed their guns into places they couldn't see, clearing the area methodically.

"Victor's suite and Fortune's suite are clear," a house guard announced aloud when they were done. He looked different, his armor heavier armor and rifle large.

"What about little Peps's room?" Mark asked the man.

Peps didn't enjoy being referred to as "little" Peps, but at least he was thinking of her. "Captain Echo, I'm over here. As soon as I heard the attack, I grabbed my kit and moved to an improved defensive position, just like you taught me."

He was at her side in an instant. "Good work, Peps. I'm glad you were paying attention during that lesson."

Peps glowed inside and maybe levitated off the ground for a second. "What do we do now? Counterattack the sons-of-bitches trying to take down our house?"

He looked at her, aghast. "You've been around my soldiers too much. Don't let your parents hear you talking like that."

"It can be our secret," Peps said.

"Sure thing, kid." Captain Mark Echo motioned toward the end of the hallway. "Granger and Hawk, take point. Amanda and Nate, bring up the rear. I'll watch over our little duchess with a mech driver's vocabulary."

"Yes, sir," the soldiers said.

Peps stayed close to Mark, watching his back whenever he aimed his pistol into one of the rooms they had to pass. Marlboro House was big, nearly fifty rooms when the barracks and workers quarters were counted.

"We're going to the shuttle bay, right?" Peps asked, knowing the answer but wanting the captain to know she knew.

"Exactly correct, Peps. Keep your eyes open. Let me know if

you see anyone with a weapon not wearing our colors." Captain Echo held his pistol at the ready, and scanned high and low for unseen threats.

He towered above her, broad shouldered and regal even if he wasn't as impressive as her father or her brother Gregory. They were almost too big—something she admitted only to herself, because they *were* her father and eldest brother.

Two full squads joined their group. Captain Echo gathered them, took roll, and assigned most of them to medium mechs, keeping only a few in lighter gear in case they needed to move fast within the manor.

"Don't stray, Peps," Echo said. "You'll ride in my unit until the crisis is resolved."

"Okay, Captain," she said, wondering if she dared call him by name.

Peps grabbed a radio from the shuttle bay and listened to the battle in the courtyard. She could hear the fighting without it, but now she also knew what her father and mother were saying as they led the counterattack.

Mark—*Captain Echo*, she had to remember—was busy coordinating the rest of the house guard and probably assumed Father's regular troops had things well in hand. Several companies of Marlboro fighters were on their way from the barracks.

"We need to help," Peps shouted, barely aware of what she was doing until Captain Echo and his sergeants stared at her. "The regular guards are fifteen minutes out."

"Your parents and the Marlboro Elites can hold that long," Captain Echo said, but he sounded unsure.

The battle in the courtyard wasn't far away. The ground shook from explosions, and Peps heard someone screaming when the noise abated.

She shook her head. "No, Mark, they need us *now*."

Sergeant Crafter frowned. "Did she just call you Mark?"

"Never mind that," the captain said, springing into action. "First and second squads, with me. We're moving to support the duke and duchess. Third and fourth squads, secure the shuttle bay. Notify our ships we may be sending up VIPs within the hour."

"It won't get that bad," Peps said, terrified that maybe... Mark was right.

Captain Echo ruffled her hair. "Of course not, little Peps."

She realized they were going to leave her, but she also knew a faster way to the courtyard. "Wait. You told me I have to ride in your mech."

"That was before it became a combat mission," Captain Echo said.

Peps climbed into his rig, strapping into the small, heavily armored passenger compartment meant for family and dignitary protection during rescue missions. "That will take too long. I know a quicker way to the House hanger."

"Of course you do," Echo said, sounding chagrined. "I've worked on these grounds my entire adult life, but every one of you Marlboros has a knack for exploration and troublemaking."

"Maybe that should be our new house motto." Peps didn't think she could be happier.

Captain Echo laughed at the head of the Marlboro House Guards. "MHG, follow us to victory. For little Peps!"

"Peps!" the soldiers roared.

CHAPTER FIVE

RON STEERED around the new perimeter, alarmed that Danestar had brought such a formidable force. They were not one of the renowned military houses, merely wealthy. The mercenaries they'd selected were the best, and there were a lot of them, but he still considered it a foolish waste.

"Captain Echo says he has Peps," Patricia advised during her own tour of the battle lines. "She's insisting the Marlboro House Guard go directly to your aid."

"Her heart is in the right place," Ron said.

"It's cute." Patricia's smile could be heard in her tone. "She loves her daddy."

Ron searched for and found his wife's icon in the tactical display. They fought well together, but often separated on the battlefield. The woman distracted him—usually in good ways—and they each had responsibilities. Mistakes were expensive during this type of power play.

"Gregory," Ron said. "What is your analysis of this attack?"

"It's too direct, even if it was supposed to be a surprise," Gregory said from a third sector of their perimeter. "You should bring Victor into this war council."

Ron agreed and sent the comm alert. "Are you here, Victor?"

"I am."

"Your mother is calling on her Wilson assets," Ron said.

His sons chuckled. Their mother had kept her Wilson assets separate after marrying Ron, an unusual practice but not unheard of. House Wilson had stood high among the minor houses, where most wouldn't have bothered with the maintenance of the legal structure to keep Wilson independently solvent within the Marlboro trust.

She'd gone a step further and maintained a well-respected military force that included Patricia's Company, made entirely of female mech warriors; Patricia's Two Hundred, made entirely of male armored vehicle operators; and Patricia's Wings, her co-ed pilots.

House Marlboro ran a strict meritocracy—the best man or woman got the job so long as they were loyal and willing to work hard. Ron teased her about the way she set up her personal force, calling them club sports. Sometimes this annoyed her, but they'd been together a long time now and had survived more traumatic marital stressors.

"Pull up your tactical maps." Ron updated unit positions and threat estimates.

"This can't be right," Gregory said. "We have the numerical advantage. With our heavier weapons, more professional fighting force, and the advantage of holding the home ground, their attack makes no sense."

Victor's voice was low but confident. "They overestimated the power of betrayal and surprise."

"What now?" Gregory asked.

Ron hesitated, aware how this would hurt Victor. His son truly adored Penelope Danestar.

"We crush them," Ron said. "Show the other houses what happens when you attack Marlboro."

No one spoke. His sons understood the harsh reality of wielding power.

"Our house has been among the top military forces since the

beginning. We have too many rivals that wish us ill. Weakness is death."

"I'm back," Patricia said. "My Company and my Two Hundred are standing by in reserve, ready to be thrown at the Danestars when we rout them."

"Good." Ron advanced, looked up and down his battle line, and checked his HUD. The only thing wrong with their position was that a lot of his landscaping and secondary buildings were going to get trashed—and the roads he was required by law to maintain would need resurfacing.

This will get messy.

"Are you ready, Gregory?"

"Yes, Duke Marlboro," his eldest said.

"Victor?"

"I am," his second oldest said. "When this is over, I intend to complete my courtship with Penelope."

"As you wish," Ron said.

"Do you think she will resent your part in her family's destruction?" Patricia asked.

"We're only eliminating their military, right?" Victor said. "Danestar will recover, and I don't believe Penelope wished for this to happen."

"None of us wish for war," Patricia said. "Focus on what we need to do now, and we can talk about the rest later."

"That's good advice," Ron said, then activated his main channel. "Marlboros, attack on my command. Take prisoners, but only when they surrender unequivocally. The military of House Danestar will not survive this day. All of their war material will be considered prizes during the Legislature and Assembly of Nobles review."

A cheer went up as mechs, armored vehicles, and air ships spread outward from the Marlboro estate, immediately putting the House Danestar regulars and their mercenaries to flight.

"Our new enemy planned this attack poorly, Father," Gregory said privately.

"Someone used Danestar," Ron said. "And they will pay dearly for the pain they have caused your brother."

"My Two Hundred has moved to the scenic heights on the border of our estate and that of House Redwine, who is mobilizing their meager forces and will likely remain on the fringes of the conflict. Our king has also activated a full division to ensure those who wish to remain neutral are allowed to do so," Patricia said. "Two Hundred, deploy the smoke screens and electronic chaff."

Other units moved forward as the armored vehicles elevated their barrels and fired large canisters of smoke. The projectiles struck near the Danestar line, quickly eliminating their ability to see the counterattack. Other battlefield technology was deployed from the smoke bombs. Electronic disrupters whirred in complicated patterns, hampering their communications and drones should they try to use them. Flares rendered infrared technology less effective and reflected from the clouds of smoke to create a new level of blindness.

"Victor, take charge of the first wave," Ron ordered.

"Marlboro mechanized warriors, 1st and 2nd Platoon, with me!" Victor charged into the smoke, visibility from his vantage point nearly normal because Marlboro tech was synchronized to the signal patterns of the micro drones causing the Danestars so much discomfort.

Spectators from other parts of the city, or from satellite footage, would be seeing fireworks on a grand scale and little else.

"Gregory, advance in close support," Ron ordered.

"Yes, Father."

"But not too close. Allow Vic his own glory."

Gregory summoned 3rd and 4th platoons, then advanced at a steady pace. "As you wish, my duke."

"But don't let him do something stupid!" Ron shouted hurriedly.

"I'm on it." Gregory's words sounded clipped. "Lord Duke Marlboro."

"And save some for the rest of us!" Patricia blurted.

"Mother!" Gregory sent each of them a formal military salute, a digital package of signals that had been traditional a hundred years before.

"Oh, you are my darling boys," Patricia said.

Ron understood that in this context, that included him. "War puts you in a feisty mood."

"You know it," Patricia replied.

If anyone heard their byplay, they were too busy to comment.

Victor and Gregory's mechs pushed the Danestar invaders back, emerging from the ring of smoke and jamming devices into public parks, streets, and fields—that the loser would have to pay for after this feud was over. One squad retreated into the industrial district, and Ron ordered the pursuit terminated. That territory ran dangerously close to the king's business interests. A brief, very dark image of Reginald Danestar, the head of their household, meeting with Gerard and his espionage corps troubled Ron.

Banish the thought. Jumping to such conclusions without proof was worse than foolish. Intuition wasn't admissible in the Decision House court of appeals.

Air support shot over Ron's head, firing a stream of glowing death into retreating mercenaries. Patricia's Two Hundred opened fire with long-range salvos from the heights, adding to the death and destruction.

Danestars and their mercenaries surrendered in droves.

Ron spotted an expensive mech that moved better than the others. The driver was an expert, which meant it had to be Carter Danestar, the young buck who probably had more to do with this power play than he should.

Ron accelerated, taking larger and larger steps, nimbly hopping over public vehicles. The last thing he wanted was to cost a working man or woman an insurance deductible—assuming said individual was able to carry battle insurance at all. Even if House Marlboro was able to identify all of the collateral stake holders in this disaster, the payment he would authorize to bystanders would be slow and probably unsatisfactory.

Carter Danestar sped down a side street with two of his bodyguards. Ron caught the first and sliced off one leg with his oscillating power-sword, shoving the falling mech aside to continue the pursuit.

The second bodyguard turned to fight. Ron opened fire with his main gun, cutting the mech in half at the waist. He dropped his shoulder, charged, and scattered the machine and its pilot cockpit across the boulevard.

Carter Danestar looked back, then increased his speed.

You're not scared, Ron thought. *You're smart enough to run.*

The chase wasn't easy. Ron's mech was larger and more powerful, which sometimes meant a greater top speed but not always.

Carter pulled away on the first curve, but turned into the Cherry Blossom District where long, winding streets displayed beautiful trees in full bloom. A breeze sent white and pink flowers up in a cloud. Carter Danestar blasted through them, and Ron followed, pouring on the speed.

He knew this area well and predicted exactly where he would catch the traitor. What he hadn't anticipated was the rocket squad. Mechs he would have detected, but these men looked like civilians until they pulled the tarps back from three work trucks.

"I should have expected a trap from you, Danestar," Ron scowled right before the first volley flashed through the air. He raised his onetime energy shield, then a mechanical shield that wouldn't sustain much additional damage. Defensive measures added a lot of weight—in power converters or armor plates—but did little to secure victory. So he only had the two layers of protection. After that, it was just the armor of his actual unit.

Explosions knocked him back a step. When the smoke cleared, Carter Danestar remained. The rocket crews sped away in three directions, breaking dozens of traffic ordinances.

Carter circled him.

"What's your game?" Ron asked. "You can't beat me even with the damage your ambush caused to my shields."

"You've never heard of dropships?" Carter asked.

"House Danestar doesn't have dropships, and mercenaries aren't allowed to use them without approval of the king," Ron said.

Three brown and white vessels swooped low over the orchards, their jets churning up cherry blossoms in huge spirals behind them. Each drop ship carried three mechs—nine medium mechs belonging to House Bull.

Not mercenaries, then, Ron thought.

"Minor houses can also make alliances, you know," Carter Danestar said.

Ignoring the punk, Ron called over his comms, "Attention, Marlboros, I've encountered a Danestar ambush and new players on the field. House Bull is en route with drop ships and medium mechs. Repeat, House Bull is in play and moving against us."

"Copy that, Duke," Patricia said shortly. "Who has resources near my husband's position—which is far outside his assigned zone?"

Letting his wife handle all that, Ron charged his opponent, taking Carter Danestar by surprise. "You thought I would run?"

"Damn you, Marlboro!" Carter shouted as they closed in the roundabout connecting several of the boulevards in the Cherry Blossom District.

Ron slammed the bulk of his mech into Carter's unit, then wrapped him up with both arms. Hefting the smaller machine into the air, he slammed it down, throwing his weight on top of his adversary.

The cockpit of Carter Danestar's mech cracked, just a hairline fracture that spider-webbed from the center. Ron stood back, aimed his primary and secondary guns, and fired everything he had.

Fragments of armor and cockpit glass-steel exploded into the air. Carter screamed but his radio cut out abruptly. Blood, body parts, and the young man's last hope of survival were flung violently away from the bullet strikes.

Ron's adversary was dead. But now nine House Bull mechs dropped near him, carelessly destroying rows of the much loved trees. *Clumsy assholes.* Furious, Ron stomped on Carter Danestar's ruined mech as Captain Echo notified the duke that he and the Marlboro House Guards were arriving to help.

But he barely cared. Rage, pain, and fatigue filtered his awareness. The center of his vision was red with vengeance, the edges dark with rage. This treacherous fool had attacked his family and broken his son's heart. This man had murdered people Ron had sworn to protect.

Two more stomps finished the machine as well as the man. No one would forget what happened to the upstart who had betrayed House Marlboro. They'd promised an alliance, the betrothal of Victor and Penelope. But they'd delivered treachery instead.

"Burn in hell, Carter Danestar!" he roared, external speakers amplifying his announcement to anyone within a square mile.

"We'll include your savagery in our report to the Assembly of Nobles," a man said over his loudspeaker. "I am Travis Bull, and these are my best fighters. Prepare to die, Marlboro."

Ron respected the man's calm, confident demeanor. House Bull might have been a better alliance than Danestar. But all of that was in the past.

Nine mechs encircled him, weapons raised. Power-swords humming and axes powering up.

"We're coming, Duke!" Captain Echo of the Marlboro House Guards announced breathlessly. A pilot had to push a unit hard to sound like that.

Ron saw the MHG first platoon racing through the orchards, sweeping along the paved boulevard to minimize public damage, but cutting corners more than once.

"You're supposed to be guarding Peps and the estate," Ron growled, picking his first target, not Travis Bull, who looked formidable, but his second-in-command, Malcom Sky, a legend in his own right.

"I brought them, Father."

Peps!

Ron glanced at his HUD and saw his youngest daughter waving at him from inside Captain Echo's mech. Each of the MHG units could take one adult or three juvenile passengers depending on age; it was one of their personnel security and rescue features.

For a desperate second, Ron's attention flipped between the advancing mercenary mechs and Peps, because even as she waved excitedly, another expression was drawing the youthful vigor from her face.

"Father, what did you do to Carter Danestar?"

"By all means, go give your little girl a hug," Travis Bull snarled. "Sky, bring me the pieces of his mech."

"Yes, Lord Bull, my father," Malcom Sky said, voice cold. His mech was scraped, dented, and moved perfectly—which spoke of money spent where it mattered, upgrades, regular maintenance, and time on the training field.

Father? What was that?

Ron went at the House Bull officer, but the man drew back patiently, inviting Ron to overextend and expose his flanks. The man had stood on the floor of a freshwater bay for three days to await a Zezner raiding party that had been plaguing One of House Bulls' client companies, Udin's Coastal Fishery and Guided Tours.

That had shown determination Ron still admired.

But it wasn't his concern now.

Stopping, aiming scatter bursts right and left at the same

time, Ron peppered the other Bull mechs with kinetic rounds and signal flares. One retreated due to cockpit damage. The other paused, pivoted, and fired in the wrong direction.

"I don't like this," Peps sniffled.

"Neither do I, little Peps," Captain Echo said sternly, "but they are trying to kill the duke and we're here to fight."

Malcom Sky shifted. His remaining mech troopers adjusted perfectly. The man was one step above his mercenary heritage, but his squad knew what they were about and didn't flinch. Lord Travis Bull was seasoned enough to allow talented killers to lead the way. He took one mech and swept wide around the flank, possibly to cut off Ron's retreat.

"Reginald Danestar won't be paying you again," Ron said, then fired a trio of small rockets at Sky.

The Bull officer pulsed an energy shield, which few non-house units could afford, and retreated another step. Ron and Sky exchanged kinetic rounds from close range as other mechs peeled away from the formation to fight the MHG.

Ron tried not to think about Peps in the armored passenger hold of Echo's mech.

Sky stepped back, touching his mech arms together, a posture that suggested he was running a systems check—like a professional. Green mech fighters rushed. Men like Malcom Sky and Ron Marlboro took care of the details. They circled each other as they checked for damage.

From farther away than necessary, Travis Bull cursed Ron. "We might be minor houses, but Bull and Danestar made an alliance that can't be broken. My lieutenant will rise another notch when he marries Penelope Danestar and is adopted into my family's house."

Ron checked Duke Bull's marker. The commander was still in the fight, but barely. The man didn't have a reputation for cowardice, but it was possible he would run.

"Now you're trying to piss me off," Ron growled, talking to

the duke but keeping his eyes on the man's dangerous lieutenant.

"I'm coming, husband!" Patricia said. "And I'm bringing the boys."

"Not all of us produce children like you do, and when we do, some lack nanites for more than base survival," Bull said, and Ron remembered that under other circumstances, they were amiable friends—sipping whiskey at the king's ski lodge and smoking cigars until late in the night.

"That's not my problem, Bull," Ron said, then took a tentative step back from Sky. He didn't care about this mercenary. He wanted to pivot and go after the man he was talking to on comms, Travis Bull.

"Of course not. You're correct, as always. But Malcom Sky will make a fine adopted son, and when he marries Penelope Danestar, House Bull Danestar will be a major military power. My strength and experience combined with their money will be formidable."

"Why are you telling me this?" Ron asked, his guts suddenly feeling like they were falling out of his mech.

"Because King Gerard scorned you on the battlefield when everyone knew you were the reason we won," Bull said. "That can only mean one thing."

Malcom Sky and the other mechs shifted but didn't attack. It was clear they had orders to give their dukes time to parley—a rare thing this deep into a house betrayal.

"You know the risk I'm taking by talking to you," Bull said.

"I do." Ron wanted to die. The man wasn't one to waste words. He clearly had information implicating a danger to both Marlboro and Bull, a threat so dire, it required this deadly subterfuge to even discuss it. "Say your piece, but make it quick."

Ron's mind worked overtime, analyzing the situation. *A battle to make us appear enemies. Death, destruction, betrayal, and heartbreak—all fair and reasonable in the game we play with the great houses.* Ron missed the Zezner threat.

"Who do you think would win in a contest between Gerard, Atana, and Spirit versus Marlboro?"

Ron said nothing.

"Same question, but against my house?" Bull asked, edging closer to emphasize his words.

"You'd be slaughtered," Ron said, "after you made a mess of Lorne—I'll give you that. You fight better than most. Beating you would cost your enemies a bitter price."

"What about Gerard, Atana, and Spirit against Marlboro and Bull?" Bull asked.

"You're forgetting House Bronc. They're loyal to the king and nearly as powerful as my family."

"Duke Bronc is on the fence," Bull said. "We had a whiskey together."

"Oh, you had whiskey. That's practically a neutrality contract."

Bull ignored his sarcasm. "Don't let your son jeopardize this alliance."

"Penelope Danestar has the final decision with any courtship," Ron said, knowing the situation wasn't so simple.

"Maybe, maybe not. But ask yourself this. What is more important, your house that has survived a thousand years or your son's fleeting happiness?"

Patricia, Gregory, Victor, and all of their supporting units arrived at the center of the Cherry Blossom District just as five large drop ships of House Bull's finest touched down opposite them.

Duke Bull retreated through the ranks of his rough but serviceable battle mechs, tanks, and landed airships. Surrounded by his best fighters, he faced Ron and waited.

"What's happening, husband?" Patricia asked as she joined him.

"We are betrayed, but not by the house we first thought," Ron said, throat rough with new damage.

"Talk to me," she said. "I don't like the sound of your voice. What's wrong?"

Ron hesitated, still on their private channel. "I'm afraid Victor was wasting his time. Penelope might look like a sweetheart, but I've learned she is already betrothed."

He started to worry when she didn't reply immediately.

"That harlot!" she hissed.

"You know as well as I do, she probably has nothing to do with the marriage proposal," Ron said, feeling more tired than he had after defeating the Zezner. "Despite the legal requirement that she approves of it."

"What now, Marlboro?" Bull asked.

"We have to fight and look like we've both taken too much damage to cause the other houses problems for a long time," Ron suggested. "Neither of us can look like a threat to Gerard after this."

"I'll send my people orders to engage in a spirited scrimmage and limp away like we fought you to a draw," Bull said.

"Good enough." Ron sent his own order.

"What is this?" Victor demanded.

"Do it, son, and don't question me again until it is over."

CHAPTER SIX

"DON'T TROUBLE YOURSELF," Patricia said. She stroked his hair with one hand and held his head against her chest with the other. A cool breeze came through the open window, just like it had on the night of the betrayal.

"I'm not," he said, relaxing into her embrace.

"Liar."

He pulled back reluctantly, propped himself on an elbow, and studied her in the moonlight. "I'm worried about Hannah and our grandchild."

"Not Victor and his broken heart?" she asked.

"Well, him too. He couldn't have known Penelope was betrothed. And she was probably ordered not to discuss the matter, which put them in an awkward situation."

"Because they have genuine affection for each other," Patricia said.

Ron waved his hand, annoyed at basically everything and not having the words to argue the point. "Victor is a Marlboro. He knows how marriage works in our society. And, according to the Danestar and Bull doctors, Penelope and Malcom have an excellent chance of producing children."

"That's important," Patricia conceded. "But when has a Marlboro not been a good match for making children?"

Ron didn't comment.

"Talk to me," Patricia said. "You're so far away right now."

"Gildain is a rich planet," Ron said, feeling her sink into him. His fascination with space exploration and what they knew of other worlds was one of his favorite topics. Although his wife had little interest in it, she humored him almost teasingly. Other husbands talked sports or mech upgrades, and their wives expressed the same type of affectionate tolerance, he thought.

"Mmm." She snuggled in closer.

"If not for the persistent Zezner invasions, we would be a peaceful race, don't you think?"

"That would be nice," she admitted. "And boring. Are you going to surrender your title and become a farmer or a craftsman?"

"Maybe I will."

"Just let me know, so I can start shopping for a new husband."

He jostled her. "Okay. Please tell me how that works out for you." He let the comfortable silence stretch out.

Ron wanted to explain his agreement with Travis Bull and wasn't sure why he held back. Perhaps he feared failure, and hoped his wife could provide for their family with her still functioning House Wilson.

Nothing is certain, he thought.

"What makes us fight amongst ourselves?"

"Was your confrontation with Bull so disturbing?" she asked, sounding sleepy. "He's not a major duke like you, not nearly as powerful, no matter how well he and his troops fight. You could have crushed them."

"Danestar will fill their war chest."

"But it will take time for them to expand their military strength, no matter how much money they have to throw at the upgrades and recruitment," she said. "And the best commanders are already in the great military houses. More of them are in ours than any other, don't you think?"

He didn't have to agree because they knew each other's minds.

"I'm worried about Gregory and Hannah, and our soon-to-be grandchild," Ron said.

"And we're back to that," Patricia returned. "As someone who has given birth, nanites and all, I can tell you we women know what we're doing. And the doctors have some degree of skill if there is an emergency."

He hugged her close with one arm. "You're so tough. Giving birth and barely even screaming or calling me names, every time."

"Don't even go there, husband."

He laughed. She joined him. Their view of the galaxy stood motionless outside their window as their shared mood mellowed.

There was little he could say that his wife hadn't heard over and over, so he pretended to sleep. It was doubtful she was fooled, but she drifted into a peaceful slumber as he stared at the ceiling, and the night sky through the window, and the Marlboro crest above the mantle.

His heart ached for Victor. He fought down his growing resentment at Penelope Danestar. She was too gorgeous by half, society's darling, a debutant seemingly as innocent as flowers in spring. But he knew there must be more to the young woman than that. No one among the nobility retained their innocence for long.

Leadership was a business and businesses failed every day, even on Gildain where there was more food than could be consumed and resources to build a hundred space fleets and ten thousand mechs.

Of course the Zezner wanted the planet for themselves.

He became uneasy. Everyone assumed they wanted Gildain for the same reasons humans valued the planet.

Send them out to make the universe fit for expansion.

Ron pushed aside the dream. He wasn't a religious man or student of ancient history. The phrase was important to both disciplines.

But why did he dream of it so often?

And how had the Zezner known to recite the phrase, and then call him a near-human?

"What does it mean?" he murmured.

"What... honey?" Patricia asked, but she didn't wake up.

The answer to one of his questions came as he saw the first meteor of the night. He knew what was wrong with the commonly held assumption that the Zezner wanted the vast resources of Gildain.

They came with massive, well supplied fleets. Is that the condition of a race that is starving and resource-poor?

They don't need our planet, not for those reasons, he thought. *There's another explanation.*

Finally confident that he wasn't paranoid or suffering from mental stress, he slept immediately. The answers would come.

———

NOTHING COMPARED to a Gildain sunrise from Duke Ron Marlboro's balcony. Side by side, arms around each other, Ron and Patricia sipped coffee and watched the city, its rolling gardens, and the farmlands beyond the urban areas.

"Shall we walk around the balcony and check the king's industry?" Ron joked.

"I'm not as fascinated with that quarter of Lorne as some people I know."

"You must admit, it's impressive," Ron said. *"Did you know...* that ancient texts complain that industrial sectors were noisy and created atmosphere-destroying pollution?"

"Look who read a book!" Patricia teased. "I'm going with friends to visit Hannah. Woman stuff."

"Of course." Ron kissed her. "I'll be in with the mechanics most of the day. If we must fix everything after back-to-back battles, we might as well hit the upgrades hard."

"You love upgrades," she said. "I'll see you at dinner."

"If you're lucky."

"Oh, I always get lucky."

He watched her go and tried not to think too much, savoring another day of life. A walk in the garden appealed to his mood, so he explored the grounds of his estate as though he'd never been there before. Working in the shop, as much as he loved it, could wait.

Others walked the paths, sat by the streams, or crouched to examine exotic flowers. A fox peeked out of a bush, then three smaller ones. Ron stayed where he was until they moved on. In the distance, beyond his estate, the morning sun reached the Cherry Blossom District, and the view that normally improved his mood tarnished it instead.

"Duke Marlboro," came the familiar voice of Doctor Stacks. "You look well, if one can see past all the bruising and stitches."

Ron smiled. "Someone patched me up rather nicely."

Stacks bowed his head, acknowledging the compliment.

"It's a good day for a walk. What brings you out?" Ron asked.

"It's part of my fitness regimen. Nothing as strenuous as what you and your warriors practice, but I put in some miles and sketch plants when the mood strikes me." Doctor Stacks held up a satchel with a worn tablet and a leatherbound notebook inside. "What's on your mind?"

"Maybe I'm just enjoying the morning," Ron said as they strolled around a pond, waving to other pedestrians they passed.

"You only stalk the gardens when restless or worried. I would know. I've been your doctor for almost a century."

Ron pushed aside thoughts of Carter Danestar and Travis Bull in the Cherry Blossom District. There were plenty of other things to worry about. "I've been thinking of Hannah and Gregory."

"You'll be a grandfather soon enough," Stacks said. "Nature will take care of everything."

"Of course. And thanks for making me feel old."

"You *are* old, Duke. And you're more fit than you have a right to be," Stacks said, expression thoughtful, his dedication to esoteric subject matter showing on his face. "Every man, woman, and child of Gildain ages unbelievably well. Except for the island people of Amern."

"Pardon?" Ron asked. "What does that mean?"

"Nothing. I ramble."

Ron gave him the look.

"The island people of Amern never leave, and never mingle with the rest of us on this planet. They're short-lived, their life expectancy rarely exceeding a hundred years. Their technology is… quaint."

Ron frowned. "What does that have to do with us?"

"Nothing," Stacks said. "Forget I mentioned it."

Ron stopped, obligating his Chief Medical Officer to do the same. "Did I tell you what the Zezner I fought near the cliff overlooking the White Ocean said to me?"

"No." The doctor still appeared nervous. He was a smart man who knew it wasn't easy to slip Ron's attention.

"He called me a near-human," Ron said, holding his gaze. "What do you think that means?"

Doctor Stacks stalled. "Well, you know that the nanites don't occur in nature. Maybe the Zezners are prejudiced against us for that reason."

"You say that, but nanites are natural to us now. They come with every infant, just like all the other body parts," Ron said, feeling a growing pressure in his skull.

Doctor Stacks also looked uncomfortable, but that was

normal for him; he spent too much time thinking on things better left to nature. "Of course. But you will admit no other creature on Gildain has them."

"Nanites can't be created by you or any of our best scientists," Ron said, aware that his thoughts would become fuzzy if he pursued this line of inquiry for long, and a merciless headache would follow. "Which means they must only be natural for us. We just don't understand them. And I've yet to see one, so they might as well be wind and wishes."

"Of course, Duke. But you must at least recognize that they're not natural," Stacks said. "Members of my order are required to view them under a microscope as a rite of passage."

"Of course... your rite of passage." Ron's head hurt, and he could tell Doctor Stacks was suffering as well. "What else could they be?"

"I don't know, but it deserves more study than we give the topic. However, there is nothing for you, or your eldest son and your daughter-in-law, to worry about. Marlboro nanites have a long track record. The child will be born safely and will benefit from your genetics... and all the other augmentations."

Ron massaged the back of his neck as they walked. Relief came the moment he pushed the troubling discussion about nanites out of his mind. "Thank you, doctor. That is reassuring."

"Where is Patricia?"

Ron smiled. "Doing mysterious woman stuff with my daughter-in-law and her ladies."

"Ah." Stacks stopped, gesturing politely. "I'll leave you to the manly vices you'll be able to pursue until she returns."

"I'm going to work on mechs with my mechanics," Ron said. "Don't start any rumors. You remember what happened that time Patricia thought I had a mistress."

"I would rather forget it. Please don't hesitate to call me if you need anything."

"Of course," Ron said. "Good day."

The conversation replayed in Ron's head, provoking more

questions than it had answered. The doctor's assurances about Hannah rang true, but his feelings of uneasiness remained. Too much had gone wrong since his victory over the Zezner.

It was my victory, he thought. *They all know it, especially the king.*

Ron, his father, his grandfather—indeed all the Marlboros before him—had faced political crises. He understood everything that had happened, and unfortunately, also knew what had to be done to keep his house and family alive.

What bothered him more and more were his doubts about why the Zezner invaded Gildain in the first place. Why spend a century waging war on a planet to gain resources you didn't need?

A flower from a distant cherry blossom tree drifted on the wind and landed in his open palm.

I can't let one day ruin all the others.

He studied the wondrous beauty in his hand for a long time, then tossed it into the wind where it danced away with perfect grace.

If I were preparing a world for… someone… would they find Gildain acceptable?

CHAPTER SEVEN

RON AND PATRICIA stepped out of their limousine in their best military uniforms, flanked by Marlboro House Guards dressed for the occasion while trying to look unobtrusive. The red carpet leading up the wide stairs was long and wide. His security detail hated moments like this because of the spectators crowding the sidewalk.

Gregory and Hannah were excused from the festivities. Her time was so close, not even the king expected them to attend.

Victor, Fortune, and Peps followed. The paparazzi took pictures and videos. Crowds threw flowers, rose petals, and colorful silk streamers. Each of the Marlboros approached the crowd twice, greeting citizens and exchanging pleasantries. Conversing with the onlookers a single time looked artificial, something done out of obligation. Three times came across to the media as attention-seeking, a behavior common to minor houses.

House Marlboro knew how to fight aliens, and they also knew their manners. Public support was going to be more important than ever if Ron's estimate of the situation was accurate.

He watched his people come up the stairs, his family along

with their security elements and other staff. It took a long time to reach the pavilion where they would watch the parade thrown to honor House Marlboro—an honor nearly equal to standing beside the king during the Zezner emperor's surrender.

"King Gerard looks spectacular today," Patricia said as they arrived at the vast veranda topped with a gold silk tent and flag poles for every house banner on Gildain. "All the women want to know if he will remarry soon."

"Why would he? It must be nice to be the bachelor king again," Ron said.

"Father," Fortune said as she joined them, crossing to a place of honor near the king. "There is a Zezner in our section."

"I see him," Ron said. Each member of his family studied the red-skinned alien. "He's tall, even for one of them. General Voth and his elite guards are with him. We are in no danger."

"We wouldn't be in danger, anyway," Victor said. "One unarmed and unarmored Zezner is nothing for us to fear."

Ron studied the conquered enemy, always curious when he encountered one outside of their four-legged mechs. When he was younger, he'd assumed the aliens had four legs like their machines, but they turned out to be more humanoid than experts had expected—taller than most men, powerfully built, but appearing lanky due to their odd dimensions. He thought their arms and legs were too long.

General Voth met them at the edge of their section, bowed deeply, and took a step back. "Duke Marlboro, it is an honor to greet you and your family here today. This parade is for you, of course, but King Gerard also wishes you to take this prisoner, a prince among our enemy, as a token of his everlasting gratitude."

"When did we become slavers, Voth?" Ron asked hotly.

Patricia held his right arm. "Calm yourself, husband."

"It is not of our doing. King Gerard knows slavery to be against nature. This is the Zezners' custom. Redion Axst is honor-bound to serve the victor of the last great battle," Voth said. The stout, powerfully built man stared straight ahead when he spoke, but at Ron's chest since Voth wasn't a tall man.

"The Zezner emperor did not surrender to me, if you remember," Ron said.

"The Zezner say you were the one who defeated them, no matter who beheaded their leader at the end."

"It seems the king has unloaded this poor soul on us," Patricia observed quietly.

Ron waved General Voth aside. The man stiffly stepped away and waited for the Marlboro procession to pass. Maybe that had been poorly handled, but Ron wasn't in the mood to tiptoe around the feelings of a man who called himself a soldier despite evidence only of administrative acumen.

The Zezner warlord presented himself with alien dignity, a mannerism that terrified humans who had not fought or parleyed with them. He was tall, muscular, and big-boned, but lean—as though all of his available sinew had been stretched to its limit just to maintain a standing position.

"I am Duke Uron Marlboro, a lord of Gildain and protector of humanity. How shall we be acquainted?" Nothing could be taken for granted with the Zezner. They thought and behaved differently from humans.

"I am Redion Axst of Zezner and the Quest. You ask better questions of greeting than your king or his war chiefs," the Zezner said.

Ron knew the aliens had "questions of greeting," but didn't know exactly how to phrase them or what level of nuance they required. But he was willing to try.

"Do you have an answer?" Ron asked.

"We are a defeated people," Redion said. "The terms your king negotiated provides many of my people new lives, but they cannot claim them while enslaved—so I am enslaved in their place, forever and without conditions, that they may live as freely as a conquered race can."

Ron sensed the disapproval of his wife and children. "You are not my slave, Redion."

"On that point we disagree, but perhaps the word means something different in the language of near-humans," Redion said.

"And I thought we might treat each other civilly," Ron muttered.

"Did I err?"

"Why do Zezner call us near-humans?" Patricia asked.

"Why do humans call us Zezner?" Redion asked, then bowed his head. "I am at your service, always."

"Are you sick or injured?" Ron asked, starting to sweat from the warmth radiating from the alien.

"I am the healthiest of my people. That is why I was chosen. Our body temperatures are much higher than yours. My advisors have told me this unnerves many people of Gildain."

"Interesting." Ron studied the individual he would now be required to care for, protect, and teach human laws and customs. Then he looked toward the king's balcony and saw the man was busily entertaining Duchess Stephani of House Spirit and her formidable entourage.

"The parade is beginning," Victor announced.

Ron clapped his hands. "Take your places. And pass the wine."

This brought laughter from everyone but the Zezner.

"Do you know how to laugh?" Ron asked.

"Of course, but the sound disturbs near-humans," Redion explained.

"Do me a favor and just shorten it to 'humans' when you're around my family."

"Of course," the Zezner said, then faced the boulevard along with hundreds of other lords, ladies, and their hangers-on.

The minor houses marched first, their infantry keeping step and standing tall. Marching bands played martial tunes. Streamers fired from popguns and small fireworks filled the air.

Patricia leaned close to him. "It's nice."

"Like a country fair," Ron said. "Maybe we should slip away and go for a hayride."

"This is in your honor." She was beautiful and obviously stroking his ego.

"Our honor."

Not all of the smaller houses could afford to maintain armored vehicles, mechs, or ships, but he admired them greatly for their earnest attempts at pageantry. House Atana didn't bother to represent their footmen and women, but began and ended their parade with tanks, mechs, and small ships on trailers.

House Bull came next, their famous house guards prancing on elegant horses ahead of their modern war machines.

Victor leaned toward Ron. "Why aren't they on bulls?"

"That is a low joke I've heard many times," Ron said, not liking the animosity in his son's eyes.

"Sure, but you have to wonder." Victor's normal lightheartedness returned.

"Bulls make bullshit," Ron said. "Who wants to clean that up, or ride behind them when they're dropping it?"

Patricia slapped his arm. "Leave that talk for the taverns."

"Gladly, if you would allow me to patronize one."

She kissed his cheek. "You don't want to be away from me for even one evening."

"True."

The parade continued. Ron watched it all, but paid more attention to his wife and family than other lords and ladies thought proper. He saw them pointing, then whispering behind their hands. Some even left. Others applauded too loudly, in Ron's opinion.

In the middle of it, he glanced at Redion who stared at the horizon as the sun set.

"Spectacular," Ron said.

"It is the most beautiful thing I have ever seen," Redion said. "My people live to see one such sunset before they die."

House Redwine's marching band passed, barely distinguishable from their soldiers. Or maybe they were the same unit. Ron barely cared. If not for Hannah, he would have little use for the mercantile family.

Patricia, his children, and many clients of House Marlboro mingled now, eating and drinking and greeting one another. Everyone clapped appreciatively when larger fireworks went off high above the city.

Ron found himself sitting with only Redion for company. "What is the Quest?"

"To free the Talgar, of course, and to learn which way the near-humans will go next," Redion said.

"That should annoy me, but it doesn't," Ron said.

"I am famously non-annoying," Redion said.

Ron laughed and his alien client—because that was what he was now—laughed with him. The sound was nearly inaudible.

"I can see how that bothers some people," Ron said.

"But it does not bother you?"

Ron shrugged and pointed at the Marlboro vanguard. "Here come my troops. I'm proud of them, Red. What do you think of my troopers? You must have faced my soldiers in battle."

"House Marlboro is strong and should have been granted greater honors at the conclusion of the war," Redion said. "You will be betrayed and slaughtered. Your battle slave, Redion Axst of Zezner and the Quest, will very likely die with you."

Ron mulled that over. Evidently his humiliation was so public, even the conquered alien could see it. "Was it that obvious?" he asked, checking to make certain no one was eavesdropping.

"To one such as me, it is clear," Redion said. "You must take action."

"What action?"

Before Redion could respond, a page approached, bowed,

and paid his respects to Ron and Patricia. Then he bowed again and held forth a sealed letter without raising his head.

At other verandas, house leaders received similar messages. Ron didn't need to open it to know what it was. The Gildain Legislature had the power to demand all members of the Assembly of Nobles convene at their rotunda, and used the power frequently.

But never during a lord's triumphal parade.

"Thank you, young man. Send my compliments to the Prime Legislative Officer," Ron said.

Patricia glared after the boy when he left, like this was his fault. She also knew what an assembly summons looked like. "How can they call the Assembly of Nobles during the celebration? We haven't served dinner or been invited to any of the other pavilions yet."

There was no answer. He held his tongue, watching the other pavilions until he was certain every house had been called. Victor, Fortune, and Peps gathered near, listening and watching for what to do next.

"It's a deliberate insult," Victor said, stiff with anger.

Captain Echo and the Marlboro House Guards lined up in their best uniforms, ready to escort Ron and Patricia to the Rotunda—the ancient building where the Assembly of Nobles, and the House of the Elected before that, was located.

"Transport by vehicle will be nearly impossible, Duke," Echo said. "We must travel by way of the undercity if we are to honor this summons."

Ron avoided Patricia's gaze, choosing to look at the miles-long parade and fireworks above it instead. Royal engineers had opened the undercity to official travel a millennium before. Citizens had sheltered there during several of the worst Zezner attacks. It was a vibrant and modern place now, despite its history—but he had no love for it.

From the looks of the other dukes and duchesses within his view, they were even less pleased.

"A summons from the Prime Legislative Officer must be acknowledged without delay, and attendance is required lest a house forfeit its franchise." Ron stood, smoothed his uniform, and nodded to Captain Echo. None of his family spoke. They knew how he felt about political intrigues.

"Captain Echo," Ron said.

"Yes?"

"Activate your second platoon. You may escort my wife and me to the Rotunda, but my family will have a full security element protecting them at all times. Do you understand?"

"Are we at war, Lord Duke?"

"Maybe, maybe not. But we must be prepared for any eventuality."

Ron gave the MHG time and was glad to see that the second platoon was on scene in minutes, which meant Echo had anticipated his request and staged them nearby—no small accomplishment given the number of people crowding the area.

"May I have the honor of accompanying you, Duke Marlboro?" Redion Axst asked.

Ron considered the alien.

Patricia looked worried. "It will anger nearly everyone in attendance."

Thinking it over, the duke said, "Redion, the honor is yours. Stand tall when you are with me."

He'd meant to ensure that the alien was conspicuous during this farce. But his words held another meaning. Redion clearly interpreted his statement to mean "stand tall, be proud, I value you as my friend and ally now," or something very close to that sentiment.

Patricia observed the transformation as well, and nodded her approval.

"The same advice goes for you," Ron told his children. "This may be an intentional slight to our reputation, but stand tall in my place and receive all the glory due to our house. Be generous and kind, be good hosts in my absence, and be ready for anything."

"Lord Duke," Captain Echo interrupted. "I've received word from the doctors. Hannah is in labor."

Ron didn't hesitate. "The hospital is on the way."

"Is it?" Patricia asked with a sly smile.

Grinning, Captain Echo said, "Definitely on the way, Duke. May I offer my compliments on your navigational prowess?" His loyal admiration practically glowed through his skin.

Redion's brow furrowed. "I do not understand this conversation."

Patricia took him by the arm as they began to move. "You *are* a bit toasty. Interesting. My husband is about to answer an insult with an insult. We will be late, but with a reasonable excuse."

"Is that wise?" Redion asked.

"No, Red. It may start a war between the Assembly of Nobles, the Legislature, and the king," Ron said.

"So soon after peace," Redion said. "I am with you to the end. Who could have guessed how little time that would be?"

Ron laughed and strode from the parade grounds to the entrance of the undercity. Patricia, Redion, and a platoon of the MHG accompanied him.

————

ENTERING the undercity was always an experience. The wide staircase twisted down for three levels, the vast stadium-like series of balconies, escalators, and elevators shining brightly as a tribute to another era of technology.

House Whiteleaf had long held the charter to maintain the place; they were fond of cleanliness, order, and chrome. Where skylights were impractical, there were powerful lamps to grow all manner of plants in the mini atriums. The place was nowhere as grim as its name implies. Elsewhere, undercity was more functional and grimmer.

They boarded a train the moment Captain Echo cleared off nonessential passengers from two of the cabin cars and secured them.

"Make sure to explain the unscheduled nature of our travel today," Ron said. "And alert me if our disruption of their travel plans causes any serious inconvenience."

"Yes, Duke," Captain Echo said.

The undercity sped by, both above and below the railcars. Most of the residential areas were full of lit apartments and people on balconies conversing with their neighbors. He couldn't hear from inside the train, but knew there was a great deal of music and laughter in such places. At least during the good times.

They entered into a tunnel that angled toward the surface and soon emerged near the hospital. Captain Echo and his men deployed onto the passenger dock, and he soon give them the all-clear. In moments, they were heading up the stairs into the hospital.

"We cannot go with you inside of the hospital," Echo said.

"Thank you, Captain," Ron said, then entered with Patricia and Redion.

A security team immediately confronted them. "He can't come in here."

"He's with me," Ron said without slowing. "Stand aside or I will knock you down. My daughter-in-law is having my grandchild; I mean to be in the waiting room when it happens."

"Of course, Duke Marlboro. We meant no disrespect. It's just that Zezners are not allowed in the hospital."

"That's a rule?" Patricia asked. "I would like to see it in writing. Please send me your supervisor."

They left the security guards near the front door. A nurse greeted them with a smile and waved for them to follow. "This way, Duke Marlboro. Good to see you and your lovely wife again."

"Does she not see me?" Redion asked.

The nurse didn't miss a beat. "What's your name, Zezner?"

"Redion Axst of Zezner and the Quest," he answered.

"Nice to meet you. I'm Bridget Reach, CNP. Right this way. I may require a medical screening to make sure you're not a health risk. You understand, of course."

"It is a prudent precaution," Redion said. "Though it has been thoroughly documented during the last hundred years of warfare that our biologies don't carry hostile biomes or viruses toward each other."

The nurse looked questioningly at Ron and Patricia.

"He's correct," Ron said.

Patricia finished for him. "There have been dozens of prisoner exchanges and battlefield injuries treated on both sides. We wouldn't allow a threat to our grandchild."

"Of course," the nurse said. "But you must understand that once we pass through these doors, you'll be in *my* house, with my rules."

"Agreed," Ron said, then looked to Redion to make sure he would comply.

"I mean to cause no problems," the alien said, ducking through the door as he followed them.

"You stay with Redion," Patricia said. "I'll check on Gregory and Hannah, then call you in."

"Don't take too long," Ron said, then stood in the waiting area while a pair of nurses took Redion Axst's temperature and performed a battery of other evaluations to make sure his presence was safe.

Five minutes later, Patricia returned shaking her head, smiling pleasantly if slightly exasperated. "False alarm. There will be no grandchild today."

"Is she okay?" Ron asked, more nervous than he had been during the final battle against the Zezner invaders.

"She is," Patricia said. "We had better continue to the Rotunda."

Ron waved the comment aside. "Of course, just as soon as we are sure. I'm not leaving so quickly."

"There will be repercussions," she said flatly.

"Do you want to rush off to play Legislature and Assembly games?" he asked.

"Not even a little."

"This is very fascinating," Redion said. "How did you defeat us when every day your world is full of such intrigue and political maneuvering?"

"My husband is very good at war," Patricia says.

"Yes," Redion said. "We have long known this."

"And everyone knows politics is war," she finished.

CHAPTER EIGHT

THE ROTUNDA of the Legislature was nearly the size of a coliseum and had probably seen as much blood on its steps as that of the ancient and long-abolished gladiatorial pits. The support pillars were precision-cut glass-steel, with every fourth pillar crafted out of local marble. Banners honoring the principles of the Legislature hung in sheltered alcoves rather than house standards used in the Assembly of Nobles or the statues of learned men and women that decorated the Decision House, the seat of the judicial branch.

Government buildings, cafés, and small businesses crowded the district around it. One mile distant, facing the building, was the Assembly of Nobles where similar trade was conducted with considerably more pomp and ceremony, but only once a year.

Lights illuminated the architecture, slowly changing colors and sometimes revealing the shadows of men and women standing guard.

"We're very late," Patricia said.

"None of them needed to wait for us," Ron said, wishing he hadn't put his wife in this predicament. She shouldn't suffer for his own impertinence.

"Wouldn't that have been yet another dishonor?" Redion asked.

"Yes, but only once—to House Marlboro," Ron admitted. "By waiting for me, dozens of houses and forty-nine senators have lost honor. They won't be happy, no matter the validity of my reasons."

"If we're attending, then let's get it done," Patricia said.

Ron bowed slightly, allowed her to go first, then escorted her up the steps. Redion followed a few strides behind.

A few civilians were out, strolling through the park and tossing coins into buskers' guitar cases. The delicious smells of food carts filled the air. Whenever the Legislature or the Assembly was in session, the vendors stayed as late as possible.

At the top of the stairs, they faced a wide floor paved with an intricate mosaic of tiles, almost like a pixelated image of the Gildain crest. The symbol was so old that only dedicated historians understood its meaning.

To the stars and beyond.

Redion held up a hand for them to stop. "Do you know what these say? I am fluent in your language, as are all Zezner battle commanders, but I cannot read this."

"Only a few words make sense in Gildain," Ron said. "We must continue without delay. Come back later if you must, then ask one of the Legislature stewards to tell the story of this place."

He entered and looked down on the crowd of politicians, lords, security guards, and catering staff. "We're so late, they're cleaning up the meal."

"They're clearing away the desserts and drinks, husband," Patricia said. "Be on your best behavior. This may cost us dearly."

Silence swept through the room as they made their descent off the main stairway. Then it was across the speaking floor and back up toward their bench among the other great lords and ladies. Heads turned. Men and women whispered behind their hands.

Carl Peterson, the Prime Legislative Officer, banged his gavel, then announced their arrival. "Lord Uron Marlboro, Lady Patricia Wilson-Marlboro, and Redion Axst of the Zezner Empire."

"That is not precisely my name," Redion said with a bow.

Peterson ignored the alien, facing the assembled lords and members of the Legislature instead. "Now that the great hero has arrived, we can vote on the funding adjustment for the Blue Sun project."

Ron tensed. Patricia led the way to their bench but remained standing. Up to fifteen people could sit comfortably in their Legislature accommodations; it was called a bench, but it was more like a booth. There were grander versions among the great lords, but Ron and Patricia had selected theirs for its superior acoustics. It was easy to hear the PLO *and* the people around them.

That also meant people could eavesdrop on each other.

"I wish I had known this was the reason for the urgent meeting," Ron said.

"There is more to this," Patricia said. "When has the Legislature interrupted a triumphal parade to vote on a budget issue?"

Redion inclined his head. "I would like to know this, as well. I certainly do not have an answer, so the question must be for you, Duke Marlboro."

"Never change, Red," Ron said.

"Are you upset with me?" Redion asked.

"No, I'm not upset. The answer is never. Interrupting a triumphal parade is unheard of."

Prime Legislative Officer Carl Peterson continued, though he glanced significantly at Ron. "Are there further arguments in favor of suspending the funding for the BSA?"

Ron stepped forward. "Why would it be suspended after so many decades?"

"Perhaps if you had arrived earlier, you would have heard the opening arguments and the debate that followed," Peterson said. "There is no one to lead the expedition, and since it requires leaving Gildain, possibly forever, I can't think of a single lord of sufficient wealth, status, and other resources to effectively manage the project."

Murmurs went around the room. Side discussions and arguments broke out.

"They are trying to pin us in a corner," Patricia said. "What is going on, husband?"

"Political intrigue, as usual." Ron wished he knew more. Guessing at who orchestrated this particular insult, or why they chose a budgetary issue for the emergency meeting, would make him appear a fool. So for now, he would proceed cautiously. "We need better intelligence."

"True," Patricia said. "But what do we know right now, for certain? With that as a starting point, we can investigate further."

Ron's head ached. "Fact one: they are trying to provoke us."

"You, husband. They are trying to provoke you. I am not the one challenging men to duels in the garden."

"That was a long time ago, and it was to win a certain duchess of House Wilson's attention," Ron said. He scanned the room, thinking of Bull's warnings, wishing his gut wasn't telling him the situation was even worse than the treacherous minor lord guessed. "Fact two: our house is too powerful to remain this close to the king, and too weak to stand against all the allies he commands."

Color drained from Patricia's face, but she forced a smile for anyone who might be watching them... and was beautiful as always.

"Order!" Peterson shouted, then banged his PLO gavel on the edge of his bench. "We're all tired. Can someone please move for a vote?"

"I move that we suspend this discussion until the ladies and gentlemen of the Legislature, lords and common folk alike, are better rested," Duke Travis Bull said in his deep baritone voice.

"House Marlboro seconds the motion," Ron said immediately.

Lord Carl Peterson glared at him for several seconds. "The motion carries, but before we adjourn, let me congratulate the Lord and Lady of House Marlboro on their most excellent triumphal parade."

Together, Ron and Patricia got up and left the Rotunda of the Legislature with Redion striding proudly behind them. Mutters and complaints of their insult to the PLO crescendoed behind them.

———

FAR BELOW THE UNDERCITY, generations of fallen men and women were preserved in geothermal crypts. It was as though, even in death, they were in stasis, preserved for a god to pass judgment upon in ten thousand years. Ron knew he was tired because his mind waxed poetic.

There were no guards. He passed through three archways, each with unobtrusive bioscanners. What were the devices looking for? Who reviewed the data? Did he care any more today than during his previous visits?

The crypts were ancient. The caretakers were automatons and not big on conversation.

Walking the underground maze could take hours and was more peaceful than the parks or gardens above ground. Ron came here when he didn't want to be bothered.

King Gerard should have recognized both his leadership and his personal valor on the battlefield. Ceremonies, parades, and certificates held a fraction of the honor standing beside him on the day of victory would have brought.

Now Duke Adams of House Atana was the Grand Marshal of the king's peacetime armies. He would not only lead, but award production contracts, land annexations, and possess veto power over the creation of new houses.

Perhaps it was the right decision. House Marlboro would remain among the most powerful families on Gildain. Had he become the Grand Marshal… what king could trust anyone in control of so much?

I overestimated our support in the Legislature and the Assembly of Nobles. Understandable, but how did I miss a direct attack by Danestar and Bull?

And then the Legislature summons me on the day of my reluctantly granted Triumph?

This has gone from mere insult to a situation where my family might be in danger. Am I at war with a greater power? Against House Atana? House Spirit? Or even the king?

He reflected on the verbal alliance with House Bull—the soon-to-be House Bull Danestar. The only factor working in his favor was the sheer unbelievability of the arrangement. Marlboro had dismantled Danestar's fighting force and sent Bull running. No one needed to know that last detail was part of their agreement.

I've made a mess of things, Father, Ron thought, ruefully remembering his father and grandfather's quiet wisdom, wishing they were alive to offer advice.

His walk was almost complete. When he emerged from the crypts, he would take action and leave brooding behind.

Lost in thought, Ron approached the next corner, not realizing what was wrong with the scene until it was nearly too late. He stopped short. Normally the crypts were cool and dry; now the air hung heavy with jungle heat.

Numerical figures came to mind the moment he focused on his environment, something he'd always been able to do. He wasn't certain of the exact temperature, humidity, or barometric pressure, but he knew what it should be here and could estimate current conditions within a few degrees.

Was that because of his nanites as Doctor Stacks insinuated, or some other legacy of his birth? The Chief Medical Officer often blurred the lines between these issues just to get academic attention. The man loved to discuss tiny details that often bored Ron.

Stacks was well trained, intelligent, and loyal not just to House Marlboro but to Ron's actual family. He believed the doctor would stay with him if, maybe when, he lost everything. That meant something.

So many pieces were in motion.

He stopped, looking over his shoulder. "Who's there?"

"I am here, Lord Marlboro." The Zezner prisoner, Redion Axst, the one Captain Echo and the MHG were already calling Red Hot, answered. His alien voice sounded deep and rough, but some of the spoken vowels were like steel sliding over a whetstone. "Is it not right that I accompany you at this distance when you require solitude to contemplate your sins against the Zezner?"

"I gave you leave to retire to your quarters," Ron said, curious now despite himself. What did he know about their traditions? It had been so long since a Zezner was defeated that no one, including Ron, had remembered this tradition of servitude. How far did it go?

"You did, Lord Marlboro."

"Call me Duke Marlboro, or my duke. Or just duke."

"Are you not a lord?" Redion asked. "My tutors insisted on rigorous memorization of your quasi-artificial culture and caste system."

"Who are you calling quasi-artificial? Our ways are genuine, and definitely not a caste system," Ron said. "The Houses have existed since the dawn of Gildain."

"That long?" Redion asked, his tone suspiciously near what a human would call sarcasm.

"Even longer. And any man can rise higher than his birth."

"Yes," Redion said. "Of course. I apologize. You must understand, the Zezner are much longer lived and view these things differently. My question remains unanswered. Are you a lord?"

"I am a lord and a duke," Ron said. "The later conveys more power and prestige."

"So, this is what you desire, power and prestige?"

Ron sighed, weary of the discussion. "What do you want?"

"I am not allowed to say," Redion said. "Please do not inquire again."

"Next time you decide to come with me, ask and we'll go together. I don't like being followed."

"As you wish, near-human," Redion said.

Ron advanced on the alien, fiercely staring him down. "Another Zezner called me that."

"I imagine he is dead." Redion didn't seem perturbed by Ron's tone or close proximity. He was behaving very differently than he had during the triumphal parade.

Ron felt a vibration in his wrist, then twisted his arm enough to read the message.

Redion stood patiently, unperturbed at being ignored.

"What are the limits of your attachment to my house, my family?" Ron asked, not sure he could get rid of the conquered alien—which was bad, given the proximity of Travis Bull.

"I must serve until I die with honor," Redion said.

Footsteps approached, nimble and quick on nearby stairs, as though made by a man younger and more agile than Bull, but Ron knew it was him. The man had always been fit and energetic.

"I'm about to have a meeting," Ron said. "Give me privacy and speak of it to no one, not even my wife."

"Of course," Redion said, then moved toward a row of crypts, peering with interest at the power displays and sealed lids.

"Good that you waited for me," Bull said.

Suddenly, Ron was glad there was a witness, and one he could count on to remain silent. Travis Bull looked ready to fight—furtive and aggressive at the same time. It was an interesting combination that made Ron wonder if he wasn't about to be assassinated.

"The parade was a farce," Bull said.

Ron didn't take the bait. He didn't want sympathy from an enemy he'd been forced to accept as an ally.

"So that's how it's going to be?" Bull asked.

"Friendship wouldn't bring anything to our alliance," Ron said. "And I haven't forgotten the details of the attack."

"Necessary." Bull removed gloves and tucked them in his belt. "I worry it still isn't enough. If Gerard or his cronies realize we're a team, they will launch preemptive strikes, from open warfare to assassinations. You know I'm not wrong."

"What happens when my son kills your newly adopted son in a duel?" Ron asked.

"Make sure that doesn't happen," Bull said.

"Why are you here?" Ron asked.

"I want to know that you're committed. Because if you're having second thoughts, I'm going to volunteer to lead the Blue Sun Armada," Bull said. "Which you should do first, then sue for control of my fleet assets—basically forcing me to leave with you."

"You want to run?" Ron hadn't realized the extent of his new ally's desperation.

"We're talking about war with House Gerard," Bull said, stepping close and lowering his voice. "That alone is suicidal, but with Atana and Spirit, we only have one chance to survive."

Ron paced.

"You hadn't considered the BSA," Bull stated.

"Searching for the Ancient People of Earth is a juvenile daydream. The BSA isn't even close to being ready to disembark. If that is where our hopes lie, we're in serious trouble."

Bull laughed. "Oh, *we are*. I wouldn't have approached you if it were otherwise. You might call our predicament hopeless—fodder for historians in a hundred years."

"I know why the king is moving against me," Ron said. "What did you do to earn his ire?"

"We've been rivals since childhood. Fostered in families that hated each other," Bull said. "I've spent a lot of money keeping our vendetta secret. Who would loan me money or sign contracts with a house in continual conflict with the king?"

"What changed?"

Bull didn't answer.

Ron pressed the question. "Why now? What did you do that's forcing you to take so many risks?"

Bull's face grew dark. He narrowed his eyes and looked past Ron. "Just a feeling. Instinct. It's saved me before. And I dream too much."

Ron wanted to ask him about his dreams, because he wondered if he heard a strange human telling him to make the universe fit for expansion. He changed the topic instead.

"Marlboro is already recovered from the attack. Danestar has no military strength left. I allowed only bodyguards and a small defensive force to remain per the laws of house warfare."

"Danestar has publicly asked House Gerard, Atana, Spirit, and Redwine for sponsorship—up to and including an alliance by marriage," Bull said.

"But they were refused," Ron said, knowing the answer and seeing another layer of Bull's plan. It would work but was less clever than the man thought it was.

"Reginald Danestar just left House Bull. He begged for me to honor the betrothal of his daughter to Malcom Sky Bull, my officially adopted son." Travis Bull laughed gruffly. "I had him on for a bit, but we signed the paperwork. As soon as they are married, we will combine our resources and build a formidable fighting force. Much of my new wealth will be invested in ships —something you should be doing as well, but secretly."

"I'll take it under advisement."

Bull turned to leave but stopped. "Have there been any new attacks?"

"Not yet," Ron said.

"Good." Bull hesitated. "We're allies now. If Marlboro is attacked, Bull will stand with you even if we aren't ready."

Ron nodded, hating the situation. "And Marlboro will stand with Bull. Don't start a fight unless we must."

"Think about the Blue Sun Armada."

Ron glanced at Redion who stood facing him from a distance. "I will consider the cost versus potential gain."

"That's good enough. I'm sorry about Victor. He was always the most entertaining of your progeny. Your oldest has a stick up his ass."

"If you don't get along with Gregory, I suggest you stay away from him. Because he's worth ten of your best in a fight," Ron said. "And also avoid my daughter-in-law and grandchild when the day comes, because I don't think you understand the wrath of an angry mother."

Bull laughed. "I hate the sound of crying children—and their parents. You won't see me anywhere near a birthing room in this lifetime."

CHAPTER NINE

PATRICIA KNEW her husband was approaching before he swept into their living room. The premonition was almost a sixth sense, like they were linked in ways no one talked about. It also helped that the Marlboro House Guards kept tabs on them both. She used this information often. When he was away from the estate, it was more difficult, but she had people for that as well. Someone needed to protect him.

This morning he came striding into their suite dressed for something other than work in the mechanic's shops. Or at least she hoped he wasn't going to ruin his crisp and fashionable attire crawling underneath a mech chassis.

Her own outfit, due to the ample warning she had procured through her sources, complemented his appearance—and his hers.

"Are you taking me on a very special date?" Patricia studied Ron with the razor-sharp intensity only a wife could manage. Something was bothering him, and she imagined it had to do with the Bull Danestar alliance he was trying to manage solo.

Stop holding out on me, Uron.

"Who is the watch commander on duty for the house guard?" Ron asked as he paced back and forth, talking on his bio-comms, occasionally looking back to meet Patricia's gaze. Less secure than a combat channel or a mech or ship, the bio-comms were far more convenient, hands-free, and were linked with hers. "Please report at your earliest convenience. We will be traveling to the spaceport today, without an escort. I'll need to provide you our route in case something comes up."

Patricia strolled around the large room until she could see Redion Axst standing in the foyer, hands crossed just below his rib cage, slightly higher than looked comfortable. One of the Marlboro House Guards, Corporal Jamie Beard she thought, stood opposite the alien looking slightly embarrassed to be losing a staring contest with the Zezner.

Her new position placed her near enough to hear the voice on the other end of the comms if he switched to an external booster, which he didn't, unfortunately.

"Are you avoiding my question?" Patricia moved in slowly, out of view of the visitor's foyer, cutting off his route and demanding his attention with bedroom eyes. "Or maybe you're going to keep me in the bedchambers all afternoon."

That stopped him in his tracks. He was stammering for words when Lieutenant Carmichael appeared in the doorway, standing at attention in that formal but relaxed manner only the Marlboro House guards could execute properly.

"Lord Duke, how may I be of service?" Carmichael said. Today, for organizational reasons rather than fashion, the lieutenant wore a mostly red uniform with black accents to represent the colors of House Marlboro. Taller even than Ron, athletic, and handsome, his black hair was slightly too long, but no one said anything. Competence earned a man leniency in such matters—up to a point.

Patricia's husband acknowledged Carmichael respectfully, but retreated across the room toward the balcony to conduct a video call—something that couldn't be handled by his bioware, apparently. There'd been a lot of such communications of late.

He thought he was being clever, but she could read him like a program code.

"Lieutenant Carmichael," she said, "what the duke meant to request was a small escort in plain clothing, with a security overwatch. There's no need to discuss the details of the assignment with him. I'm sure you can manage and keep me updated. Do we understand each other?"

"Of course, lady," Carmichael said. "Patterson and Walkin are on the schedule and well-suited to nontraditional guard duty. I believe the pair of them should be sufficient for an escort. Overwatch Team Alpha is staged and ready as well. Will that be sufficient?"

She touched his shoulder. "That's perfect, Lieutenant."

He nodded and retreated from the room.

"Are you holding out on me, Lieutenant?" she asked.

The man's poker face was good, but she had everything on the line. Duke Uron Marlboro was not only the love of her life, but the protector of her family and all families aligned with or sworn to House Marlboro. With so much at stake, she wasn't about to back down.

Nothing could be left to chance. If that meant spying on her husband, so be it. If that meant guilt-tripping a young officer into spilling the beans, well, it had to happen.

She stood very close and faced the same direction he was, watching her husband, making it clear they were talking about the duke. "No one is a better warrior than my husband, but he's not wired for intrigue. I need information, Lieutenant Carmichael, to protect him and to serve the honor of our house."

He swallowed hard. "It might be nothing, ma'am, but I was wondering if he was talking to Lord Abnercon again."

"I see," she said. "Thank you. That is useful. I had thought Abnercon was done selling the Blue Sun expedition to my husband."

"They couldn't find a better person to lead the expedition than the duke, if you don't mind me saying," Carmichael said.

"Let's not bother him with our little conversation," Patricia said, smiling appreciatively.

"Of course," Carmichael said. "It isn't an officer's place to speculate on rumors."

She nodded. "Unless said officer is asking a direct question in service of the house, your secret is safe with me, Lieutenant."

Ron finished his call and returned to her, sighing and spreading his hands apologetically. "I'm sorry, love. Running our house feels more like managing an uncooperative corporation sometimes."

She gently patted the side of his face and kissed him without saying anything about Lord Abnercon. "But you do it so well. I think I'll keep you."

"Outstanding," he said. "I will alert the gossip news and send them some compromising pictures."

"Why are we going to the spaceport? Don't tell me your wanderlust is aiming you toward the stars again," she said.

"The way things are going, I think we should consider the expedition to Blue Sun. They'll need a strong house to lead it, and if the king values us so little, perhaps it's time to change history."

"I understand you, husband. But perhaps don't speak of that where people can overhear us," she said. Was this her husband talking, or the influence of Lord Abnercon? "I always enjoy an outing to the spaceport."

"You assume you're invited."

"I distinctly heard the pronoun 'we' in your conversation with Lieutenant Carmichael."

"I could've been talking about one of my many mistresses or a visit to the Duke's Club, which is near the spaceport, as you may recall."

She punched him in the gut, hard, not like a lady at all, but he was ready for it, taking it without complaint.

"Oomph!" he grunted, then attempted to act aloof. "You strike like a prizefighter."

She smiled sweetly. "Finally I get a compliment out of you." She headed for the door as though she didn't care whether or not he followed. "And I know you, Uron. If you were going anywhere, it would be to the machine shop or the gym."

"That's where you *think* I'm going," he teased. "Do you have problems like this with wives among the Zezner?"

"We spend one year with our betrothed, and then never speak to one another again," Redion said. "I have had forty-seven unions, each more successful than the last."

"Are you bragging, Red?" Patricia asked.

"Perhaps a little."

Ron stepped through the front door, strode across the sidewalk and onto the driveway with Patricia on his left and Redion following slightly behind. "Sounds like a pretty good system."

"You're full of it," Patricia said. "You'd be miserable without me. And probably forget to put on your pants in the morning."

"My mistresses would remind me," Ron said. "Mistresses, plural."

Patricia pursed her lips and gave him a mock kiss from arm's length. "You're so manly."

Patterson and Walkin waited at the car, causing her husband to frown slightly. "I distinctly remember saying we would drive ourselves."

"You took too long on the phone," she said. "I made other arrangements. Now get in before I have Patterson and Walkin report to Carmichael."

The drive to the spaceport was easy, though it took nearly an hour. Lorne was a large and sprawling place, with many green areas—parks, public gardens, and fountains.

Redion never stopped looking through the window, no matter what Ron or Patricia talked about.

A voice came through her bio-comm. "Overwatch Alpha for Wilson One, how copy?"

"Excellent," she said.

Ron pulled his attention back from the window to gaze at her. "Pardon?"

She patted his hand where it rested on her knee. "Nothing, dear."

Overwatch Alpha laughed pleasantly. "I'll keep the comm traffic to a minimum, Wilson One. We're maintaining a comfortable orbit and have eyes on your vehicle. No need to answer."

Neither Patricia nor Ron spoke as they neared the spaceport. It took up more land than the entire city but looked very different—more polished steel and concrete, less artwork, sculptures, and walking gardens. There were token attempts at landscaping, but anything near the many launch towers and raised loading platforms would be incinerated by a surface-to-orbit operation.

This wasn't done often, as most of the Gildain fleet was kept in orbit for obvious reasons of economy and resource management. Brute force blastoffs of the largest ships burned enormous amounts of fuel and filled the atmosphere with unwanted rocket exhaust.

With the Zezner War concluded and the chance of ships getting blown apart eliminated, there was talk of building a better and more permanent fleet—including the long talked about Blue Sun expedition.

The idea frightened her, but she knew it fascinated her husband. Maybe it would cause her less anxiety if she spent some time studying the history, or legends more like, of the distant star and its relationship to the people of Gildain.

A delegation—one naval commander and a young man wearing a fleet jumpsuit—met them at the entrance to the shipyard. The younger of the pair appeared to have crawled up from belowdecks, yet had a cheerful look on his smudged face.

Patricia greeted each of them as Ron stared distractedly at several poorly maintained ships. Patterson and Walkin hung back, watchful but careful not to draw attention to themselves.

Identical twins, the young men were two of the quietest soldiers serving the house.

"Is there a problem, Duke Marlboro?" the commander asked.

"Who are you?"

"Commander Heinrich Dale, as I said when you arrived." He looked Redion over, but said nothing.

"Remind me of the fleet rank structure. Does a commander outrank a captain?" Ron asked, steel in his words.

Patricia saw where this was heading but couldn't stop it.

"No, sir. Of course not," Commander Dale said.

"My visit didn't rate the attendance of a captain?" Ron asked.

"My apologies, Lord Marlboro. We are very short-staffed. I am the highest-ranking fleet officer at the spaceport today," Dale said.

"I see."

Patricia moved in. "We are surprised there are so few ships, and they seem half finished. Isn't this one of Lord Abnercon's pet projects? He certainly pesters the budget committee about it often enough."

Commander Dale nodded. "I've heard that, but commanders aren't generally invited to budget committees. All of our best ships are in orbit. We haven't had much of a budget during the Zezner Wars. Most of the fighting has been on Gildain."

Ron turned away. Patricia continued the conversation.

"Of course, Commander Dale. How hard will it be for us to tour the fleet that is in orbit?" she asked.

"No problem at all," Dale said. "We need two days' notice to perform safety checks on the shuttles and summon a captain of sufficient prestige to perform the tour."

Ron eyed him.

Patricia felt some of the same heat. "Be careful, Commander."

He bowed his head, then stood unrepentant. "The morale in

the fleet has suffered due to budgetary neglect and the constant delays. There would be a delegation in the Blue Sun system by now if not for the Legislature and the Assembly of Nobles dragging their feet."

"That may be changing, Commander," Ron said.

The man's posture transformed. He stood straighter, less defensive but far from smiling or inviting them to dinner. "Midshipman Isaac Sage is one of our engineers with an impressive curriculum vitae related to ship design—he obtained several civilian degrees and is largely hated by his peers in the fleet. Makes everyone look bad."

"Apologies, sir," Midshipman Sage said. "My commander consistently asks for my best; I endeavor to follow orders."

"*I'm* your commander," Dale said.

"Of course, sir," Sage said. "Very good."

"Mr. Sage will be your guide when you return for the orbital tour," Commander Dale said. "He will send you, or your staff, instructions to best prepare for the launch. You've no doubt made several, but leaving the atmosphere of Gildain should never be taken for granted."

"Our thanks," Patricia said.

Ron pulled his attention away from the midshipman, then offered to shake Commander Dale's hand, which the man accepted as appropriate between ranks and services, and a compliment coming from the duke of a major house.

Sometimes Patricia's husband made her so proud, she wondered what she'd ever done to deserve him. The moment was too good to let go. "Commander, could we borrow Sage for the afternoon and have a more detailed tour of the spaceport?"

"Of course," Dale said. "Please return him when you're done. As difficult as he can be, we have a lot invested in him."

"Of course," Patricia said, then faced Midshipman Sage. "Shall we?"

"What would you like to see first?" Sage asked. He too studied the Zezner but said nothing. Patricia wanted to believe this was out of respect for her husband, but it might have just been an awkward social situation no one knew how to handle.

"Basic infrastructure first," Ron said. "But not in great detail. I'm not interested in what remains behind, but in what is needed to get new ships launched and ready for an expedition."

Sage transformed immediately, his eyes showing a mischievous hunger for adventure Patricia knew her husband would respect. What was more interesting was Commander Dale. The man, several strides away by this point, looked back like he was seeing Ron and Patricia for the first time.

There had been a lot of intrigue since the final battle of the Zezner War, and she worried that she read too much into small details—but this was something. She pulled Ron close as they walked so she could whisper privately.

"What is it?" he asked.

"The fleet, and its people, have been neglected for a century," she said. "They may have been looking for someone like us."

"My thoughts exactly," Ron said. "This may be an opportunity. But only if we commit to Blue Sun." He paused. "There are risks."

"Agreed."

"Watch over me, wife. I need your help more than ever," he said. "I'm glad you tagged along."

"Because I'm saving your ass as usual?"

"Because you're gorgeous," he said. "And you look out for me."

She hugged him as they walked, then stepped aside to maintain a more publicly appropriate distance. Midshipman Sage gave them an excellent tour, causing her to wonder about Commander Dale's complaints.

"Your commander has a good sense of humor," she said, watching the young man carefully.

He smiled, then waved the comment politely away. "He is an outstanding officer, very observant. There are many people in the fleet who crave a return to glory. Others who wish to maintain an easy, predictable life that requires only reasonable efforts and sacrifices."

"What's wrong with that?" Ron asked, tone neutral.

"Nothing good comes from *reasonable* effort," Sage said.

Ron's eyes lit up. "I'm going to like this one."

Sage hesitated, then looked nervous. "May I show you something, Lord Duke Marlboro?"

"No need to be quite that formal, Sage," Ron said. "What do you have for me?"

"We could tour the hangars. Would you like to see the ships that will be launched if the BSA project moves forward?"

"Mr. Sage, that is exactly what I want," Ron said.

The young man looked questioningly at Redion. "What about the Zezner?"

"He's with me."

"Good enough. Let's take a motor cart."

Ron, Patricia, and Redion climbed into the vehicle and held on as Sage raced down access roads, then a ramp leading under the launch pad. Below the metal and concrete surface was another world—a place full of scaffolding, partially constructed ships, and teams of workers that spent half their time sipping coffee and gossiping rather than doing actual work.

"The lighting is inadequate," Patricia commented. "Could be a safety concern."

"We've brought that up more than once," Sage said. "I can also show solid numbers that prove better lighting, climate controls, and increased staffing levels will increase efficiency by double-digit percentage points."

"Keep those reports handy, Mr. Sage," Ron said.

"Duke Marlboro, you can call me Sage. Or anything you want, I suppose. But I'm not in your chain of command, and I like you and Lady Patricia more than any of the nobility I've met."

"Do you rub elbows with the nobility often?" Ron asked.

"More than you would think, Duke. They come, look around, then leave and never come back," Sage said. "You'll be back, though."

Ron chuckled. "You think so?"

"I could be wrong. But that doesn't happen often."

"I see." Ron turned his attention to the partially completed ships and detected an obvious theme—they were incomplete and collecting dust. There were also a lot of people getting paid for doing a whole lot of nothing.

The mood changed and they rode in silence for nearly an hour, barely speaking except when Ron or Patricia had specific questions. Sage looked uneasy when he returned them to the security area.

"Thanks, Sage," Ron said. "That was informative."

"Am I going to be wrong this time?" Sage asked, looking even younger than he was.

Ron didn't know how to answer, and Patricia didn't bail him out like she normally would.

Redion stepped forward. "I might be able to help with the ship designs, Mr. Sage. My people came a long way to fight for possession of Gildain."

"And lost," Sage said.

"Yes, we were defeated. But the fact remains, we have more experience with long voyages than you do at the moment," Redion said.

Ron stepped closer to the midshipman. "I'll be back, even if we decide not to commit to the project. Don't tell anyone what I'm considering. Do you understand why that might be important?"

Sage nodded. "I heard about the Danestar treachery. Are you going to consolidate their assets into House Marlboro?"

"That's a question for another time," Ron said. "Tell Commander Dale that we have concerns, but also interests in the BSA and the fleet in general."

Sage's face lit up.

"No promises," Ron said. "But even if I cannot invest directly in the Blue Sun expedition, I will advocate for the fleet and the shipyards the next time the Assembly of Nobles convenes."

"Very good, sir." When Midshipman Sage left them, he was in high spirits.

Patricia said nothing until they were alone except for Redion. "Concerns? Like the fact that this fleet couldn't leave the system if our lives depended on it."

"And they do," Ron murmured. "More than ever."

He settled into his seat and drank a bottle of water. "How much better are Zezner ships than ours?"

"Not much, if yours were in good repair and your people were practiced in their use," Redion said. "The final battles for Gildain were terrestrial. You had the advantage of fighting on your home soil."

"What if I had ships sufficient to transport my house, and allies, away from the planet. Could you help me keep them safe?"

"It would be my duty to do so," Redion said. "A word of warning, Duke Marlboro. Fleet actions will be horrifically costly in the beginning because you and your rivals will make deadly mistakes."

"The idea is not to have a fleet action," Patricia said. "We merely want to be prepared for the worst-case scenario. An attitude of strength may prevent needless violence."

Redion nodded. "Your words are wise, and I pray this strategy works."

CHAPTER TEN

RON LEANED BACK in the seat, unwilling to slouch but too exhausted to maintain a more alert and energetic posture. Patricia, on the other hand, was as erect and ladylike as ever. He smiled to think of her in battle, or other places. But that didn't make the day any shorter or his worries any less severe.

"Patterson, take us to the Elegant," Ron said.

"Coffee this late?" Patricia asked.

Redion made a nervous hiss. "I may not partake of coffee. My teachers warned me that it will make my head explode."

"Literally?" Ron and Patricia asked at the same time.

"I am unsure, but it is best not to tempt fate where the ballistic expansion of one's cranium is at stake."

Ron gripped his shoulder. "Of course. No coffee for you."

"Not that I don't appreciate this spontaneous trip to the Elegant," Patricia said, "but it is out of our way and it's late."

"I told you I had to meet someone."

"You better pray it isn't a mistress, Uron Marlboro," she warned.

Ron leaned conspiratorially close to Red. "When she uses my legal name, I'm generally in a lot of trouble."

"My thanks for the explanation. I thought she was affecting

formality for the sake of an apology," Redion said. "I will endeavor to remember this nuance."

Patricia crossed her arms and narrowed her gaze, bouncing her crossed leg in a steady rhythm.

"Who do you think we're going to see?" Ron asked. "I saw you talking to Lieutenant Carmichael."

Patricia made her most innocent face. "I'm sure I don't know what you mean."

He let it go. She didn't want to get the man in trouble, and it didn't matter. His Marlboro House Guards were supposed to know his habits. That's what made them good at their jobs.

They rode in silence to the Elegant, then stepped out onto the sidewalk of the fashionable district. More than a few people noticed them. Some pointed at Redion, then talked behind their hands. Scores of pictures were taken.

Ron opened the door for his wife and motioned for Redion to also enter, but the alien hung back.

"It is not right for me to enter before you, unless it is in combat, in which case it would be my duty," the Zezner said.

"Have it your way." Ron followed his wife, and his over-heated alien companion followed him. The café was busy, but not crowded. That was one of the things that made the establishment exclusive. There was no bouncer or security guard to be seen, but they were there, and they handled the flow of patrons expertly. Even now, a group was being upgraded to a private room to make space for Ron, Patricia, and the alien in the trendy patio section.

A man summoned them to his table, then motioned for them to sit. "Duke Marlboro, I'm glad you could make it. And it's an added bonus that you brought your wife and the Zezner guest of honor."

"That is not what I am, precisely," Redion said. "In fact, it is nearly the opposite of my condition."

Patricia held out her hand. "Lord Abnercon, I've heard so much about you."

"Have you? I hope it is reasonably scandalous," he said. "But I fear I live a boring, academic life when not embroiled in the fast-paced world of ship financing."

"I'm glad you brought that up," Ron said. "I've taken an interest in ships lately."

"Have you? At last, my persistent nagging has borne fruit," Abnercon said.

"You understand my reputation would be at stake. I need the newest, best vehicles available," Ron said. Patricia held his hand under the table and gave it a squeeze.

"I'm not sure who you spoke with at the spaceport, but I would like to give you a personalized tour. There are many older, but high-quality ships I can broker for you at a very reasonable price," Abnercon said, opening an ornately decorated data book.

"I'll have a look at those, Of course. But listen to me. I want new ships, the best available, including foundry ships that can build more during a long voyage," Ron said.

"That *is* ambitious. As wealthy as you are, such an investment must be underwritten by the Assembly of Nobles," Lord Abnercon, "and that could be a very delicate trick."

"Leave that to us," Patricia said.

Abnercon summoned a barista, greeting the young woman by name when she arrived with a digital server pad. "Heatherstar, I would like something special for my important guests."

"Of course, Abner. Perhaps a shot of highland scotch would bring the coffee around to your likening." She gave him a wink.

"It would. You are simply the best, as always."

She smiled at the old lord of finance and went to fill the order.

"You're a regular here," Patricia observed. "That one seems nice. She knows exactly what you want."

"She does a fine job, and I tip well."

"And she's carrying a pistol under her apron," Redion said. "Is that normal for a server of the food and drink?"

Ron laughed, once again glad for his new friend. "She's a security officer for Lord Abnercon. Normally, these types of arrangements aren't spoken of, even if observed."

"My apologies. I have erred," Redion said, head bowed.

Abnercon shifted uncomfortably. "I see that conversations may become unexpectedly forthright with your Zezner charge in attendance."

"You'll get used to him," Ron said. "How many foundries are in space dock?"

"I'll consult my records," Abnercon said.

Ron shook his head, lifting one hand slightly to forestall the finance lord's delay. "I'm not asking for specifics. Just how many exist and their approximate readiness."

Abnercon paused, staring at his barista security operative on her way back with a tray of drinks. "Three in reasonable, if outdated condition. Several more that might be better used for parts. And don't forget their crews. Skilled fleet personnel are not easy to come by. You might need to recruit from unlikely sources."

"Such as inoperable foundry ships or private companies," Ron suggested.

"Yes." Abnercon accepted his coffee, waited for the others, and spoke when Heatherstar had retreated. "You may even consider those with criminal records, if their skills are valuable enough."

Ron felt sick. He hadn't thought of that option and wanted to kick himself. Such a tactic might be necessary, and even useful in some instances, but it was also a true sign of desperation. What kind of expedition was he planning? What was he getting his family into?

CHAPTER ELEVEN

PATRICIA PUT her head on Ron's shoulder during the drive back and fell asleep. He looked through the window, watching the nightlife with detached fascination, and marked the changes from his youth.

The music seemed more upbeat, the crowds louder and more cheerful. He supposed that was a good thing, but it made him feel old. The martial tunes of his youth seemed more patriotic than what he heard now. These melodies were light and airy and had grown more popular as the victory over the aliens looked certain.

The power structure of Gildain was also changed.

Why else would I be considering the Blue Sun expedition?

His father and his grandfather were considered the greatest of the Marlboros line. All he'd ever wanted was to make them proud. Outshining them had seemed not only impossible, but dangerously arrogant.

Now, as his wife slept on his shoulder, and their alien companion meditated sitting straight up in his seat, Ron watched a city that suddenly seemed strange pass the windows of his private vehicle. The driver, Corporal Kenton Storm, respected his silence and drove with pride in his work. That was the House Marlboro way, from the duke to the humblest servant.

Several of the towering buildings flashed with neon lights and high-resolution video screens. He didn't recognize the video programs that were popular. Even some of the advertisements were for products he'd never heard of.

Patricia woke up as the car slowed.

"You ought to be in the infantry," he said.

She quirked an eyebrow at him. "Because I can sleep on command?"

"I'm just jealous. I wish I could."

"So do I, husband," she said. "Then you wouldn't wake me up in the middle of the night with your worrying."

Corporal Storm slowed but didn't stop yet. "We're here, my duke."

"Go ahead and park," Ron said. He looked at Redion.

"What now?" Patricia asked. "Are we ever going to return home?"

The words affected Ron strangely. He imagined himself thousands of light-years from Gildain, asking the same question. If she sensed his mood, she didn't show it. He quickly refocused his thoughts. This was supposed to be a fun surprise.

"Three hundred and ninety-three days ago, or nights rather, you brought me here and told me I couldn't beat the neighborhood champion at night boards," Ron said. He saw that she remembered instantly, her face lighting up with excitement. "Don't look so amazed that I remembered."

She turned to Redion to explain. "He didn't even know what night boards were. Thought it was a sporting event he could just dominate with his natural athleticism."

Redion leaned forward. "May I ask what this mysterious event is?"

"A strategy game, played on the board with sixty-four squares of opposite colors," Patricia said.

Ron smiled and let her enjoy the moment.

"When he learned it was the game of strategy and intellect, he again thought he could win," she said.

Redion looked confused. "Even my people know that he is very intelligent, and a master of strategy and tactics. Why wouldn't he assume he would emerge victorious in such a game?"

"It turned out to be much harder than I thought," Ron said. "Some people believe it is an ancient tool as old as humanity."

"Are we going to play, then?" she asked.

"Assuming there's anybody out tonight and up for a game," he said. "Tonight, I will redeem myself. I have been practicing in secret since that fateful night that you played the prank on me."

The three of them strode along the walking path while Patricia's bodyguards and airship overwatch kept a respectful distance. Ron saw these, of course, but said nothing. There were plenty of people out. The nightlife in Lorne was active in more places than just the bar district. Music drifted across the park. Trees and archways were brightly lit, and the city skyline was fantastic at the far edge of the green space.

Again, he watched some of the buildings outlined with brilliant lights and images. Civilian aircraft flew in their proper zones. Satellites winked in the upper stratosphere. His thoughts drifted to their tour of the spaceport, but he didn't allow his mind to dwell on those things now.

They reached a collection of picnic tables and gazebos. Men and women of almost all ages faced each other over small tables and battled each at the night boards.

"This appears to be a fascinating game. The first rank of pieces seem to be identical, and small, as though they might be cannon fodder," Redion observed.

"He's going to catch onto this game quickly," Patricia warned. "You better beat him while you can. In a year, he will probably thrash you."

Ron looked at his tall alien friend. "Do you see what I put up

99

with?"

"Yes, I do."

Ron and Patricia laughed.

"Come, I will teach you the game," Ron said.

They played for longer than he planned, and he learned that Patricia had been studying the game as well. The locals sometimes watched, sometimes challenged them, and always seemed friendly. He hated to leave all of this behind, even to explore the stars—and prevent a civil war.

Staring across the water during one of the quieter moments, he picked out a mural on a building depicting the ancient people of earth as most Gildainians imagined them. To Ron, the images resembled men and women he knew, which made it hard to believe they were from a civilization lost in the stars.

Just before it was time to leave, he made eye contact with his wife when she looked up during her final game with their Zezner ward. He didn't have to speak. She knew his heart, and he was probably especially transparent now. Happiness and contentment did that to a man.

The game ended, the three of them bid farewell to the night players and walked back to the cars with their security element trudging a safe distance behind.

"What was the purpose of this delightful excursion?" Redion asked.

"No reason. I thought it would be enjoyable," Ron said.

Redion frowned. "You say there is no reason, then provide one."

"Most people wouldn't consider it a good reason for a duke," Patricia offered by way of explanation.

"Who are those people? I will correct them," Redion said. "But until then, perhaps you will share the rest of your burden. Clearly, you have more on your mind than games."

Ron took his time, more certain of what he was about to say than ever. "I decided we will take command of the Blue Sun Armada."

CHAPTER TWELVE

RON HATED TO ADMIT IT, but Travis Bull was a better equestrian. The man had grown up on horseback. Even now, he spent most of his time on his country estates and ranches exercising his horses. Ron visited Elondale, House Bull's central property, often to assess assets and equity for reparations to be paid to House Marlboro for Bull's part in the failed house war.

Or that's what they told everyone.

Travis Bull did pay monthly installments awarded in the lawsuit, because a royal audit was definitely coming, and they didn't want to draw attention to their true purpose. If it was learned House Bull had only been pretending to transfer the funds, everything came apart. Their alliance would be revealed. House Gerard would crush them swiftly.

The riding trail twisted upward. Ron adjusted his position in the saddle to avoid an embarrassing fall. He'd learned to hold the reins gently in his left hand and keep his right hand free for emergencies, or like in the old days, to use a weapon.

Bull, astride a great bay stallion, waited for him at the top.

"This must be our last strategy meeting for a while," Ron said. "Hannah is due any day now."

"I'd say she's overdue," Bull said.

Ron thought about the false alarm during the triumphal parade. That would've made the birth early, but not dangerously so. A month later, he was anxious to see the child born on or near the due date.

"This is my favorite location for espionage," Ron said. They had several covert meeting protocols. Coming out here could be done often, and he enjoyed it a lot more than the dockyard inspections of ships half built. This was more like a vacation than plotting against the king.

But that wasn't what they were doing, of course. No one could survive direct treason. There was no place far enough from Lorne to run. Ron and Bull were preparing to defend themselves, nothing more. In a perfect world, they would outmaneuver their rivals and slip away before a real house war could erupt.

"Leaving this place behind will be like cutting out my own soul," Bull said. "But if I stay, I'll see war tear it apart. We need to build the fleet faster."

"Agreed. And it must be the best fleet. Because once we leave, these will be the only ships we have, possibly ever again," Ron said.

"You're putting your money into research and development at a time when you should be buying anything that can navigate the stars. I would take old, tested, and reliable over new and experimental."

Ron didn't disagree, but he'd made his decision. "It's a delicate balance. I've had my engineers opt for the simplest designs when possible. But we must be able to sustain an entire civilization on these ships. That means foundries, resource miners, and the means to protect them from unknown threats."

"I don't disagree with you, Ron," Bull said. "Just think you should focus on our timeline. We should've already been gone."

The two men sat astride their horses on the ridgeline overlooking the rolling green meadows of Elondale. For a moment, Ron was envious. He imagined his family stretched across this part of the continent, each manor house barely within view of one another, each of his children lords and ladies in their own right, with complete autonomy apart from the court politics that ran so rampant in the capital.

"It's breathtaking, isn't it?" Bull asked.

"It is, sir," Ron said. He felt an unusual degree of solidarity with this man born of another class but who was cut from the same cloth as he. A man too stubborn to completely bend the knee to the rightful monarch of Gildain.

"I have not been able to inspect the production lines with the spaceports as much as I would like," Bull said, finally getting to the purpose for this meeting. "I must rely on you for that. And, if this is the case, we must be on the same page."

Ron nodded. "Then perhaps you should default to my opinion, since I have the best firsthand knowledge of what is available."

"You make a good point, Marlboro. But I'm not ready to concede it."

There were other aspects of the secret alliance he needed to discuss but didn't want to. The marriage of Bull's adopted son to Penelope Danestar was foremost among his concerns. Victor hadn't forgotten his affection for the young woman. In fact, Ron thought it was growing more intense. No prize was more enticing than one that was out of reach.

Travis Bull didn't care about the delicate sensibilities of young couples in love, so he spared Ron the indignity of discussing it. Only one of them had biological children to consider. Instead of talking, they walked their horses forward, closer to a trail where they might ride at a more vigorous pace.

High above, floating like ghosts in the clear blue sky, were the outlines of several space stations. He couldn't see the ships moving to and from them but knew they were busy. Since the end of the Zezner War, all forms of trade and industry had spiked. There was even talk of returning to the asteroid belts where there had once been legendary mining facilities.

The horses cantered to a stop on Bull's front lawn, between the manor house in the stables. As soon as they stepped down from their mounts, grooms hurried forward to take the animals.

"I've had an idea," Ron said.

"Heavens help us," Bull said, walking in step with Ron toward the house.

"Perhaps we can compromise. Some of the fleet must be industrial, and those vessels might require fewer bells and whistles."

Bull canted his head, his expression doubtful. "I wouldn't be too quick to say that. Industrial ships can fail and kill their crews, just like anything else in the void."

"Agreed," Ron said. "But you won't need weapons and shields, not the type for battle, anyway. And their crews will be slightly less diverse in terms of their duties."

"I'll concede that point as long as we agree not to underestimate the complexity of the ships, equipment, and skill sets needed to build vessels during a long voyage, not to mention planetary exploration."

"Well said. We're closer to agreeing than you realize, which is refreshing."

Ron waited until they were inside. The foyer was massive, with high ceilings and wide, expansive floors decorated with tiles much like those of the Legislature rotunda and the great house of the Assembly of Lords. He was curious how long the dwelling had been in the family, because while the mansion was robust and elegant, it did not align with modern fashions—and that was an important status symbol for great and minor houses alike.

"So what's your idea?" Bull asked.

"Asteroids. Mine the asteroid belt," Ron said.

Bull laughed. "Next thing you know you'll be looking to recover the lost fleet of the *Exactas Meridias*."

"The *Exactas Meridias* isn't real?" Ron asked with a laugh as he accepted refreshments from the house staff, who were friendly and courteous. Everything seemed to taste better on this country estate. Perhaps if they found a new home world, he would try a similar living arrangement.

They spent the afternoon drinking tea with a splash of scotch and worked out details—the supply lines to be constructed, agreements and contracts to be honored, and what tactics they would employ to keep their secret alliance from being discovered.

"You have a large and excellent staff here," Ron said.

"Don't worry," Bull said. "They're loyal, and I have people to watch my people. You should know by now that I'm not a fool who takes chances."

CHAPTER THIRTEEN

WHEN RON FINALLY LEFT, he was satisfied with the arrangement but exhausted. He rested in the back of the official House Marlboro car and ignored all the speed violations his best driver, Corporal Kenton Storm, committed. There were few vehicles on the road today, just as he'd planned. Less traffic meant less attention. Anyone trying to follow them would be easy to spot.

And even if a rival attempted surveillance, he had an excuse for being there. In fact, it was a scheduled meeting available for public scrutiny—if someone knew where to search for the bureaucratic paperwork that House Bull and House Danestar were required to sign as part of their loss in the house war.

His wrist band chimed. When he looked, the name read *Stacks*.

"What is it, Doctor? Has Hannah gone into labor?" Ron asked over his bio-comm, then activated a video screen in the back of his driver's seat.

"No, Lord Duke. There's been an accident. Vehicle crash. The duchess was involved. They're rushing her to the hospital now," Stacks said. His tiny image appeared stiff, which meant the man was worried about Ron's reaction.

"How bad, Doctor?"

"She is in serious condition, but it's too soon to tell. A broken leg at least," Stacks answered. "Please don't make me speculate while you are still en route."

"As always, Dr. Stacks, you're thinking of my family's best interest." What Ron said and how he felt were at odds. Self-control was important for a leader, something Patricia had told him often. His face flushed red. He clenched his jaw before saying anything else.

Dr. Stacks signed off, but Ron barely heard him. His driver Storm changed course immediately and picked up speed, pushing beyond the legal limit but not dangerously so.

"Thanks, Storm."

"No problem, Duke. I'd fly across the city if this thing could take wing."

Ron laughed despite himself. "Make sure you let me in on that patent if you unravel that kind of technology. I'll get Marcos Dillinger to integrate it with our mechs."

The car raced along the highway, its speed edging ever upward. Storm drove in the far left lane with red and blue lights flashing in the grill and bumper. Other motorists wouldn't know exactly who he was, but they would understand this was an official car.

Ron watched the city rush by. The Cherry Blossom District was several miles on the other side of the urban sprawl. He could see each of the great houses that kept their residences in Lorne and wondered if they were all plotting against his family.

The thought sickened him, because that's not where he normally directed his mental energy. It wasn't like him. Somehow, he thought the world would be a better place after the Zezner invasions were put to a stop.

The House Atana training grounds came into view. A few months ago, he would have delighted in the spectacle even though their mechs were inferior to Marlboros. Most of the Atana models were bulkier than necessary—like they wanted to appear intimidating. Tanks and specialized infantry units were Atana's main strength. But even Atana mechs were glorious to see in action.

The highway curved around the northwest section of the Atana training grounds, hundreds of acres of open space that included storage bunkers, access roads, runways, and… a launch facility under construction.

Ron had heard the rumors. Every major house was expected to build and maintain a launch facility to support King Gerard's defense fleet. But most dragged their feet, an easy thing to do during decades of war on Gildain. Resources had been needed to support the ground war—not flights of fancy.

If the people of Gildain could have stopped the Zezner from coming to the planet, they would have done so a long time ago. Space superiority had always been an unattainable dream.

He wasn't sure how he felt about this revelation. House Atana was actually building ships. If their vessels were anything like their mechs and tanks, they would be over-armored and slow, but they might also be first into void service.

Ron's private efforts had barely begun due to the need for secrecy. The ships he had assembled—begged, borrowed, stolen, and built from scraps—could do little more than navigate away from the planet at this point. His hopes were pinned on the Blue Sun Armada—which he still had to be selected to lead.

The trick there was to appear as though he didn't want the job.

"Lord Duke, there's trouble at the ATG," Corporal Kenton Storm said.

Ron shifted his attention to a nearer section of the Atana Training Grounds and sat straighter. A mech had slid into the statutorily required water barrier separating the ATG from the public roadways. There was also an earthen berm and a hundred meters of open field.

"I'm not sure the rescue crew knows what to do, Duke,"

Storm said. "I will of course continue to the hospital as planned."

"You will do no such thing. Drive to the mech crash. I will handle the consequences of damaging the highway retaining wall," Ron said, hand already on the door to open it.

"Yes, Lord Duke," Kenton Storm said.

The Marlboro official car slammed through the chain-link fence, careened over a concrete retaining barrier, and sped toward the water's edge while emergency crews moved ineffectually to attach tow lines to the sunken mech.

Ron jumped from the vehicle, his door swinging wide as Storm parked so abruptly the suspension complained with a groan. Ron scanned the terrain sloping toward the water. Bubbles streamed up from the back, indicating that it was losing internal atmosphere. That had to be from damage or operator error. He wouldn't expect a Marlboro pilot to panic, but Atana trained their people differently.

Storm bailed from the car and ran to catch up. "What do you need me to do, Lord Duke?"

"Stop calling me Lord Duke. We need to move quickly," Ron said, then waved his arms to get the attention of the site supervisor across the water. It was about fifty meters. The man didn't notice him immediately. "Poor situational awareness," Ron muttered.

"Why aren't they sending divers or drones to assess the problem?" Storm asked.

"I was wondering the same thing." Ron moved along the shore, finally catching the site supervisor's attention.

"Lord Marlboro, what are you doing here?" the supervisor shouted through cupped hands.

Ron shouted back, "Do you still have a pilot trapped in that mech?"

"Yes!"

"Does the escape hatch use a standard safety code?"

The man hesitated. Each house was required to have standard safety codes for this type of situation, but many commanders restricted access for perceived security threats. Ron didn't understand this, because none of his people would want to steal an Atana mech. What would be the point?

"Yes, it should be the standard safety release sequence," the man shouted back but didn't sound confident.

Ron stripped out of his shirt and handed it to Storm.

"I'll go, Duke."

"No offense, Storm, but I'm a stronger swimmer than you are. The weight of that mech will drive it into the muck at the bottom, putting it several meters deeper than that salvage crew on the other side realizes," Ron said. "Hold my pants."

Wearing nothing but his skivvies, Ron dove into the water, shocked by how cold it was. He should've expected the frigid temperature, but things were happening fast like they always did in a life-or-death crisis. Stroking for the bottom, Ron pushed everything out of his mind. There was no time for thoughts of betrayal, or aliens, or even Patricia's injuries. His imagination resisted, however. Was this an accident, or had someone sunk the mech on purpose? And to what purpose?

He kicked with his legs and speared his arms through the water ahead of him, then struck forward in smooth, powerful motions. He barely saw the mech in the murky water. Bubbles streamed up from the back where there were several mechanical systems that shouldn't be leaking air. That was a problem, but what was worse was the fact that no bubbles came from the pilot's cockpit.

The man had either attempted to open it prematurely and vented all of his atmo or his preparation crew hadn't secured the hatch properly. Either way, the pilot was a goner.

Ron grabbed the front view shield and peered inside. The man, it turned out, was a young woman. She'd done everything right, except her safety harness had failed to release. To his surprise, she was still conscious, still holding her breath, her eyes pleading for help.

She hadn't completely lost her cool, but panic was on the way. When it arrived, it would be a party. She'd nearly reached the limit of her endurance, holding the one last breath that had kept her conscious this long.

He swam to the back, searched the control panel, and popped it open. His lungs burned. Holding his breath was one thing; holding it while swimming aggressively and trying to figure out a complex problem was another thing entirely. As soon as he could, he punched in the code from memory.

It didn't work.

By the stars!

He punched in a universal override that only the leader of a house could possess. It was supposed to work on everything but royal vehicles. He would have to make a full report as to why he used the code, but this would be easy to justify.

When the hatch unsealed, it still refused to open because of the water pressure. Grimacing as he jammed his fingers into the small gap, he wedged it wider, bit by bit, only able to get it done because the interior was also full of water. Instead of being impossible, the exercise was only difficult. He swam inside, irrationally worried that the lid would close and trap him with the young victim.

She lost the last of her air as she struggled again and again to get the safety harness to unlatch. Her violent thrashing forced him back, just for a moment, and he thought he could hear her last scream.

Frustration competed with his other miseries. This was a simple skill that any pilot should have mastered before they took their first steps in a mech.

Assuming the straps weren't defective or damaged.

He pushed her limp hands away and went to work, but the straps wouldn't release for him either, and he didn't have a knife.

Red spots pulsed in his vision. He was running out of oxygen and the young woman was unconscious.

He searched the cockpit for tools, thankfully finding a locker that opened with a latch rather than some sort of security code. Nanites tingled in his bloodstream, maximizing the efficiency of his cardiovascular system—not a bad sensation, until he pushed too far and started to pass out.

Shadows flickered above him. Rescue divers had finally arrived and were attempting to manipulate the hatch, trying to widen the opening, but they worked against each other. When the mech sank deeper, they bumped the hatch shut. The water-muted *thunk* of the latch sinking into place sounded like a death knell.

Trapped. He was trapped.

From the inside, he couldn't push it open. One diver pulled it, while another attempted to work the emergency gearbox. The way he was positioned blocked the other diver's effort and vice versa. He wanted to scream at the incompetent fools but couldn't.

Out in the murky water, another shape emerged.

Storm.

He appeared nearly as desperate as Ron and the now unconscious mech pilot, but that didn't keep the Marlboro corporal from taking effective action. Ron's driver shouldered the two divers out of the way, grabbed the edge of the hatch and yanked it up by brute force. Veins bulged in his neck, shoulders, and arms. Ron waved and pointed. Storm was pulling at a bad angle. To the man's credit, he adjusted, and soon had the hatch open.

Somehow Ron popped the safety harness, and dragged the pilot toward the surface, swimming for all he was worth.

The divers stayed below, possibly attempting to salvage damaged equipment before it was waterlogged. Mechanized Electro-Nuclear Combat Hulks could stay submerged for a long time if their air supply wasn't compromised, provided they had sufficient oxygen on board for the mission and they didn't take water into their electronic components. Ron made a mental note to make sure the interior of his Marlboro mechs were as water-resistant as possible, just in case.

Limbs trembling with exhaustion, he crawled onto the muddy shore, vomiting water and forcing himself to his knees. Looking up, he realized he was on the Atana side of the waterway. And that was good, mostly. This was where the medical teams were. But it also put him in his enemy's territory, although no outright war had yet been declared between them.

Paramedics began abdominal compressions on the pilot and soon had her puking out water. Ron looked to the shore and saw Kenton Storm bursting from the surface, water spraying everywhere, and profanity following shortly thereafter. Eventually, the rescue divers emerged and mingled with other members of the House Atana emergency response team. None of them showed their faces to Ron.

"That was a disaster," Ron grumbled.

Storm plopped down beside him. "Sorry I dropped your shirt and pants in the mud over there."

Ron just laughed.

The site supervisor marched forward, pointing an angry finger. "I had this under control!"

Corporal Kenton Storm jumped to his feet, shoving the man backward. "You're talking to Duke Uron Marlboro of House Marlboro! Watch yourself."

"Oh, yes. Of course. I'm sorry. My apologies," the site supervisor said as everyone looked on in confusion.

Ron ignored the confrontation and went to the ambulance gurney where the pilot now sat, bleary-eyed and miserable but alive.

She looked up. "I was saved by a Marlboro." Her words dripped with disdain.

"Sad, but true. I've been saved from Zezner swarms many times by your comrades in House Atana, so let's just call it even," Ron said, attempting to set her at ease. It was an exaggeration, but seemed like the diplomatic thing to say.

He faced the crowd of chagrined onlookers, including the site supervisor. "Well, this has been fun, but I will require clothing for myself and my driver so that I can go to the hospital and check on my wife."

No one moved, possibly because this was a more difficult request than it seemed, or maybe they didn't have the imagination to deal with the rapidly changing situation.

Ron held up one hand. "Never mind, we swam over here. Getting back to my car should be simple by comparison. Good day to you all."

He dove into the water and free-styled his way back to his wet clothing on the banks of the freeway side of the waterway. Once he pulled up his pants and tugged his shirt down over his head, he spent a final moment considering the scene across from him. Men and women worked frantically to prevent the expensive battle mech from sinking farther. On the periphery of the operation, one of the rescue divers stared balefully at Ron.

"Do you think that man tried to kill you down there?" Storm asked, handing Ron his shoes.

"Perhaps," Ron said, turning away and striding toward the car. "Or maybe his incompetence makes him bitter."

In the back seat, Ron sat in his wet clothing and pondered the disaster as his equally soaked driver maneuvered through the midday traffic rush.

CHAPTER FOURTEEN

RON DIDN'T WAIT for Storm to open the door to the Official Marlboro Car. He stepped out at nearly the same time his driver was popping out on his side. "Take it home and get cleaned up. Bring me a new suit if it's not too much trouble."

"Of course, Duke. Please give Gregory and Hannah my best and remind them it wouldn't be wrong to name the child after a limousine driver."

"I will relay the advice and throw in what a strong swimmer you are," Ron said.

They exchanged salutes and Ron rushed into the hospital. A group of doctors, anesthesiologists, and nurses gathered near one room, reminding him of an infantry squad getting ready to storm an enemy trench. Once their plan was in order, they entered, ready to do battle.

Ron wondered what emergency required such a large team, but didn't have time to linger and find out. He'd often visited injured soldiers and their families here. He knew his way around. Right now he needed to find Patricia before the voice in his head started whispering.

She'd be okay. It was just an accident. Just like the Atana

mech submersion had been an accident and the rescue divers had inadvertently shut Ron in the cockpit without air.

Exactly like that, because who would want to hurt the leaders of House Marlboro?

"Duke Marlboro?" a vaguely familiar voice asked.

"Bridget Reach, right? CNP?"

"You remember me," the woman said. "I'd always heard that about you. Remembers people."

"How can I help you, Bridget? Or maybe you can help me. My wife is around here somewhere—car accident."

"Oh, no. I'm not here for that. Hannah just went into labor. Isn't that why you came?"

"No, it isn't." Ron struggled to catch up. Something else was happening here.

"You wouldn't be, I suppose, since we're still trying to get a hold of her husband," Bridget said. "Let me locate your wife's room so I can send you word in the event there is an emergency."

In the next hallway, two patients were brought in from the ambulance bay and quickly surrounded by emergency room personnel.

Accelerator gun wounds, Ron realized.

The paramedics had taken the time to put on a neck brace. He couldn't say that was wrong, but blood loss seemed more likely to kill the young man. The red fluid was everywhere.

What is happening to Lorne?

"This way, Lord Marlboro." Bridget led him through a set of double doors right as several people came the other way.

"Why is it so busy today?" he asked.

Bridget narrowed her gaze. "We've been busy since you defeated the Zezner. Or didn't you know? I don't know why there is so much unrest and drunkenness this long after the victory celebrations."

Ron wasn't sure what she was talking about. He'd only been to the hospital once since the war ended, and that was for

Hannah's false alarm. He'd assumed everything would go back to normal for most people with the war over. The brief house war between Marlboro, Danestar, and Bull hadn't created many casualties. There had been some that first day, but with no additional battles, it amounted to little more than a skirmish. Barely a news item compared to celebrity scandals and impending elections.

The people of Gildain were used to war and politics. Regular life was much more novel to them, he imagined. He made a note to spend some time in the city talking to people, just to get a feel for society beyond his area of influence.

"My apologies, I've been distracted by business," Ron said rather lamely.

"At first, things were slow. But people are bored and behaving badly. Crime has actually gone up since the war ended, and we see more and more accidents coming in. Today, to be honest, we're much busier than normal." She looked down at her personal comm device, apparently reading a news alert. She didn't have bio-comms. "There was an accident at the House Atana training field. Sorry, I was checking to see if we're going to get even busier, but it seems the injuries were not critical there."

Ron kept his comments to himself.

They walked quickly to the intersection, then turned right. He memorized every corridor and doorway to the best of his ability, a habit from too many close fights with Zezner raiders. Was it ridiculous that he knew the best way to advance or retreat if there was a shoot-out in the hallways of the Lorne Medical Center, East Campus?

"Do you want to go into the maternity ward, or continue to check on your wife?"

"How far to my wife's room?" He was worried. If she'd been in an accident and not badly hurt, he would expect to find her in the lobby perhaps, or maybe in one of the emergency rooms almost ready for discharge.

"Not far, if you know the way. But I can't take you there now. I need to attend to Hannah," Bridget said.

Ron wished he had one of his soldiers to send to Patricia's room with a message, or a LMC staffer, but everyone in the hospital had their own jobs to do. They didn't need to babysit a worried duke. "Take me to see my daughter-in-law, if you would."

He sent a text message to Gregory asking him where he was and telling him to hurry up. Bridget escorted him into Hannah's room. He went through decontamination protocols that had become standard several years before, and stepped into the observation area.

"One moment, while I check to see if she wants to admit you into her suite," Bridget said.

"Of course." Ron checked his bio-comm, finding no messages or alerts.

Bridget looked back, unsure. "I expected you to be indignant, and to demand to see her at once."

"You should remember from our last contact that I'm not like that."

She furrowed her brow like she wanted to say something else, but turned and went through the door.

Gregory didn't respond to his message. He was about to call Victor or Fortune when Bridget waved him inside.

There were two nurses, a security guard, and another man he thought was a doctor. The obstetrician made introductions, confirming his assumptions.

"Uron," Hannah said, opening her arms for a hug.

He immediately obliged her, then stood beside her bed. One look at the instrumentation and the assembled staff told him they were ready to go. "Call me Ron, daughter. I told you before."

"Okay, I'll try to remember. Did you get ahold of Gregory?"

"He's on his way," Ron lied. He didn't want to tell the woman her husband was missing in action right now.

120

Hannah was hugely pregnant, and gorgeous. Her dark skin glowed with vitality and the light in her eyes spoke of confidence. She was, he remembered, keenly intelligent—which was the trait that had drawn Gregory to her. His son was strong as an ox but also quick and nimble as a cat. But what truly separated him from other mech commanders was his exquisite intellect. Exquisite—as in nuanced, delicate, and beautiful—not at all the bruiser he appeared to be.

Hannah was the only woman Ron had ever met to match or exceed his eldest son in natural gifts, even if she was from a house known more for its mercantile abilities than war.

"There is something you are not telling me, *father*," she said, then raised one eyebrow. "You asked me to call you that after I married your son. Will you lie to me as I'm giving birth to your grandson?"

"Patricia had a slight accident—"

Pain flashed through Hannah's expression and she cried out, surprising the medical staff.

Ron had witnessed numerous births, but had seen nothing like this. The raw misery and terror in Hannah's face refused to end. He pointed the doctor. "You! Get a surgical team ready."

The man just gaped.

Ron locked eyes with Bridget. "Take charge, Bridget."

"Of course," she said. "Now get out and kindly inform the charge nurse at the end of the hallway to prep a surgical team and nanite support package."

Ron sprinted into the hallway, dodging around medical staff headed elsewhere, reaching the desk as though he had been teleported there. "Nurse Bridget Reach, CNP ordered a surgical team for Hannah Marlboro's suite and a nanite support package."

"Only a doctor can authorize that, Lord Marlboro."

"Then consider me a doctor!"

In every direction, up and down the hallway and into some of the rooms, faces turned his direction, staring at him wide-eyed. A few seconds later, the largest medical team in the history of childbirth was surging toward his daughter-in-law's room. Groups of doctors and nurses, specialists pushing machines, and other professionals he didn't recognize, rushed by him.

He took a cleansing breath, pretending he was calming himself during a battle, and faced the charge nurse he'd shouted at. "I find myself in an awkward position."

She glared. "And what is that?"

"I've treated you poorly, and must ask a favor. First, I must apologize for shouting."

The woman shifted, checked something on her work terminal, then blinked in surprise. "You're apologizing to me? You're a duke. Of a large house."

"That is no excuse." Ron looked down the hall, not sure which way to go—back to Hannah's room or in search of his wife? "It won't happen again."

"Apology accepted. What can I do for you?"

"I need to find my wife. She was in a car accident."

"There have been several car accidents," the charge nurse said. "One moment. Oh, no. That was a bad one. You can't find her because she came in on the auxiliary campus due to the number of people involved. Security has... had trouble with the Duchess of Wilson-Marlboro, I'm afraid."

"What does that mean? Where is she?"

Ron was getting worried, and couldn't stop looking toward Hannah's room. There were a lot of people inside, and more outside her door—an entire team of what appeared to be senior doctors.

A commotion came from the other end of the hallway. An angry high-pitched shouting. Duchess Patricia Wilson-Marlboro was giving some poor security supervisor hell.

"That would be my delicate flower," Ron said, causing the charge nurse to laugh.

He strode toward the commotion and found Patricia driving

a small uniwheel down the center of the hallway. "You can't drive that thing in here."

"How else am I going to see my daughter-in-law with this broken leg, Duke Uron Marlboro?" Patricia snapped.

Ron looked to the security supervisor. "Where did she get that?"

"Sir, I mean, Lord Duke, the lady requisitioned it from one of my guards," the man said.

"Is the guard okay?" Ron asked, holding back a laugh.

"He'll recover."

"Move aside, Ron," Patricia said, then steered past him. "What are all of these doctors doing? I need to see Hannah."

Ron took hold of her arm. "Something is wrong with the pregnancy."

"What do you mean? Tell me everything."

Ron got the supervisor's attention and pointed toward a room. "Is there somewhere we can talk in private?"

"There is a lounge for family members. I will clear it out."

"Thank you," Ron said.

"What the hell is happening to us, Ron?" Patricia demanded as he helped her from the uniwheel into a regular wheelchair.

He wasn't sure where to start.

"Why do you smell like a drainage canal? And why are your clothes wet?" she asked.

"It's been an eventful day. I'll explain all of that once we find Gregory and get him here."

"I thought he was with you?" Patricia looked worried.

"Get situated here and talk to the doctors when they come in. Bridget Reach... you remember the nurse from the false alarm after the parade?"

"Yes, of course."

"She's with Hannah now. She's been very helpful." Ron pulled out his comm.

"I'll talk to her."

"I'm going outside for better reception. If Gregory doesn't

answer, I'll send the MHG to search for him." Ron left feeling more tired than he had in weeks.

The parking lot was busy. He saw people from every walk of life and wondered what crisis had brought them here. He called Gregory three times. On the third attempt, his son finally answered.

"I'm here."

"Where the hell have you been and what do you mean, here? At the hospital or on the call?" Ron paced back and forth.

"Coming across the parking lot now," Gregory said. "I see you."

Ron scanned the area until he spotted his son striding toward him with a pair of bodyguards flanking him. "Don't tell me you were in an accident too. Where is your vehicle?"

"Accident?" Gregory asked.

"Your mother was in a car wreck and I stopped to save an Atana mech pilot from drowning during a training accident. But forget that. We need to get to Hannah."

Gregory grabbed his arm hard. "What's wrong?"

Ron reversed the grip and guided the bigger man toward the hospital entrance. "None of the doctors have stopped long enough to explain. She was in pain, so I ordered a more robust medical team."

Gregory relaxed but continued to move quickly. "Labor is painful, last I heard. You should know that."

"I never saw Hannah make that particular expression. She looked scared," Ron said.

This made Gregory nervous. "That's not like her." He strode ahead of Ron, taking charge just as Ron hoped he would, not because he was the eldest son of House Marlboro, but because he was Hannah's husband and now a father.

Ron quickened his pace to catch up. "Gregory."

His son stopped, listening but impatient to get moving again.

"Where were you?"

Gregory hesitated, unreadable emotions crossing his expression. "Some of my men were attacked. Lorne police say it was random. Bumping and shoving getting off the subway, but it got ugly. They were outnumbered and hurt badly. I had them taken to our field medics instead of LMC, due to reports of higher-than-normal caseloads here."

Ron fell behind as his son marched into the hospital. He typed on his forearm, sending text messages via bio-comms to Victor, Fortune, and even Peps—then to each of his commanders.

Alert status, yellow. Return to the house. MHG, 1ˢᵗ Squad, report to the LMC birth care center immediately.

CHAPTER FIFTEEN

THE LOUNGE WAS dark when Bridget tiptoed to his side. "Duke Marlboro?"

"What is it, Bridget?"

"It's a girl. The mother and father are sleeping," she said.

"Can we see her?"

Bridget looked toward Patricia's sleeping form. "Are you going to wake your wife?"

"I should, but this may be the only time I get to hold my granddaughter for long. Show me the way." He left quietly but made sure the Marlboro House Guards were alert and at their posts. No need to take chances. Then he followed Bridget to the recovery room where a very sleepy Hannah held a not-so-sleepy baby girl.

"Hannah," Ron said. "I'm glad you're all right."

"Thanks for everything," she said. "I don't want to sleep. I just want to hold her forever."

"You will, but first you need your rest. Let Grandpa Marlboro take a shift."

"As that what you want her to call you?"

"Eh, she can call me Lord Grandpa."

Hannah laughed. "You're a good man. That's why you have

such a good son, Lord Grandpa. That's all I wanted from this marriage—a good man. Someone to cherish my children and protect them."

"Gregory will do all of that," Ron said. "The Zezner Empire couldn't harm this girl with my son protecting her."

Hannah smiled again, very sleepy. "True, because you already defeated them. I'm going to sleep, Lord Grandpa. Her name is Amelia—but I am sure you will call her something else."

"Sweet dreams, Momma," he said, then faced the room, gently bouncing Amelia. "What shall I call you, Amelia the Great? Chubby Face? Amelia the Most Beautiful Baby Girl in all of Gildain? Maybe I should call you Storm after the man who saved my life the day you were born?"

The conversation was one-sided, but she wouldn't stop looking at him with wide baby eyes.

"There are going to be some rules, little miss," he said as quietly as possible. For a moment, he considered going into the hallway but didn't want to expose the child to sick people. He knew no one in this wing was contagious with anything remotely dangerous, but decided to stay put. He was content, and no one seemed to be waking up from his pacing and baby talk.

"Rule one, Marlboros stand together. Two, victory arrives by way of hard work, dedication, and unity. Three, Lord Grandpa is a far better equestrian than Duke Bull, no matter what anyone tells you."

———

PATRICIA'S sleepy voice came into Ron's ear via his bio-comms. "Where are you?"

"With little Amelia. Don't be jealous." Ron whispered, hoping the earpiece picked it up.

"You know she will love you best. Enjoy your time with the

little princess now, because her mother and grandmother will have their turns." Patricia sounded awake, and in pain.

"How are you?" he asked.

"They moved me to a room down the hall when the pain came back," Patricia said. "They were supposed to let me see Amelia first. I'll never forgive you for crowding into my territory. You know that, right?"

"I'll make it up to you."

"You bet you will. I'll be down there as soon as these drugs wear off," Patricia said.

Ron talked to her for a while, making quiet jokes at her nonsensical rambling. Medication wasn't her friend and they both knew it.

Some of his good humor slipped away when she mumbled words he had heard in his dreams many times as of late, "Send them out to make the universe fit for expansion…"

"Get some sleep, wife."

"Okay. Night, night."

Ron returning to the reading material he held in his left hand, reviewing the report a third time, still pacing the maternity room with his granddaughter in one arm. He tapped one corner with his thumb to thank his accountant for sending it to him. Cordell was good at what he did, a thoroughly competent man. If he detected financial mischief, he was quick to alert Ron.

Duke Travis Bull had filed "relief from the Crown" papers, what in more archaic terminology was considered bankruptcy. It was a way of absolving debts, but also of suspending his eligibility to secure credit. This type of financial maneuvering was public record, though most people didn't pay attention to such minutia.

His blood pressure spiked, causing Amelia to complain with baby noises.

"I'm sorry, princess. What should I do with the Bull?"

Ron wasn't certain, but he thought his granddaughter had just answered by filling her diaper. He couldn't remember what kind of schedule babies were on when they were this young. He was still debating his options with Amelia the Great when Gregory woke up from the chair he'd been sleeping in.

For a second, Ron was stunned by his son's resemblance to a younger version of himself. It made him uneasy for some reason. Gregory was big, broad shouldered, and radiated confidence even as he shook off sleep. His hair was a bit thicker and solid black, lacking Ron's streaks of steel gray. It was an easy comparison, but he knew that his eldest son was bigger, stronger, and excelled in skills Ron had struggled with during his own youth. It was every man's dream that his sons and daughters would exceed him; Gregory Marlboro was a study in generational progression.

"Father, how long have you been here?" Gregory asked, holding out his hands to take Amelia from him.

"Long enough for this little princess to do some work in the diaper area," Ron said.

Gregory looked horrified, glancing first at his daughter, and then for Hannah or a nurse.

Ron laughed a bit too loudly but didn't wake his daughter-in-law. "What's the matter, are you afraid of changing diapers?"

Gregory looked up, delightfully innocent. "Is that something we do?"

"It is today," Ron said. "Over here at the changing table. I'll show you."

"I don't know why I'm so nervous. Fighting a Zezner four-leg would be easier," Gregory said.

Ron coached his invincible warrior of a son, pretending more confidence than he felt. Truth be told, it had been a very long time since he'd changed a Marlboro diaper—usually just to avoid waking up Patricia. She allowed their nannies to do their jobs, but rarely in the middle of the night.

And if he was being honest, there was something extra fatherly about taking care of a baby. He didn't like a crying infant any more than the next person, but he was proud of his ability to calm the little monsters—not that anyone gave him the credit he deserved.

"Good job, son," he said, then made his exit. On the way to Patricia's room, he read the notice from Cordel again and clenched his teeth. If Travis Bull couldn't afford to run his household, what kind of ally was the man?

Patricia was awake when he arrived, reading a tablet of her own. He took a moment to just look at her and think. She understood the complexities of house politics. His alliance wasn't so much a secret from his family as it was something they didn't talk about. Right now, he wanted to tell her everything but that would expose her and his offspring to the legal repercussions if he failed—or if House Bull, soon-to-be House Bull Danestar, betrayed him completely.

As things stood, Patricia could denounce him, sue for her part of House Marlboro, and carry on as the matriarch of House Wilson as though nothing had happened.

King Gerard could execute or banish him as he chose, but Ron's family would survive.

"Dark thoughts?" Patricia asked.

He hugged her, prompting her to sit up higher than her doctors had recommended in order to return the embrace. Leaning down, he held onto her until his back ached and his arms went numb.

"Do you want to talk about it?" she asked.

"I held Amelia the Great for most of the night," Ron said, changing the subject.

"You've already loaded her with a nickname? I should be furious. That is a grandmother's right."

Ron chuckled. "I knew I was taking my life in my own hands when I did it."

"You don't seem repentant."

Ron sat in the chair closest to her. "I never am."

"Isn't that the truth." She put away her reader. "The doctors agree with me; I don't need bed rest. So I'm asking them for release paperwork so I can spend the proper amount of time with Hannah and Amelia. And our son, of course. How is he doing?"

"You'd be proud of the lad. He just changed his first diaper."

"As he should. Now, I was just reading," Patricia went on, "in the *Lorne Financial Report*, that Lord Travis Bull has sought relief from the Crown."

"Neither he nor Danestar can escape what they owe us," Ron said, not sure if he wanted to continue the game. Life would be easier if he could truly confide in his wife.

"Of course. Yet it doesn't seem that all of these reparations are finding their way into our accounts. Are they actually paying?"

"I will check with our accountants," Ron said. "Not to worry. We don't need their money."

"But it *is* owed us," she came back quickly, her tone lacking emotion. Despite her fiery personality, this was just business— and she was testing him.

"All in good time."

"Duke Uron Marlboro, you are walking very close to the line."

"As dukes are wont to do. Let's not talk of house business here." He took her hand, held it, and wished things were different. Two broken legs and not once did she complain. Her accident wasn't an accident, he was sure of it. The incident at the ATG had been an attempted assassination; House Atana had crossed the line this time, but he didn't dare tell Patricia.

She'd declare open war and Lorne would become a battlefield. Maybe House Marlboro would survive. Many of their allies and vassals would stay the course, but he would be doing them a disservice to demand such loyalty.

"I miss the Zezner War," he finally said.

"Is there some place you need to be?" she asked him.

"Yes, wife. I'm afraid there is."

"Then take care of business," she said.

He went to the door.

"Ron."

He turned back, not trusting himself to speak.

"I understand what you're doing and I don't like it. Make a decision. If we are not going forward together, if we are not standing side by side and taking on all comers, then I will take our children to my parents' estate until it is over."

He stared deeply into her blue eyes, traced the outline of her face with his gaze as he had done before many battles, just in case it was the last time he saw her. But he didn't confess the depth of his alliance with House Bull or apologize for his decision. When he tried to find the words, nothing sounded right. And he had to admit that he barely saw the path directly in front of him.

Forgoing his civilian comm device, he tapped the base of his ear to activate the House Marlboro tactical channel via his bio-comm. This was his preferred method of communication. He used it during mech fights, when piloting a ship-to-ship fighter, or on infantry missions. War was what he knew, and the tools used to wage it had become his home away from home.

"Storm," he said. "Bring the car around."

"Right away, Duke. Lieutenant Carmichael wants to know if he should deploy a lead and chase car with combat squads," Storm replied.

"Just you and me," Ron said. "Pack our combat kits."

"Should we take mechs, Duke?"

"Where we're going, mechs aren't allowed." Ron strode into the brightly lit parking lot.

"No offense, but if mechs aren't allowed, then our combat kits aren't allowed, either," Storm said.

"Don't tell anyone what we have in the trunk," Ron advised. "What is your ETA? How long to load up?"

"It's already loaded. Like always. Hope that's okay."

"Make sure I put something extra in your holiday bonus," Ron said. "That's quality work."

The car pulled through the official lane, parked, and Corporal Kenton Storm was out and pulling the door open for Ron in one fluid series of movements. He climbed in, and his driver dashed back to his side and pulled into traffic.

City lights outlined streets, highways, and monorails running from residential areas to the manufacturing, service, and training districts. Fewer men and women were traveling to mandatory enlistment billets than they had during the Zezner War.

Ron saw prosperity and happiness, despite the spike of civilian violence and unrest. Lorne was the shining jewel of Gildain. With the Zezner defeated, everyone but a few warlike houses were looking forward to peace. He pretended it was for him, that King Gerard and his vassals weren't planning a purge of everything Marlboro touched. For ten minutes, he allowed himself to feel like a normal person.

The intoxicating sensation evaporated when he arrived at The Bold Pitcher, one of Duke Bull's favorite haunts. Storm parked the car, took a ticket, and came with Ron into the club. Normally he waited in the car, but tonight he entrusted it to the valet. A driver was first and foremost a bodyguard, and he was one of the best in Lorne.

Music filled the main floor. Men ate dinner with mistresses in booths near the walls. In the center was a large bar, a dance floor, and a section of billiard tables.

"Busy tonight," Ron commented.

"It's always like this," Storm said. "Not that I come often, Duke."

"Of course. You are a man of good character and high moral attributes," Ron said.

"That's generous, Lord Duke." Storm held up a hand to a pair of ladies rushing toward him with smiles and arms spread to hug him. "I'm working, ladies. Another time."

"Oh, Stormy! That makes us so sad," the brunette said while the blonde pouted.

Ron headed up the stairs, straight for Duke Bull's table. Six men, minor lords and skilled mercenaries, populated his booth —each with a girlfriend or two.

"This is not how I imagined you spending your time, Bull," Ron said once he stood before the big man.

"I'm a man of many wants and needs," Bull said, leaning back to spread his arms around two attractive young women.

"I read something interesting in the *Lorne Financial Report*," Ron said. Storm watched the other men and steadfastly resisted the attention of their dates—who seemed to like Ron's bodyguard a lot.

"Bah, what a scandal rag," Bull complained. "Whatever you read… it means nothing."

"I have an interest in your financial wellbeing." Ron was ready to duel the man right here but maintained his decorum— better to catch him off guard if there was going to be violence. Duels required a challenge, but that didn't mean he wanted to give the man too much time to prepare.

"You mean my ability to pay for my loss in our little house war? Correct?" Something in his gaze warned Ron to keep up the ruse, to not allow anyone to realized they'd made a secret alliance against the king and all the great lords and ladies of Lorne.

Ron shifted gears. "Don't imagine for one instant that you can escape your debts to me!"

"Relief from the Crown protects me from creditors and tax assessments, not paying fines for a lost war. If you came here to rub salt in my wounds, you've wasted your time. I'm too drunk to care," Bull barked.

This had to be an act, because while Travis Bull was well known for patronizing less reputable establishments, he wasn't known for drunkenness. A song ended. Someone downstairs shouted for another round and more music. Ron ignored it all, his focus locked on Bull.

"Why did you come here, Ron?"

Storm stiffened at the casual use of the duke's name, but stayed where he was, ready to fight. His job was to act only when his lord initiated something.

"Let's talk in private," Ron said. "For your sake, not mine."

"Oh, how noble. You don't want to humiliate me further? Is that it? Then why not just release me from my debts and get out of my life," Bull said, leaning forward to place his elbows on his knees. This caused one of his dates to adjust her skirt or risk flashing everyone at the table. She lost her balance, nearly falling out of the booth before her patron caught her with one hand. So he wasn't that intoxicated.

"That's not how it works, and you know it. A private room. Now. We have things to discuss that doesn't concern your lackeys and bimbos."

Two of the four lackeys stood up, puffing out their chests and clenching fists. Ron ignored them. Storm adjusted his position slightly, better to defend his lord if he was attacked. Bull hesitated, shook his head, then slammed down his drink.

"Fine. Let's have a talk. If I don't come out again, all of you are witnesses." Bull led the way, sneering at how his loyal friends seemed less interested in this last part. None of them wanted to be tangled up in a murder investigation.

Bull, Ron, and Storm cut through the crowds on the upper level, eventually reaching the back of the establishment where an employee let them into a room without asking any questions. Inside, it was dark. The walls were obviously well insulated, because he could barely hear the loud music.

"Is this where you normally do business?" Ron asked, angry, but calmer than he had been on the drive over here.

"No. I scouted it and set this up, knowing you'd come when your accountant read the report," Bull said. "We have problems."

"We do." Ron crossed his arms, not willing to initiate this exchange. How much did his ally know? Was Bull suffering similar attacks on his family and resources? Ron could ask these questions, but the information would be of a higher quality if he didn't have to.

"I thought you'd betrayed me when the bomb blew up on Elondale. Two of my horse trainers were injured, and there was significant damage to the stables." Bull folded his hands together, looking down momentarily. "My men were fools, rushing into a burning building to save animals, but they did. I can't fault them, but neither am I happy about their condition."

"What's their prognosis?" Ron asked.

"Survivable burns. Lots of surgery and rehabilitation. They may have to be left behind when we leave the planet, assuming we ever do. I'm starting to doubt your commitment to the Blue Sun project," Bull admitted.

Ron let the moment draw out but relented. "Recent events have made me more committed than ever. I have been steadily, but quietly acquiring ships and the best crews in the fleet. I agree we must step up the timeline. The question is how to do it successfully."

"That's not all," Bull said. "Several of my men were attacked on the subway. The police said it was a gang war, and my men were in the wrong place at the wrong time."

"Gregory had two men that were attacked on the subway, as well. The police investigated it as an argument of some sort," Ron said.

Bull regained some of his confidence. "What else, Duke Marlboro?"

"Patricia was in a multi-vehicle accident and badly injured," Ron said. He felt Storm tense in anticipation of revealing the ATG incident. Hesitating, Ron measured his unlikely ally, trying to decide how far to trust him. If the man sensed he was still holding back, it would weaken their partnership even further. But if he told everything, it might prompt the man to do something rash.

"We're in this together," Bull said. "Neither of us wanted it. I thought we were starting to trust each other. But no matter what happens, when the fighting starts, we're going to be back-to-back whether we like it or not, facing enemies from all directions."

"I rescued a submerged mech pilot from House Atana. Divers came too late to help, but not too late to lock me in a damaged cockpit without air."

"That was you? I knew something had happened. Afterward, there was a huge, very public argument between Duke Adam Atana and Duchess Stephani Spirit." He let out a long breath, almost wistfully. "If only House Atana and House Spirit would go to war. That would solve two-thirds of our problem."

"Why would my attempted assassination cause them to fight?"

Bull shook his head. "It could have been unrelated. My sources believe Spirit sold Atana defective mech computers, and Adam was furious at nearly losing one of his favorite pilots."

Ron ran several scenarios in his head, including one he like better than others—second thoughts by Duchess Stephani of House Spirit. They'd been friends in their youth, almost more than friends, but politics and the needs of their houses had gotten in the way. "Or one of them is having second thoughts."

"Pray that we get that lucky," Bull said. But it didn't sound like he was praying.

CHAPTER SIXTEEN

WHEN STORM DROVE AWAY from the club district, there were fewer vehicles on the streets. The pedestrians he saw appeared very drunk and possibly full of regrets. Work crews rolled trash cans into alleys and dumped them. Lorne City Police vehicles cruised the area, looking for people who needed to go home or to jail.

Ron's mind whirled. So much had happened. Information constantly changed. The most steadfast player in the post–Zezner War situation was, surprisingly, Duke Travis Bull. Ron constantly doubted him, and then grew more convinced they were not only on the same side, but stuck together until the very end.

Which was coming.

If I'd had my druthers, I would have chosen different allies.

He called Patricia first, then checked on each of his children, vassals, minor allies, and unit supervisors. The only person who didn't answer was Victor, which worried him more than all the others combined.

"Take me to Victor's apartment," Ron said.

"You got it, Duke." Storm altered course. With no emergency imminent, he drove so smoothly, Ron could have sipped a whiskey had he been in the mood. Contrary to the events of the previous day and his confrontation with Duke Bull, he wasn't angry. Not now. He was contemplative.

"Five minutes," Storm advised. "Do you want me to call ahead and confirm your son is there? He could be out with his single friends. Lorne has been festive lately."

Ron nodded. "As long as the festivities don't include dueling or tavern brawls, I'm fine with it."

"Of course, sir. Dueling and brawling are straight out." Storm had been at Ron's side in both situations, even though he'd only been the Marlboro driver for a few years.

Ron studied the apartments as the car rolled to a stop. Unlike many lords and ladies of Gildain, he allowed his sons and daughters to live away from his primary and secondary estates. Problems could arise, but even Patricia agreed they needed to get into, and out of, their own trouble from time to time.

He was about to rescind the liberty until the current crisis was over, just as soon as he could decide on a publicly justifiable excuse to circle the mechs, so to speak.

"Wait in the car, Storm."

"As you wish, Duke."

Ron strode through the lobby. Both the security guard and the chief doorman recognized him, bowing their heads politely and stepping back the moment they recognized he didn't desire small talk.

To the left was a check-in area, and beyond that a lounge with virtually every creature comfort available. In the other direction was a bar and a piano player. He enjoyed the ancient instrument if it was played well, but there was something off about the musician tonight, his glissandos inconsistent and poorly timed.

The elevator hallway was equally grand, resembling the royal palace or a ducal manor more than a public apartment building. The attendant recognized him and gave a polite head bow, but nothing elaborate. They'd had that conversation already, and the man understood Ron didn't expect bowing and scraping.

In some parts of the city, citizens treated him just like a regular man, but most of the time, this made them uncomfortable. Even if they understood Ron accepted the casual interaction, the reality was that others might observe the interaction and become judgmental.

That was Lorne. That was the world he and his family lived in.

But not for long. Joining the Blue Sun Armada, leading it, was all but inevitable.

Armada, he thought. That's what it would have to be, but the biggest armada ever created, and more than just a military deployment. Normally, it was referred to as an expedition or just a project. His imagination drifted over his last visit to the space docks—rows and rows of ships, large and small, some nearly finished, others barely begun.

He stepped into the elevator and took it to the top floor, fourteen levels up.

When it opened, Victor was waiting for him, ready to go out, dressed fashionably, but not looking particularly happy.

"Father."

Ron embraced him, a father to son hug that made the younger man uncomfortable. He stepped back.

"What was that for?"

"No reason. I've had time to reflect, recently. Family is what matters. Friends and allies. The strength of our house."

"All good things," Victor agreed. "I've been thinking about your briefing. You didn't say it during the video conference, but we all know the vehicle crash that put Mother in the hospital was no accident, and that someone tried to kill you at the ATG."

"There's more," Ron said. "Some of our soldiers were attacked on the subway."

"I'm aware of that also."

"As were some of Duke Bull's soldiers."

Victor turned away quickly, striding across the elevator foyer. He owned this floor, and they had complete privacy. Still, his son, who was clearly furious, controlled himself and resisted the urge to shout and curse.

Ron respected that but knew his son's self-control was finite. "Do you understand why I cannot speak of the details?"

"You're trying to protect us, like always. But you know House Bull is just trying to pay off their debts and rebuild their military with Danestar's wealth."

"Of course they are! That's the way it is done. I'm sorry we couldn't be a normal family. Nothing grieves me as much as this farce. I know you have feelings for Penelope."

"Feelings! It's more than feelings. I love her more than the air I breathe! There is no way she wanted this. I can tell her love for me are real. Or do you think I'm simple?" Victor asked.

"You're not the first young man to fall in love with a young woman when it went against house alliances," Ron said. "I was extremely lucky with your mother. That almost never happens."

Victor shook his head.

Ron couldn't interpret the expression. He wanted to know his son's heart, but something was off.

"None of us can be like you and Mother," Victor said. "You choose happiness somehow. No one can duplicate your marriage. I thought I could, but obviously I can't. Maybe Gregory and Hannah, but they have everything so easy. They're not passionate like the rest of our family."

"The eldest sons are often the most sensible, steadfast, and levelheaded," Ron said before he thought about his words.

Still pacing, Victor turned to come back. He laughed ironically. "You have me there. I'll not argue. Gregory is much calmer, and stronger, and more successful than I will ever be. But I am not him."

Ron considered his words carefully, not wanting to misspeak again. "I don't want you to be Gregory, or me, or even your grandfather. But no matter what course you choose, I need you. There are hard times ahead. Remember that when you make decisions."

Tears welled in Victor's eyes. It took him several moments before he could talk, but he did stop pacing. "Of course, Father. Now, if there's no official business to address, I had plans for the evening."

"It's late," Ron said, but kept his tone neutral.

"It is, but I'm young. And my generation is wont to go out all night in search of entertainment and new experiences," Victor said.

"Who's going with you? I am very close to issuing body-guard mandates and recalling everyone back to our central estate until I figure out who is behind all of these attacks."

"Kilo and Marsten, and some of my friends," Victor said. "Please leave the MHG out of it tonight. I promise I will call for assistance at the first sign of real danger."

Ron nodded. "We never even went inside of your apartment. Maybe lobbies are where we best communicate."

Victor laughed. "Well, perhaps we have time for one drink. Come in. You haven't seen the renovations. It's quite fashionable."

CHAPTER SEVENTEEN

FORTUNE PUNCHED THE AFTERBURNERS, shooting away from Lorne. Three airships followed her, spread out in a three-dimensional fork maneuver, two high and one low. *Like in a game of night boards, caught in a corner where I can take either the knight or the rook, but in the next move, one of them will take me.*

Normal dogfight doctrine said the two above were the most dangerous but warned against an unexpected strike from below. Physics might be against this adversary, but the lurker was often a surprise winner.

Her vision flicked over supplemental view screens. In VR competitions, the eye movement was acceptable. But those were just really expensive gaming consoles. For some reason, in an actual ship, watching the cameras put too much strain on one's vision and could be a fatal mistake. Microseconds mattered, and she was only *nearly human* like the Zezner kept telling her father.

Laughing crazily, she waited for the simulated auto cannon strikes to hit, but so far, she'd avoided every single one.

Three ships against one. It had been a stupid bet against veteran pilots who respected her enough not to go easy on "the Girl from Marlboro House," as they called her.

"Fortune?" Peps asked from the backseat. In this atmo-void fighter, the copilot sat directly behind the primary pilot.

"What?"

Peps squeaked. "I'm feeling a little sick."

"You've never been sick when we flew before." Fortune climbed, banked to the left again, and then leveled off, adjusting each engine for the maximum thrust. This was a far better aircraft than those of her adversaries, something she wasn't proud of. In fact, her acquisition of the ship was the main reason she was so distracted and about to get smoked.

"You wanted to come," Fortune said, tightlipped as she gripped the steering yoke and banked the airship down and to the left.

Get them used to circling left...

"Sorry!" Peps squeaked.

Fortune pushed aside concern for her sister, who was protected by multiple safety systems, and focused on the real question of the day—why had Martin Gerard, the Zezner-cursed-king, twice her age, bought her a billion credit AT-VO ship?

Damn, this thing can move!

Right now, in the middle of her favorite activity, Fortune was on edge—distracted by the memory of how Gerard had stared at her during the triumphal parade. Her mother and father believed the summons by the Legislature had been a deliberate insult—and maybe it had—but Fortune spent the evening trying not to make eye contact with the king.

He'd toured all of the major Houses at the parade, paying his respects and giving small gifts. But the gift he'd given to Fortune wasn't so small, was it? And he had lingered far longer than was proper. Fortune's eyes still ached months later from staring at the lame parade with every ounce of her attention—desperate to avoid conversation with the king of Gildain.

"I didn't know you'd be flying like this," Peps complained. "Are we supposed to be dogfighting other trainers?"

"This isn't a trainer, little Peps, and neither are our adversaries. We're in a real fighter, rated for both atmosphere and void travel." Fortune hated the ship and almost wished this were a real battle so it could get shot down. A gift from the king, she'd begged Reginald Cordel, the family accountant and business manager, to list it in the regular Marlboro inventory as a purchased asset rather than a favor of the widowed monarch.

If her father learned the king had given her a gift of such value, there would be blood.

She began an obvious trick, diving for the surface in a fairly predictable vector. Building up more speed than her pursuers could match, she then pointed the airship straight for the upper atmosphere, climbing like a rocket.

Power to spare!

Peps swallowed so loudly that Fortune heard it over the ship comm. "I'm really not doing so good."

"Just keep it in a second longer," Fortune said. "We're about to lose these bogeys."

"Aren't they hostiles?" Peps asked. "The book you gave me said 'bogeys' are unidentified and *possibly* hostile."

"Yeah, yeah. You're right, but I'm just talking and trying to out-fly three of the best combat pilots on the planet." The strain of the maneuver made it hard to speak, and she definitely wasn't thinking about the words. "Just don't puke or pass out. That's the ticket."

She loosed a war cry as she veered hard to the right, then down, and then spiraled her way through her pursuers, launching virtual rocket signals to represent her attack had this been a real fight.

Klaxons blared alarms and soon her opponents were cursing and veering away.

Three hits. More than she had expected.

"Yeah! In your face!" she barked.

Leveling off, she enjoyed the feeling of normal flight. Peps started laughing, her sickness apparently forgotten. Fortune soaked in the moment. Sometimes, even though she never said anything, it felt like it was just her and her little sister against the world.

No one could possibly understand.

Inspired by the euphoria of victory, she cranked the void-capable airship through several maneuvers that should have broken it. But when something came directly from the Crown's aerospace engineers, it was as perfect as such a machine could be and made from the best materials—much better than the barely serviceable junk Gerard issued his enlisted ship and mech pilots.

"I don't like this right now," Peps grumbled. "I thought we already beat them."

Fortune relaxed, spotting Lorne on the horizon and heading back toward the city. "I'm sorry, kiddo. I just got carried away."

"You do that a lot."

Fortune laughed and it felt good. She'd intended to take her sister to one of the upper atmosphere spaceports, the one dedicated to the Blue Sun project, but the site of the Cherry Blossom district and horsemen galloping through a clearing changed her mind. She swooped down and looked for a place to land.

"What are we doing now?" Peps asked.

"I thought we'd see what Captain Mark Echo is up to," Fortune said, resisting the urge to tease her little sister about the obvious crush she had on the dashing officer.

"Really? That sounds like fun. Then maybe we can fly some more, because I know you like to," Peps said, embarrassingly happy.

Fortune almost forgot about her problem with the king and what would happen if her father found out the direction of the man's attentions.

———

MARTIN GERARD STROLLED to his expansive, multi-level balcony and stared across his realm. With its sparkling skyscrapers and sprawling parks, Lorne shone like a jewel. Business, industrial, and residential districts had been well balanced by his family planners, many long centuries before.

A cool breeze ruffled his silk robe. He allowed it to hang open so that his mistress, if she awoke, might see his muscular chest and battle scar. He only had one, but it was more than enough proof of his bravery. She couldn't get enough of his physique, or his salt and pepper hair, or his dominance of this world.

He turned his attention to the sky, watching three of his best fighters wheel and dive after a fourth ship, Fortune's gift. She despised him, probably for the disrespect he'd shown her father at the end of the Zezner War. Or maybe she thought he was responsible for the attack on her mother and father, and many of their key soldiers.

Mariah DeLene tiptoed behind him. She wasn't as quiet as she believed, but he accepted the farce and soon felt her hands snake around his body from behind, touch his chest, then his abdominal muscles. Her bare breasts pushed against his back, and he wished he wasn't wearing the silk robe, sheer as it was.

"You left me in bed," she pouted.

"As I often do."

Her hands explored, then, as though she could read his nanite-boosted mind, pulled down his robe so she could put skin to skin. His arousal came quickly, despite his age, despite the distractions of the cloud-slicing dogfight miles above the planet.

Or maybe because of it. Images of Fortune Marlboro filled his imagination as Mariah touched him everywhere. His other mistresses were no doubt watching from the apartments he provided them, either plotting the fall of his current favorite, or secretly thanking the woman for providing them a vacation from his attention.

He didn't enjoy that thought, even though he knew it was true. None of them adored him with constant and absolute devotion. His wife had been that woman, though he hadn't appreciated her passion and loyalty at the time.

Now he was a bachelor and the most powerful man in the world... the most powerful man in the galaxy.

Because Duke Uron Marlboro crushed the Zezner invaders.

Mariah whispered hotly in his ear, "Come back to bed, my king."

He lingered a moment, gazing toward the Cherry Blossom District where the Marlboro House Guard rode fine horses. The sight amused him, and his confidence increased. Marlboro wasn't so perfect after all. The man had fallen to competing with minor houses in a gentleman's hobby rather than war. Gone was the constant mech training, strategy sessions, and reviews of every battle in the Zezner War.

Duke Ron Marlboro was spending his time touring Elondale and trying to outride Duke Travis Bull and his men.

Gerard turned quickly, catching Mariah by surprise. Flinging her over his shoulder, he slapped her once on the ass, hard.

"Oh!" she squealed.

He strode into the bed chambers, not bothering to pull the curtains, and threw her on the mattress. Before she could flirt or stroke his ego, he was inside of her, thrusting away his frustrations over Fortune.

"Oh, my king!"

Sometimes, he hated the way this woman giggled.

———

PEPS STARED at the horses prancing through the Cherry Blossom District. "They're beautiful!"

"So are their riders," Fortune said, confusing Peps just a little. Captain Mark Echo rode straight in the saddle, but also relaxed and in control of the muscular, cream-colored gelding. His troopers were stiff, but also skilled. They'd been practicing for reasons no one explained to Peps.

She concentrated on the luxurious braids and ribbons, the polished hooves and brightly shined tack rather than her sister's confusing insinuations about the attractiveness of the riders. The black leather of the bridles, saddles, and stirrups appeared soft as silk. "Surely our Marlboro House Guards are better horseman than any of the Bull's troopers."

"Ah, Peps... your blind faith is refreshing," Fortune said, standing with one foot up on the tree she was leaning against. Arms crossed, she never stopped looking at Captain Echo.

Peps heard something in Fortune's voice she didn't like, something that warned her not to trust anyone from House Bull. Turning, she saw her sister was pale—hiding her pain again. "Fortune, we can go back to the house, if you want."

Fortune, not much taller than Peps despite being ten years older, stepped away from the cherry blossom tree and put one hand on Peps's shoulder. She liked that, but still worried about her big sister—even though Fortune was fearless and happy all the time, and probably would be right up to the moment she died.

Tears welled in her eyes.

"Peps, I'm okay," Fortune said.

"We should go home. I'm tired." Peps didn't like this, no more than she had liked the battle that had taken place not far from here. She couldn't forget how her father had smashed Carter Danestar. Of course, after what he did to her brother Victor, she wanted to smash the jack-hole herself.

Looking nervously towards Captain Echo, she reminded herself no one could hear her thoughts. She'd promised him not to swear like a foot soldier, but it was hard. Because people made her so mad.

"We're not going home. There won't be many chances to tour the Blue Sun ships. You know, the ones they're going to give to our father if they know what's good for them," Fortune said.

Peps was excited about that, seeing all of the big ships that could go through space to the stars. She had learned about the Blue Sun expedition, and how it had been a dream of the great houses of Gildain for many generations, in school. It didn't make a lot of sense, though, because if her science teacher was right, going so far away meant never coming back.

And how could that be right? Was there a way to beat time dilation? Or was it dilution? She didn't care, because the point was, leaving forever didn't sound good.

"Come along, little Peps," Fortune said. "If we wait too long, Captain Echo and the MHG will be done with their equestrian pursuits and free to follow us everywhere."

"Isn't that what Father wants?" Peps asked.

"Yes and no." Fortune gave the horsemen one last look, frowned at how their formation faltered, and turned toward Marlboro House. "It's been months since the attacks. Mother is walking better than ever, and baby Amelia is probably the healthiest baby born on Gildain for a generation. I think we can take a guided tour without an army dogging our every move."

"If you say so." Peps hurried to catch up, then matched her sister's stride. Fortune's favorite airship was parked in the next clearing, breaking several minor laws. "Father won't be happy if you get cited for the landing infraction."

"He won't find out," Fortune said.

"Why do you have to break all the rules?" Peps asked.

"The rules would have me dead at birth, but I'm a rebel." Fortune looked back, and for a second it seemed she longed to get caught—but Peps couldn't be sure.

Captain Echo and the Marlboro House Guards continued their training. None of them were assigned to Fortune or Peps at the moment. Landing in the CBD to watch them ride had been fun, but now Peps was thinking about getting in trouble. She didn't want Mark to know she was a rule breaker. He had checked on her every day since the Danestar attack, even when he was off duty. The man was like another big brother, or something else she didn't understand.

"Why does Father spend so much time with the Bull if they're enemies?" Peps asked as they climbed into the airship and started it up.

"Duke Travis Bull owes our family money. Father has to keep tabs on the man's assets to make sure they don't default," Fortune said. "But there is more to it than that."

"Like what?"

"You're too young to understand."

Peps bit back several of the swear words Captain Echo's men used when they didn't think "little Peps" was listening. The ship banked hard to the left, because Fortune always flew like she was racing someone. "I know more than you think."

"Okay, Peps. Sure you do." Fortune climbed higher than she normally flew when over the city.

"The king is trying to destroy our house. I hate him."

"Who told you that?" Fortune snapped.

Peps didn't like her sister's angry tone, but she wasn't backing down this time. "I figured it out myself because no one will tell 'little Peps' anything!"

Red-faced, Fortune exhaled a long breath and leveled off her flight path. They were high above Lorne now, heading to one of the orbital stations Father and Mother had promised to take them to but never did. Fear tingled through Peps's spine. She shivered.

"We can't go there."

Fortune shook her head. "This ship is rated for limited-duration void travel. I talked to Isaac Sage and secured clearance. I told you we're going to have a proper tour."

Peps didn't know what to say, so she simply watched the space station grow larger and larger as they approached.

She thought it looked like a top, bulbous in the middle with a long tail stretching downward to the surface. Like everything else in Gildain's space program, the dockyard in space was under construction—part of that was the tether that would eventually attach it to the surface so supplies, and maybe even people, could be raised and lowered to the surface without the use of ships.

But that was years away. According to her teachers in school, the Blue Sun expedition would be gone before then. Peps wasn't sure if she wanted to be part of that adventure—despite her daydreams of exploring alien worlds. Her friends said it would never happen.

If she hadn't overheard her mother and father arguing, she would've agreed with her friends and continue to dream with no fear of actually having to go.

"You're quiet," Fortune said.

"I was thinking about what my teachers say." Peps waited for her sister to ask the obvious question and, when she didn't, answered anyway. "Mr. Burghouse says the project will never happen. It's just a way for rich industrialists to sell things to the king and his lords."

"I have to talk to flight control," Fortune said, leaning forward in her seat. "Fortune 18-Adam-X-Ray for Nanstrom Station flight control, how copy?"

"Loud and clear, Fortune 18AX. We have the flight plan we filed and a landing berth prepped. May I ask how you got this approved?" the flight controller asked.

"No, you may not," Fortune said in a friendly tone. "I am on my final approach and will touch down in five minutes."

"Outstanding, Fortune 18AX. A refueling crew is standing by. I've also got a note from Midshipman Sage that he's been expecting you."

"Thank you, Control."

Peps watched breathlessly as her sister flew straight to the landing deck and touched down on the first try.

"You're really good," Peps said, unbuckling once the ship was stopped. "I want to fly like you do."

Fortune roughly finger-combed her hair the moment it was free of the helmet, looking like the coolest big sister ever. "I'll teach you, Peps."

"One last thing," Control said over bio-comms now.

"Go." Fortune sounded annoyed.

"Midshipman Sage will be arriving shortly with two important individuals who are very much interested in your presence here today."

"Copy that."

Fortune and Peps exchanged confused looks. "Who would be up here waiting for us?"

"How would I know?" Peps shot back.

"Hold still, let me fix your hair. It's a mess. Too much wind at the CBD. We shouldn't have stopped for that."

"You wanted to stop!" Peps said.

"I didn't hear you complaining. Now hold still. Okay... good enough. Now check my hair." Fortune bent down so Peps could groom her short bob, which she didn't need, but it made Peps feel important.

They stood in front of the hatch, took deep breaths, and then stepped out together when it opened.

The sight of their parents took them both by surprise.

CHAPTER EIGHTEEN

PATRICIA HID HER SMILE. It wasn't often she saw her husband frustrated, but their daughters were normally the cause when it happened.

"What are you doing here, Fortune?" Ron asked. He looked at Peps, then at Patricia, then back to Fortune, unsure where to direct his frustration.

"What... are *you* doing here?" Fortune asked.

Patricia cringed. Their eldest daughter could be rebellious, but this sounded like a quasi-joke. Success or failure of the gibe was in the delivery. Fingers crossed, Fortune had nailed it.

Patricia's husband gathered himself, then let out a long exhalation and shook his head. "I don't want members of our family, or our representatives, inspecting the Blue Sun platform unless they check with me first, understood?"

"Yes, Father," Fortune and Peps said at the same time.

Patricia bit her lip, trying not to laugh as he held his stern gaze on them for several more moments.

"Very well," he said. "Let's get this over with. Mr. Sage, I hope the growing armada is in better condition than the last time we were here."

"We're doing our courageous best, Lord Duke,"

Midshipman Sage said cheerfully, then handed him a sealed bundle. "Here are digital copies of my reports, as well as a dozen patches."

Sage pointed to his own shoulder patch. "There wasn't an insignia for the BSA, so Tobias Luther took the liberty of designing this one. It's unofficial until approved, of course."

"There are significant similarities to the Marlboro crest," Ron said.

"Of course, Duke. It only seemed right," Sage said.

Fortune examined one of the patches. "I like the design. Very clean."

Isaac Sage bowed theatrically. "Thank you, Fortune Marlboro."

Patricia watched Fortune's reaction to the interesting young man and wondered. Sage was not attractive in a traditional sense—too tall, too lean, and his hair was a tangle of red locks that wouldn't quite go into a buzz cut. He'd apparently quit trying to maintain a strict military style. All that aside, his personality was infectious, and Patricia saw that her oldest daughter wasn't immune to his charm.

Fortune slowed her pace, allowing Ron, Peps, and Sage to continue forward several strides. Walking next to Patricia, the young woman eyed her suspiciously. Patricia knew what was coming.

"What?" Fortune asked.

Patricia feigned complete ignorance. "What, what?"

"You're watching me. I can feel it."

"I was your age once. You seem completely uninterested in being courted, but I know you're human."

Fortune laughed a bit too loudly. "Or near-human. Where is the Zezner? I rarely see Father without him lurking nearby."

"Redion is performing a ritual in our gardens," Patricia said. "But you're right. He does shadow your father with outstanding loyalty. I've grown accustomed to it."

"Everyone's noticed. There's lots of gossip."

"There always is." Patricia pointed towards Ron and the others. "What do you think of Midshipman Sage?"

"He looks like someone who might be fun to have a beer with. He'd probably make me laugh."

"That's not a bad thing."

"No, Mother. Not at all." Fortune hesitated, looking more unsure than normal. "What happened to the king's wife?"

"That's a strange question."

"Is it? No one talks about it, and it was before I was born."

Patricia cringed. "You make it sound like the king and your father and I are ancient creatures."

"You totally are."

Their conversation stopped when they drew close enough to hear Sage discussing several ship parts that were obviously destined to become one much larger vessel. Stout cables connected to each piece but looked insufficient to hold their bulk. Work crews moved quietly from section to section, checking readouts and making notes on portable devices.

"These will not be assembled until they are moved completely into the void," Sage said. "Commander Dale requested a second facility in true orbit, but was denied by the Assembly of Lords."

"I remember the debate. They are stingy with financing, despite how they support the endeavor publicly," Ron said.

"They're attempting to exhaust our fortunes on this project," Patricia said.

"Or they are being frugal," Ron said.

Patricia sniffed. "They're cheap and trying to destroy our finances."

Ron addressed their guide. "What would be the advantage of a truly orbital construction yard?"

"Contrary to popular belief, there is still quite a bit of gravity this high off the surface of the planet," Midshipman Sage explained. "It's less, which makes much of this construction possible, but we're still using—and don't tell anyone this—

slightly unapproved technology. The gravitational propulsion patent is held by a minor house without the funds to push it through the Assembly."

"Which house?" Patricia asked.

"Hawk."

"That *is* a minor house," Patricia grumbled. "They don't have a manor or land beyond one laboratory on the coast."

"Good people, if reclusive," Sage said.

"Perhaps they need a sponsor?" Ron suggested.

Patricia gave him a smile. "I'll handle it through House Wilson. Quietly." She turned her attention to Sage. "I need a moment with my husband. Would you mind escorting my daughters on the next phase of the tour?"

"It would be my pleasure."

Fortune shot her a "thanks a lot, Mother" look.

She waited until Ron quit staring at the half-built ships and the others were some distance ahead. "I don't see nearly enough progress, do you?"

He'd been leaning on the railing overlooking the construction process below. Now he stood and stepped back. "No, I don't. They have more people here, and they're more energetic, but they're still working on the same ship parts we saw last month."

"What are we going to do about it?" Patricia wasn't a nervous woman, but her heart fluttered, missing a beat. She was sick of the act, tired of pretending Ron was working alone. He thought he was protecting her, but she knew better than anyone that the Assembly of Lords and the king would blow through that legal defense like it was a weak Zezner line. In the meantime, the Blue Sun project was floundering.

"Two things," Ron said. "We need to convince everyone that our taking official control of the Blue Sun project is in their best interest. Then, we must leverage the full backing of the masses, drum up their support of the idea of a homeward fleet."

"Homeward," she said. "That's not a word used often."

"Doctor Stacks says that is the true purpose of the Blue Sun Armada. He's not a religious man, but he does believe there is such a thing as a home world, some place humans existed before Gildain," Ron said.

"I wouldn't call it an 'armada' in public," Patricia said. "That sounds militaristic and might threaten the tender ego of our king."

Ron nodded agreement but said nothing.

"So, how are we going to get this wildly enthusiastic popular support, and then how will we convince the Assembly to send us to the stars?" Patricia asked.

"It's risky."

Patricia's heart no longer fluttered. She was built for conflict and this was just what she needed—the ultimate conflict. "How so?"

"We must threaten the king and his allies." Ron placed his hands behind his back, not one of his more common stances, but it made him look taller, like a commander. "God willing, they'll find it easier to send us away than fight us."

Ice poured through Patricia's veins. Her heart pounded quicker to prepare for battle. She concealed the fight response, watching Ron with an intensity that made it impossible to blink. "Explain, husband."

"Nothing seditious. And nothing different from what every house does on a regular basis. Strive for greater commercial, social, and military success every day. Become a force of *one* like the king himself. Do everything better than everyone and make sure the people of Gildain love us like celebrities."

Patricia controlled her breathing, and if she was being honest, her excitement. She wanted Ron to do all these things, not out of pride, but because he wouldn't abuse success like the womanizing, power-mongering liar King Martin Gerard had become. "Your big plan is to just keep doing the same thing we've always done, but try a little harder?"

"No, damn it. We must change everything."

"How? What do you want to do right now? Give me something specific." She crossed her arms.

"I want to build three Blue Sun ships for unattached citizens and run a lottery. I'm not the only man to dream of the stars. But how can a shopkeeper in Lorne, or a poet, or a plumber ever leave this planet on such an adventure?"

"They pledge fealty to a house that has the resources and show their worth. They compete against others and are selected," Patricia said. "That has always been the way on Gildain. You want to invite men and women not attached to a house to travel in search of the home world with no strings attached?"

"Yes. I'm not King Gerard, who believes every creature on the planet must bend the knee to his sovereignty."

"You're making every man and woman a house in their own right."

"Aren't they?"

"Where do you get these ideas?" She felt something warming in the core of her body. Waves of mild but very real euphoria spread through her, like when she heard her favorite song or watched a deeply engaging play. Her emotions were all over the place. Something was changing inside of her, and it was both exciting and terrifying.

"It only makes sense," Ron said. "The difference between me and a stranger on the street is the luck of my birth."

"Which gave you better nanites at birth than they could dream of. You can defend them against Zezner attacks or whatever else comes at us. How many shopkeepers and musicians can withstand gunshot wounds and power-sword slashes and keep fighting? Were the roles reversed, they would die in battle before they could thank you for your egalitarian ideals." She didn't like her words but couldn't deny the truth of them.

"Perhaps," Ron said. "But I don't believe that is how it was meant to be."

"What the hell are you talking about? How could it be a mistake? It's not like a mech design that an engineer got wrong. We're talking about nature, something totally beyond anyone's control. All we can do is play the cards we are dealt."

"Not according to Doctor Stacks. He doesn't believe the nanites are natural… thinks they are more like…" Ron gasped. His body, then his face, clenched. He felt as though he was being ripped apart, burned from the inside, or that his blood had turned to acid. Halfway through his words, he started to crumple toward the ground, obviously in pain, but finished his thought like it was a battle he fought against the gods. "… the mechs we drive into… battle."

She covered him protectively with her body, searching for a wound despite knowing exactly what had happened. "Ron!"

"Ahhg!" He roared like a beast, forcing away his agony, standing, lifting her with him, and scaring the hell out of her.

"Ron! Stop this! Forget Stacks and his theories. You're scaring me!" She hugged him around the waist and refused to let go as his feet slid out from under him and he gripped both sides of his skull.

"Gods!" he choked.

Patricia shook him, then shouted in his face. "Stop angering the nanites!"

Memories of their life together, from the first time she'd seen him to right now, blurred through her thoughts. It was like reliving the last fifty years in a heartbeat.

"I'm sorry, Patricia." Ron's body relaxed almost to normal. Several deep, shuddering breaths later, he let go of his head and put his arms around her. "Something is wrong with us. I dream every night. I hear the words: *Send them out to make the universe fit for expansion.* And I see a human standing like a god asking horrible questions."

Tears leaked down Patricia's face. She pressed into his chest, refusing to let go.

"There is a reason I have the nanites, and the desire to defend the people of Gildain, and it isn't just for the glory of our

SCOTT MOON

house. We're tools for the greater good, but some have forgotten that truth completely."

"Gerard."

"Gerard and others," Ron agreed. "But we mustn't forget, or we are damned."

They held each other for long moments.

"Ron?"

"What, wife?"

"What other questions does the figure in the dream ask?"

He tensed, but she held him until he relaxed enough to answer.

"Sometimes it's a man; other times, a woman. But they both ask only one question. *And then what do we do with them?*"

"I don't like it. Those dream assholes treat us like last year's mech upgrade," she said.

"Exactly like that." Ron kissed the top of her head, then released her.

She looked up, feeling like the young woman who'd been terrified this man wouldn't love her as much as she loved him, even though they'd just met and she hadn't known anything about anything then.

He looked deep into her eyes. "Tell me not to contract the building of the citizen ships. Forbid me from making the announcement that we will run a lottery for able-bodied men and women, and their families, to join the BSA freely, without obligation to our house or any other."

"I won't." She realized her blood was neither frozen nor boiling, and her heart beat a strong, natural rhythm synonymous with contentment. "I can't. Make your crazy proclamation, and know that I'll stand with you at the gates of hell if I must."

He chuckled. "You'd like that. I imagine there'd be a lot of fighting in such a place."

"Uron Marlboro, you know me too well."

He clapped his hands together. "All right. One revolutionary announcement coming up."

"Bull won't like it."

"He won't have a choice. We're in this together, a fact he's pointed out to me more than once," Ron said, then checked his uniform, hair, and flushed face, attempting to shake off the nanite episode.

"We should wait to talk specifics until we get back to the surface," Patricia said. She didn't need time to think, and there was very little chance of a spy eavesdropping in this environment. Her suggestion was merely practical. They needed to complete the tour and learn every possible detail of this facility's production capacity.

Sage led Patricia's daughters back to the beginning of the tour, all three of them laughing at some joke. The young man really was a charmer, and charismatic too. She'd have to keep an eye on him for future promotion.

"I've given them an abbreviated version, Duke," Sage said. "If you're ready for details, I have reserved my entire day for this tour."

"Thank you, Mister Sage. That's my intention," Ron said. "Perhaps my easily distractible children will want to return to their games in the sky."

"That is an impressive fighter," Sage said, looking toward the landing platform out of view.

Fortune's face reddened. Her entire body tensed. "It's just a ship, and Peps and I will stay as long as our boring and tedious parents will stay. We're up to the challenge of ultimate boredom."

Sage looked hurt by the joke.

Fortune touched his arm. "You're not boring, my parents are."

He laughed awkwardly. "Ah, well. Thanks. Means a lot to me coming from anyone able to fly an AT-VO fighter like that beauty."

165

"Of course it's an outstanding machine," Patricia interjected, not sure what was going on but knowing she needed to stop the conversation in its tracks. Instinct was a powerful tool, especially when survival was at stake. She marked the incident for later reflection, because something about Fortune's ship was important.

"It's the best we have in our fleet, such as it is," Ron said, appearing distracted by a large crane moving a ship part on the other side of the hangar. "To be honest, I didn't know we had it in our inventory. If it's useful to you and your development team, I'll have it loaned to the project. Perhaps you can duplicate it and build more of them."

Patricia listened but watched Fortune carefully. Her daughter's reaction was confusing, a mixture of tension and relief. It seemed like the young woman wanted to get rid of the ship that had become her favorite but didn't want to talk about it—at all.

"That would be excellent, Duke," Sage said.

"Then consider it officially part of your inventory. Now let's finish this tour. I'll offer my progeny one last chance to abandon this fascinating collection of facts and production timelines," Ron said.

"We're having loads of fun, Father," Peps said, clapping her hands together and bouncing on her toes. "Aren't we, Fortune?"

"Sure," Fortune agreed. "We can leave my AT-VO fighter here and ride back with my delightful parents. I'm sure it'll be way better than having fun."

"Excellent," Ron said, slugging his tomboy daughter in the shoulder, then striding forward and motioning Sage to pick up the pace. "Let's get to work. I have a long list of questions."

"I will endeavor to answer them, or find someone who can," Midshipman Sage promised.

CHAPTER NINETEEN

"PENELOPE," the family steward said with perfect dignity. "Victor Marlboro has come to call. Shall I show him in, or call the officer of the watch?"

Penelope put down the biography she'd been reading, mentally bookmarking the page she would return to when this was done—even though she knew she wouldn't be in the mood to read. Which was too bad, because the satisfaction of holding a real book had gotten her through rough times before.

Seeing Victor would be a bad decision. All her good sense told her that. But she just couldn't resist. She went to the window and looked down, and, as if on cue, he looked up and smiled.

Her heart melted. Why did he have this effect on her? Sure, he was handsome and daring, but nothing like the dream husband of her imagination. Looking at the young Marlboro's stunning blond hair and bright blue eyes, she realized her daydreams had been vague and not all that interesting—certainly not considered deeply or with any kind of plan for the future.

Which wasn't like her.

Victor was a male version of his mother, taller and stronger of course, but not as robust as his father or his elder brother who had black hair and green eyes.

"Come down and see me," Victor mouthed toward the window.

She retreated, dropping her shades.

Subtle, Penelope. Very subtle. And mature.

She hugged herself and paced her room.

I can't put him through this.

Heart beating madly, she called the doorman. "I am not feeling well. Send him away."

"I shall inform him straight away," the doorman replied. "Perhaps a walk in the garden to take in some air and sunshine would enhance the lady's wellbeing."

"Ah, yes, of course," Penelope muttered, hardly listening. She paced for the better part of an hour, unable to focus, unable to read.

And then she donned a jacket and went to the garden. The walls were too near together, the vines too thick. Normally, the cozy little space was like heaven, but her thoughts wouldn't stop hopping. Victor. Her house. Malcom Sky. Alliances. Her father's halfhearted schemes. All of the things she would do better if she were in charge.

Perish the thought.

She sauntered along the outermost path, practically brushing the tall stone wall with one shoulder.

At the back gate, a voice startled her.

"Penelope, forgive me."

The moment she saw Victor, her heart skipped a beat. In a romance novel, that would be a good thing, but she found it terrifying—almost painful.

"But I heard the doorman mention the garden and my feet took me here."

"I do *not* forgive you, Victor Marlboro," she snapped. "Your presence puts me in a terrible position. How long have you been standing there?"

"Since the doorman turned me away. I had to see you." He smiled mischievously. "That peek from the window wasn't enough."

Penelope blushed, then calmed herself. She squared her shoulders, raising her chin proudly, not wanting to appear weak or flighty. Her heartbeat returned to something like normal.

Victor Marlboro looked good as he matched her pace. His smile pushed away her worries. She felt lighter. She felt *happy*. Would he follow her around the entire perimeter of the Danestar garden? She kept her chin high and walked briskly.

"Are you going to say something? Give me a single word to make the night worthwhile. Just one little—oof," he exclaimed as he stumbled into the hedgerow just beyond the modest gate.

"Be quiet, Victor Marlboro!" Using his full name should have expressed her stern disapproval of his actions, of his presence scarcely more than an arm's reach from where she stood. Instead, it sounded cute—like one young lover teasing another.

"I'm sorry," he whispered. "Something's got me all tangled up. Oh. What's this here? A guitar strap? How'd that get here? And this is a fine instrument. I wonder if it's in tune."

"You can't play music in the middle of the night," she hissed, moving right to the gate so he might hear the seriousness of her tone.

"You're right, Penelope Danestar. Someone might call the watch," he said, then tuned the instrument with a flourish.

"Stop that!"

"I must play now," he said, starting a lively melody. "The music is calling me!"

He's better than I remember. The fool has been practicing, she thought.

"A sunrise between lovers—"

"Not that one. I am betrothed to Malcom Sky Bull, and you know it."

He hummed a bar to find the tune. "A sunrise begins but the cold moon waits for night…"

Penelope unlatched the gate, stepped through, and put a finger to his lips and a hand across the strings. "Please stop."

Silence gripped them. The night sent a shiver up her spine.

"For you, anything," he said.

You hopeless romantic. She thought of the book she'd been reading and wondered if she were daydreaming instead of risking a scandalous incident within sight of her own window.

They stood so near each other she could feel his warmth, smell his hair. Only the neck of the guitar remained between them, and she knew that meager testament to their chastity couldn't last. So she took his hand and led him into the park—the same park she'd been watching the night her family attacked his.

Cool air touched them as they hurried down the nearest path, out of sight of any manor house, apartment building, or skyscraper apartment around the perimeter of the lush, manicured forest. She laughed without really understanding why.

This was dangerous. And it filled her heart with joy.

Am I so faithless to my betrothal vow?

Victor led her over a narrow bridge, across a clearing, and onto a large boulder worn from hands and feet that had climbed it over the centuries. A pond circled two-thirds of the rocky island. Across the water were spectacular beds of flowers and roses. Softly lit walking paths gave every approach a magical resonance.

Once, not long ago, it had been her favorite place to read, day or night. Here, Victor Marlboro had first stumbled upon her while gallivanting with a group of his friends.

With a flourish, he pulled a book from his coat—the same book she'd been reading that day almost a year ago. "In case you misplaced your copy."

"Have you read it?" Mischief prompted her to grab his wrist and hold his gaze, ready to scold him if he proved to be a shallow trickster.

"Repeatedly," he said, undaunted.

I've miscalculated. Suddenly, she had no idea how she could get back to her room without making one horrible decision after another.

She was thinking through this as she turned slightly toward him. Unthinking, she had moved a fraction of an inch closer.

And that was when he kissed her for the first time.

It should have been a short, chaste kiss. That's how the first always is, isn't it?

But he dropped the book and let the guitar fall away. It clanged with a dissonant cord. She didn't want to let go, or embrace him, or feel what she was feeling. Joy surged through her chest as tears ran down her face.

"I'm glad you came," she said, her lips against his.

———

PENELOPE DANESTAR WALKED BRISKLY across the busy downtown street, her long, stylish coat matching her hat. Her shoes and handbag offset the look nicely—bold but not ostentatious, she hoped.

"Good morning, Miss Penelope," an old man with bad knees said from his stool by the soup kitchen's front door.

"Good morning to you, Mr. Olson. There is a long line today," she said.

"There always is when the Carter sisters are making the stew. They put in extra, is what I think," he said.

It was an old call and response they did every time she visited. "Extra what, Mr. Olson?"

"Love, Miss Penelope. The Carter sisters put extra love in every pot."

They exchanged smiles. She touched him on the arm, and he glowed with pleasure.

Inside, she found a place to hang her things and tied back her hair. She rolled up her sleeves and took her place in the middle of the serving line. Today, Kathrine Little worked on her right—handling mashed potatoes, gravy, and green beans. On her left, Henry Gabriel sliced roast beef from a block of meat.

Her job, as usual, was rolls. Probably because they assumed that was all she could do. At least they stopped assuming she just came to drop off a check and then leave with a clear conscience. Of course she did make a donation, but spending the time seemed to do more good.

Everyone at the soup kitchen was friendly, though some were less clean than others. As long as everyone behaved and didn't steal from one another, the rules were flexible.

She didn't know why there was poverty in Gildain. What confused her more, was that it was getting worse now that the Zezner War was finished. Shouldn't things be improving?

Thoughts of Victor's serenade made her blush. Katherine, three times Penelope's age, caught on immediately and teased her right in front of everyone.

She hoped she could be as perceptive as the older woman someday. Not once did Katherine assume Malcom Sky was the source of her good mood. In other social circles, that was the first thing men and women said to her. *Congratulations on your betrothal to Malcom Sky! He's so handsome*—he wasn't actually —*and dashing*—maybe, but not like Victor.

The only good trait she'd witness in the up-jumped mercenary was that she often saw him working at the soup kitchen, unloading pallets of food and general supplies from a delivery truck. Thirty years old, he was. Only ten years older than Victor, but twice as serious. Maybe life had dealt him hard blows on and off the battlefield.

But so often, the man was in a sour mood, swearing at the other guys helping him unload, calling them worthless more than once. He seemed ready to strike, but never did.

Volunteers for that type of heavy manual labor were hard to find, and the facility supervisor tolerated Malcom's unpleasantness because he came early, stayed late, and worked harder than any three men combined.

"Are you all right, Miss Penelope?" Katherine asked.

"I was just thinking."

"You must have been thinking really hard. Smile, young lady. What is a day without a little light?"

"Thank you, Katherine." She did smile, and before long, was able to put thoughts of both men—Victor and Malcom—from her thoughts.

———

NIGHT IN DOWNTOWN Lorne was far different from the sunny morning where she began her day of volunteering. Restaurant performers played music—keyboards and nine-string guitars most of the time, but occasionally xylophones, drums, and flutes. Excellent aromas wafted into the street to mix with the sights and sounds of nightlife. The subway seemed even busier than during normal working hours.

Penelope passed a group of dock workers who eyed her but said nothing. She did not greet them. It wasn't expected. On the contrary, talking to these strangers might be construed as an invitation.

Trains stopped and were unloaded. In a few places, airships landed and took off. Usually lifting smaller—but still significant —bundles for destinations unknown. Trains, trucks, and cargo lifts weren't much to look at, but the amount of raw work they accomplished did fascinate her. None of her friends would understand. Maybe that's why she had so few.

At the end of the street was a large, square, three-story building with lots of tall windows from a time before air conditioning was required by union contracts. This entire area was a far more humane place to work than it had been a hundred years before.

A security guard admitted her. She waited for exactly fifteen minutes in the lobby, just like every other time before. Only then did Miles Gafferty, the Tri Union president, greet her personally.

"Glad you could make it, Miss Danestar," he said, shaking her hand like the old mech driver he was. It took getting used to, and she knew he'd first done it to intimidate and test her, but now she expected it and did her best to return the grip firmly.

Right, wrong, or irrelevant, she'd learned her handshake was firmer than her father's. He had an aptitude for business optimization, but not the heart to negotiate the best deals. That showed in the sub-par alliance he'd made with her betrothal. In his defense, her father had avoided wedding her to men she would despise. So while she hadn't been allowed to marry for love, and the alliance wasn't the absolute best in terms of wealth, prestige, or military power, it was adequate.

Like House Danestar—good, but not great. She knew her family could rise far above the minor houses. Until then, she pretended to be indifferent. Stoicism, she'd learned, was one way to remain aloof from petty schemes. Her way was to watch, learn, and be ready. Someday it would be her turn to run the house and she was determined to make her family strong. When she was the matriarch, House Danestar would depend on no one.

"Thanks for meeting with me," she said.

He led her from the lobby into the offices, passing several cubicles where no one was working this late. The place smelled like cheap floor cleaner, vinyl tiles, dusty old computers, and bad coffee. She wondered what it was like during the day when people were working for their livelihoods.

Gafferty showed her into the boardroom. No one else was here yet. "I put back the general meeting thirty minutes. Thought you might have topics that needed covering before everyone starts groaning and complaining."

"I didn't realize the Union board was so contentious," she said.

"You're a kind soul," he said. "But they're a bunch of

disgruntled asshats. Have been their whole lives, and I've known most of them that long. Trust me."

"Of course, Mr. Gafferty."

"What's on your mind, Danestar?" he asked.

"I want to talk to you about House Marlboro and the Blue Sun expedition."

Eyes wide, he turned his head like what she'd said was really something. "Oh, just that. I'm glad none of the boys and girls are here yet. That's pre-rumor-rumor stuff right there."

"Perhaps," she conceded. "But you're a smart man who knows what large orders of certain parts means for his finances."

He crossed his beefy arms. "True. But what does that have to do with you? Last I checked, you were betrothed to that Sky Bull kid."

"Let me worry about my own motivations. I've always worked with the Union regarding Danestar contracts. Do you deny it?" Heart beating madly, she concealed the surge of adrenalin. The moment he sensed weakness he would treat her like a girl.

"Not at all," he said. "Labor relations have been greatly improved since you took an interest."

"If Marlboro hasn't come looking for workers, then they will. I want you to give them your best people."

He chewed that over. "What does it matter to you?"

"The Blue Sun expedition is important to everyone on Gildain. To humanity, even. And I will soon be part of House Bull."

His eyes widened, then he covered his interest with the cunning expression she liked least. "And tell me why that matters, or should I guess?"

She cursed inwardly at her slip. There was no proof of a Marlboro Bull Danestar alliance, but she knew it existed. Too many things fit her theory—and if they didn't have such an

175

alliance, then there would be civil war before long. All evidence pointed in that direction.

"My house, and the house of my betrothed, owes the Marlboros a fortune. It would be best if they left on an expedition and never returned," she said, careful not to say too much.

Gafferty scrutinized her. "Yeah, that's probably it, isn't it?"

He doesn't believe me.

"Here's the thing, Miss Danestar, you're not mean or vindictive. If you came to request the best workers I have for the Blue Sun project, it's because you want it to succeed. And you want people to prosper and explore the galaxy to glory and back."

She held her tongue.

"You've always played me honest. I'll keep your request private and attempt to fulfill it. But take my advice and don't bring this up again."

Lowering her gaze, she nodded. "Of course. Thank you."

Others arrived. The general meeting went as it always did. She studied men and women who were so different from those friends, family, and teachers who had shaped her life.

Near the end of the meeting, people chatted with their neighbors. Gafferty handed her a cup of coffee.

"Why do you come to these meetings? What's the real reason?" he asked.

She smiled. "How bored would you get if you were in my place?"

"I'd get fat and lazy. Like I am now."

"You're not lazy," she said.

He guffawed, slapping his belly. "Not lazy, she says!"

"Well, I meant it as a compliment, sir."

"I'm sure you did," he chuckled. "You're good people, Miss Danestar."

———

GAFFERTY DIDN'T GO home after the longer than usual meeting. After the Danestar girl left, he did what he promised—met with industry leaders, scouted for workers likely to perform well on an extended space expedition, and made arrangements to contact them privately. He'd need to learn all about them, gauge their interest, and get them to apply for contracts with Marlboro while believing it was their idea.

And then he would need to review contracts to be sure Big Ron Marlboro wasn't taking advantage of them. His reputation for fairness was annoyingly consistent, but that didn't mean he was a good man. Of course the duke was watching out for his own interests. And for him that meant paying decent wages and granting overtime pay when needed, rather than using it as a way to draw workers into more shifts than was good for them.

Mariah DeLene's apartment was small but lavishly furnished. Her status as King Martin Gerard's favorite mistress had perks.

He should be jealous. Hell, he was jealous. But she'd loved him first, since they were teenagers. And she probably didn't love his Royal Ass-ness at all. Money solved a lot of problems for people like Gafferty and DeLene, and the king was a good person to get it from.

"You came," she said when he dropped his coat on the couch and swept her up in his arms. "I was starting to wonder if you found another tart you like better."

"There aren't no tarts with a posterior like yours," he said.

"I hate it when you talk like that," she said. "Don't be like the others."

He held her for a long time, unable to apologize though he knew he should. "Things will be different someday," was all he managed to say.

"How, Gaf? You've said that since we were cutting class." She held his gaze with her amazing eyes—cool gray with flecks of lavender.

"A lot of opportunities in the Blue Sun citizen ships."

"Pfff. That doesn't affect us."

"Big Ron Marlboro is building a dozen ships, maybe twenty, for anyone who wants to reach the home world," Gafferty said.

"What are you talking about? That's dumb."

"Marlboro, the arrogant jerk, is letting people join the expedition even if they're not part of a noble house, and even if they don't have the money to buy their way onto a ship. Very egalitarian."

Mariah DeLene's voice dropped to a near whisper. "Why would he do that?"

"He wants to be more popular than the king. But you know what, if he plays stupid games, he's going to win a stupid prize. I'm tempted to sign up, start my own house in the Blue Sun system—assuming it's real and that ragtag fleet of junkers can make it there."

"Why don't you?" she asked, head on his shoulder, lips touching his neck as she spoke.

"I wouldn't go without you," he joked. But he wasn't joking. That realization had to remain unsaid. If she knew how head over heels he was for her, she'd lose interest in a hurry. No challenge in bedding a besotted, lovestruck middle-aged dock worker.

"Take me to the stars," she said.

He drove his gaze into her enchanting gray eyes, looking for mockery, a joke, or, God help him, sincerity.

A tear rolled down one of her cheeks.

"I'll take you to the stars right now," he said playfully.

She slapped his shoulder gently, then wiped her face. When she took his hand and led him toward the bedroom, Gafferty knew he only had one chance to say the right thing. As a man who could argue with lawyers and judges and corporate officers, he was surprisingly tongue-tied now.

"I'll take you anywhere you want to go, Mariah DeLene. But you can't breathe a word of it to the king," he said.

"I won't."

He waited for assurances, promises to keep their new secret private, because if any part of what he told her reach the ears of Martin Gerard, there would be civil war. And men like Gafferty would die without anyone even knowing or caring they'd ever existed.

CHAPTER TWENTY

RON STRODE to the tiny spaceport on the coast, pleased with the crowds of onlookers awaiting the spectacle. He had to admire their fortitude, because the action wouldn't start for several hours. And as with any complex training operation, there was a better than average chance it wouldn't start at all.

"Are your people ready, Victor?" he asked.

"I have four troop transports staged one mile out in a simulated camp with their mechs on flatbeds," Victor said. "When you give the go, they will move into this area, secure a perimeter, and load onto the launch vehicle. They'll run a safety check to make sure no personnel or spectators are close enough to be damaged by the thrusters, then head for space. It's a basic drill. Straight out of the book."

"Basic, but rarely performed in the last one hundred years of fighting Zezner on the planet," Ron said. "Hopefully the crowds will enjoy it."

"Are you intending on making your announcement? I don't think this is the right place for it," Victor said, keeping his voice low so none of the other soldiers could hear him. "You should throw a big event in Lorne, then rub it in the faces of the other great houses if this is what you want to do."

"Maybe," Ron said. "But this message is for regular citizens, and to be honest, I'd like to gauge their support before provoking every major household on the planet."

Victor shrugged, casual and cool as only a young buck can be. "Or you could just scrap the whole idea. You know, not commit political suicide."

Ron smiled dangerously. "What fun would that be?"

Victor laughed out loud, something Ron hadn't heard enough lately. "On that point, you have me. I'm bored with peace. Frankly, it's been too long since we've been in a fight."

"I can't argue with that, and I think your mother is even more ready to punch someone in the face than you are. But the goal is to garner support that is irresistible. A miscalculation will mean our complete destruction."

Victor swirled one hand in the air to signal his people to begin the operation, then faced Ron. "What could possibly go wrong?"

Ron gripped his son's shoulder but said nothing. His commitment to his plan grew hour by hour, but there were still moments of doubt and worry. He was only human, or near-human, after all. Turning toward Red, he realized how much influence the alien had on him now. The idea of only being near-human didn't faze him like it once had.

"Keep your eyes open, Red. I'm interested in your assessment of our operational readiness," Ron said.

"I imagine it will be terrible," the tall Zezner said. "How long has it been since you launched mechs into space? And have you ever deployed them from space to a planet? Your people have never been invaders of our world or any others, so you cannot understand how difficult this maneuver is."

"Someone experimented with the tactic and read a book on it," Ron said. "I'm confident that our deployment will be a hundred percent, totally error-free, and probably a stellar example to all future planetary assaults."

Victor and the alien laughed, which was an interesting

scene to say the least. Red modified his expression of mirth to be less damaging to human ears, lowering the pitch and volume. Now when he belly-laughed, it sounded like an ethereal flute playing a circus tune gone wrong. Which made Ron chuckle.

He stood back, crossed his arms, and studied the scene. The crowd watched the road leading to the small spaceport as if they were at a rally race. Decision made, he strode toward the group and found Mayor Keith Moore standing on a raised platform.

They exchanged handshakes. Ron slapped him on the back like they were old friends.

"I have an announcement I'd like to make," Ron said. "But I'd like to hear your thoughts on the idea before embarrassing myself publicly."

"Duke Marlboro, I'm flattered. Your house is respected in these parts, especially since your son Gregory gave us so much assistance during the last storm season," the mayor said. "What's on your mind?"

Ron swallowed, pushing down his last-minute nerves and endeavoring to hide his emotions. Instead, he gave the man a warm country smile that he'd learned from spending time at Elondale with Duke Travis Bull. "I volunteered to lead the Blue Sun expedition, and will make a serious push to be selected for the role."

The mayor grinned. "Well, I and the people of Ice Bay wish you the best of luck. Personally, I am very confident that you are the right man for the job."

"Thanks, but there is one other thing. And this is where I need your input. I'm building three ships that I intend to open to unattached citizens who wish to participate in the expedition."

The mayor stared at him. "I'm sorry, can you repeat that?"

"Not everyone can be or wants to be attached to a house," Ron said. "The Blue Sun expedition will take the best minds and hands that Gildain has to offer, and many of those people live in places like Ice Bay."

"Well, Lord Duke, that is a greatly appreciated compliment. I have concerns that this will start a fervor among the people, and they'll be unhappy if such a promise isn't fulfilled. In fact… that's an understatement. We are a simple, hardworking people, and not prone to sedition in any way, so I'm not saying there would be violence. But should you fail, your popularity among unattached citizens would evaporate."

Ron held his gaze. "If I say I'll do a thing, I will. I intend for all citizens to have a chance to make this journey. There will have to be a lottery, or something of that nature. I may even require a skill and knowledge test to enter the lottery, but that's only practical."

"Oh, yes. That's fair. But think about what I said. You can't say something like this lightly, because by the end of the day, everyone in Gildain will know of your offer and not through official media channels."

"That's the idea," Ron said.

"Well, you ready, then? I'll introduce you. Good luck."

"Thanks, Mayor."

"Attention, everyone," Moore said into the microphone. "Duke Ron Marlboro has something he wants to say before his soldiers get here to launch their mechs."

A cheer for the pending launch went up, jovial but not passionate. This was great entertainment, a rare spectacle in these parts.

Moore stepped back, indicating with one hand that Ron was welcome to use the microphone.

Ron adjusted the stand to his greater height. "Thanks for having us, Ice Bay. I just want to ask you a small favor. If we botch this launch, go easy on us afterward."

Laughter rippled through the crowd.

"There is one other thing," he said, and then suddenly felt like all of his words were stilted and wrong. Public speaking held no fears for him, no more than fighting an alien invasion did. But at the last second, stage fright and doubt hit him like hammers. He pushed forward, because that was the only way he knew how to deal with adversity. "I've contracted the construction of three ships." That was wrong, out of order. "Well, this would all make more sense if I started at the beginning. I have volunteered to lead the Blue Sun expedition and will be dedicating a large part of my personal assets to make sure the project is a success. What I need from you, and from your representatives, is support in the Assembly of Lords and the Legislature. But that's not what I came here to say."

The crowd stared at him, completely silent. A breeze came up the ocean, ruffling hair and clothing.

"I've dreamed of seeking the home world, of exploring any part of space I could, since I was a boy. I'm sure many of you have the same fascination with what's out there. But I'm lucky, and I know it. Even if I'm not selected to lead the expedition, I could take my family and go by myself, though it would be much more dangerous. So what I'm saying is this: I'm building three ships for unattached citizens of reasonable qualifications and good character to join the expedition."

Surprised, the crowd exploded with questions and cheers.

The mayor stepped forward, grabbing the mic. "Settle down, everyone. I don't have to tell you what a big deal it is. House Marlboro has always been good to Ice Bay. Listen to what he's saying and try to act like adults. This isn't the time to spread idle rumors or speculation."

"Tell us the rest!" a man from the back shouted.

Ron thanked the mayor, then took the microphone again. "A wise man very recently warned me that making promises like this without following through would be in bad form. So I promise you this: my offer is real, and I will do everything to make it happen fairly. The ships I build for regular folk will be equal to the ones I built for my own family. There will be a lottery, with the only prerequisite being a knowledge and skills test so that I know everyone accepted to the voyage will be able to pull their weight."

"That's reasonable," someone said.

Another person shouted, "Wins the lottery? How do we put our names in?"

"Who else knows? Why are we always the last to be told about things like this?" someone complained.

Ron held up a hand. "Listen up, if you will. I've not spoken of this publicly until now. By tomorrow, an official statement will be made on regular news bulletins." He wished he hadn't called them regular folk, because some resented the label. "House Marlboro has all due respect for the other houses, the king, and the people of Gildain, but I consulted no one on this project. It's a personal fault. I make decisions based on what is right, not on the popular will of my peers." This part was exceedingly dangerous. "The only thing that can stop this endeavor from going forward, would be getting blocked by the Assembly of Lords, the Legislature, and the king. I respect them and wish to serve them, just as I wish to serve you. But do me a solid, if you can. Support me loudly and often in this venture. That's all I ask. The mandate of the Legislature is to ensure the will of the people be known and respected by the laws and the powers that be. Talk to your representatives and voice your support."

Silence spread through the crowd, and he wondered if he hadn't doomed his house, his family, and all his allies with this strategy.

Mayor Keith Moore stepped forward again. "It looks like the duke's troops are almost here. Let's see what they're made of. I've always loved a good launch."

The crowd remained distracted, but many turned toward the highway where armored troop transports were speeding toward the exercise with flatbed trucks carrying mechs in the center of the column.

"Thanks for coming out today," Ron said. "If you have ques-

tions about my announcement, please contact my public information officer. Honestly, he needs the work."

That sparked laughter, but then something else happened.
Someone started a chant that quickly took hold until hundreds
of people shouted "Ur-on!" and stamped their feet.

"Uron! Uron! Uron!"

Ron hadn't expected them to use his birth name. He
wouldn't have been surprised if they had chanted "Marlboro"
or "Blue Sun." This, he hadn't expected at all.

Victor and his officers lined the edge of the launch platform,
waving the squads towards their signposts. For one second, it
looked like some of the lead elements had confused their roles,
but they quickly recovered and took up the correct positions.

The flatbed trailers arrived, and crews piloted the mechs
perfectly. This was the one thing House Marlboro did better
than anyone, mech driving. The war machines unfurled themselves from the flatbeds, strode toward the launch shuttles, and
climbed into individual pods where they were strapped in by
industrial-strength restraints, then filled with foam to keep
them from shifting.

Ron's heart swelled with pride.

The rest of the support crews and squads collapsed their
perimeter around the ships, then boarded, just as if they'd left a
combat zone while under fire. Safety teams cleared away any
bystanders and set up the blast shields with only a few hesitant
mistakes. This only cost seconds, but to Ron it felt like a huge
deficiency.

The crowd, almost a mile away from Ron, didn't seem to
notice or care. Their cheers continued unabated.

And then, engines ignited, and four ships fought their way
toward the stratosphere.

CHAPTER TWENTY-ONE

VICTOR, his body armor attached to the wall of the assault ship, looked up and down the line of his mech pilots. Launching from the surface of the planet to the orbiting assault ship, then completing the safety inspection, had taken far longer than he'd hoped. His officers and noncommissioned officers had grumbled, but everyone knew the performance was adequate.

Adequate…

He wrote his report in his head over and over, trying to justify the mediocre results of the exercise.

"Moving mechs from the planet to a ship would be a post-battle event in almost any scenario," Marsten said. "This drill is contrived."

"As drills tend to be," Kilo said. "It's called practice." He smacked Marsten's helmet. "Practice launching from the surface, and practice assaulting enemies on the surface. It's a two-for-one. Efficient."

"I was just saying we shouldn't expect it to flow seamlessly on our first try. When was the last time we did any of this?" Marsten asked.

"Never in my lifetime," Kilo said.

"My point exactly." Marsten popped his knuckles and

leaned back, outwardly cool and confident. Victor's friend was from a minor house pledged to Marlboro. They'd fought side-by-side since they were kids, earning true warrior status in the final few years of the Zezner War. Just like Kilo, his other battle companion. The three of them had always been eager to take on all comers.

"He's right," Kilo said.

Victor nodded and waved away the conversation, preferring to focus on what was ahead. "As long as the assault goes well, I'll consider the day a success. We need practice in both missions. This isn't the Zezner War anymore. We've got new challenges ahead."

The fourth member of this drop squad said nothing, just stared at them with the hard, cold eyes of a mercenary who'd climbed high above his status.

Malcom Sky, the adopted son of Duke Travis Bull. The man who'd stolen Penelope.

This has to be a test, Victor thought. *My father wants to see if I can follow orders, remain professional, complete the mission even with this son of a Zezner dog in my squad.*

Drop squads consisted of four mech units. The shuttle would release each of them in a pod just inside of the atmosphere, then circle to provide air support. On the planning screen, it looked elegant. He hoped it worked as well as he'd been taught. No one had done this, even in training, for at least a decade, and probably four or five decades before that. Instead, everything had been geared towards the defense against Zezner assaults on the planet.

Victor and his companions were novices once again.

Confidence, Victor.

Malcom Sky stared at him wordlessly. The man didn't fidget, shift his weight, or recheck his gear like most men and women did at this stage. The slightest equipment malfunction, or even misalignment, could mean death, even in a training

scenario. Victor would hate the man less if he wasn't so competent as a warrior.

A mercenary. Just a mercenary who got lucky. Bull needed a
son to execute his political maneuvering with House Danestar.
The entire situation was embarrassing. He wished his father
hadn't become so friendly with the Bull.

In a squad shuttle, the copilot was the drop controller until
they deployed the team and moved into an air support role.
Warrant Officer II Sarah Kane came over the intercom. "One
minute. Close off your individual chase pods, then tandem to
your mechs."

Victor climbed into the armored pod and synchronized its
computer with his mech's computer—what drop specialists called
digital tandem. The theory, based on safety concerns, was that the
pilot of a mech always dropped separately from, but in close proximity to, his vehicle. That way at least one of them would survive
if something went wrong. It was unclear whether the mech or the
pilot had a better chance of walking after landing. Either way, the
tandem protocols maintained an invisible link all the way down.

He wondered, not for the first time, what the warrant officer
looked like. He'd only seen her in passing, but she had a posi-
tive energy that he thought, just maybe, might pull him out of
the dark places his mind went these days.

But he didn't have time for that. And he hadn't given up on
marrying Penelope yet.

He snapped into his pod and ran a systems check. One
minute wasn't a long time to prepare for a life-or-death activity.
He had fifteen seconds to spare as the drop light turned from
red to yellow. When it went green, the assault shuttle would
become much lighter without four battle mechs aboard, and he
would be plunging towards the surface, looking for the landing
zone.

It was a small target, but larger than it might be in an actual
combat mission. Precision won battles. In this case, a perfect

landing of four House Marlboro war machines, even if one of them was secretly piloted by the adopted son of Travis Bull, would go a long way toward impressing spectators.

"Thirty seconds," Sarah Kane said.

Victor controlled his breathing, pushing aside all his anxiety and frustration that had accumulated over the last few months. He wished he could see the face of Penelope Danestar, but his attention was focused on his drop pod and the mech he would soon be climbing into after the landing. Hopefully, right in front of a cheering crowd.

"In three, two, one—pods away," Kane said. "Have fun storming the castle, gentlemen."

Her final words sang in his ears as his pod plummeted toward the surface.

"Checking descent vector," he said to his computer. A poor-quality image of his mech pod heading almost straight down appeared on the screen. He bumped the side of the monitor, hoping to jostle the resolution. It flickered on and off. "Computer, check electrical systems for connection integrity."

"Connection integrity adequate," the bland voice said.

Adequate. There's that word again. I want excellence.

He ignored the crappy image, concentrating on the vector lines that showed he was in pursuit of his mech, at least. On one side of the screen, six icons, three pilots and their vehicles, fanned out in a V formation with him and his mech pod in the center. At least something was going right.

When his pod—designated as the command unit—altered course, its computer compensating for atmospheric changes, the rest of his drop squad adjusted their trajectories accordingly. He imagined dozens of squads heading toward objectives like this was a real battle. From up here, he fully appreciated the size of a battlefield. Everything seemed smaller during an actual fight, the space containing just you and the opponent right in front of you.

He thought about his father wrestling the Zezner champion

off the cliff and nearly dying with his enemy in the White Ocean. He glanced toward the horizon, a hundred kilometers away, where the ice-flecked sea loomed.

"Why don't you keep your eyes on the objective, Marlboro?" came Malcolm's voice.

Victor checked the link. Private. *At least he's not a total fool.*

"We're looking pretty good," Victor said, glad that things were finally going right, but also annoyed that he had to share the moment with his rival.

"Initial deployment was a circus," Malcom said on the private link. "Your boys bumped into each other on the way out, which shouldn't be able to happen with computers controlling that part of the process. But somehow they managed it."

"We'll check the systems." Victor didn't want to talk to this man.

"Of course. I didn't mean to insinuate your buddies were overeager or unprofessional… sir."

Victor checked the clock. In seconds, the mech pod would deploy four giant chutes to slow its fall. His own chute would deploy simultaneously, and if it didn't, then he would puncture the canopies below him and probably die in a tangled mess of mech parts and blood.

"Hold on," Victor said.

Seconds ticked by.

FWOOMP.

The massive chutes burst into the air below him as his own pod deployed its canopy. A quick check of his side screen showed the rest of the squad had successful parachute openings as well.

As always, this was where trajectories were randomized. Atmospheric conditions and wind were hard to predict and not as easily adjusted for. Everyone's chutes were steered by computers, with the option to exert manual control if needed, but it was a slow process compared to the high-speed plunge immediately preceding this part of the maneuver.

193

"Ugly," Victor said, realizing at the last second he was still on the private line with Malcolm Sky.

"That might be the first thing we agree on," the upstart mercenary said. "Maybe it's a start."

"The hell you mean by that?"

"We are on the same side, like it or not. You think I'm worthless because I wasn't born into a house like you. No, I had to fight for money to stay alive. But I learned something doing that. I figured out how to fight for idiot leaders and get along with people who made me want to choke 'em every time they opened their mouths. I can get along with you, make this farce of an alliance work. The question is, Marlboro, can you get along with me and put your hurt feelings aside?"

Victor didn't answer. They were too close to the ground and he needed to concentrate. Or that's what he told himself. In reality, the final seconds drew out for far longer than seemed possible.

"We're fifty meters off target," Victor said, hiding his annoyance. "We'll be touching down behind the spectators. Priority one, don't crush any little kids running around playing tag behind their parent's backs. Priority two, let's try to look sharp even though we are in the wrong place."

No one spoke. Victor could feel the tension. Marsten and Kilo, practically his brothers, knew better than anyone how this failure was going to humiliate him in front of his most bitter rival. Malcolm, for his part, said nothing. A lesser man might have rubbed it in.

His mech landed hard, throwing dirt fifty feet into the air. His pod cut through the debris and touched down harder than he expected, jarring his teeth even inside his shock resistant helmet. Slamming his palm on the release button, he jumped from the crude vehicle and ran to his mech which was tipped on its side, just outside of the larger deployment pod.

Annoying, but I can deal with it.

Victor, like any good combat pilot, knew how to stand up a

194

fallen mech. He wasn't like the dumbasses in House Atana who preferred tanks to mechs because they weren't good at staying on their feet. Marlboro had tanks too, for certain situations, but the blocky tracked vehicles couldn't climb the obstacles that the Zezner had been fond of placing in their path.

Malcolm Sky jogged to his vehicle, not in a hurry, but was in the cockpit at nearly the same instant Victor dropped into his seat and strapped in. The guy was so cool and professional that it irritated Victor, even though he knew he should respect the man for his competency.

Marsten and Kilo were a beat slower.

Victor waited for fifteen frustrating seconds before giving the order to assemble. "Form up, let's salute the crowd."

Malcolm stepped to his side in one easy movement, the Marlboro mech he piloted responding to his perfect control. Victor's friends were a beat slower, but soon completed the line. They stood straight.

The crowd had faced a new landing site while watching the drop. Some of them were jostling for a better view, because the bleachers were slanted in the wrong direction. Some came around the edges of the stands, others crowded the back row. A large group of teenagers gathered in a nearby field and Victor was glad he hadn't landed on them.

"On my mark, salute!"

All four mechs pounded their chests simultaneously, one time, and bow their cockpits for a full second. When they released their right mech arms, they stood at attention. Victor's father strode up and down the line, hands clasped behind his back, his emotions completely unreadable.

Victor did his duty, but he understood his father's look. They would be training hard, every day, until they literally couldn't mess this up.

Assuming Victor didn't challenge Malcom Sky to a duel first.

CHAPTER TWENTY-TWO

PATRICIA LEFT THE LEGISLATURE ROTUNDA, making eye contact with no one. Lieutenant Carmichael walked beside her and two of his soldiers followed. After the attacks on various Marlboro staff and family members, no one from House Marlboro left the manor without a security element. Except for Fortune, who continued to make unauthorized flights at will.

The young woman was her most spirited and troublesome child.

"The car is en route from the parking garage," Carmichael said. "Do you have a destination in mind?"

"Yes, anywhere I might find Lord Abnercon." Patricia needed a solution, and thus far the financier had been little help. All he'd done was sway her husband toward the Blue Sun project. It was time to deliver an ultimatum.

"I will make inquiries and secure an appointment with the man," Carmichael said.

"One other thing. Locate Fortune. I require her presence at this meeting. It is about time the girl makes herself useful," Patricia said.

"I will see to it immediately."

The moment Patricia was in the car, she leaned back and

closed her eyes. *I haven't been this tired since I was pregnant. Perish the thought.* It could happen, but she'd rather it didn't.

Carmichael climbed into the front passenger seat. The two soldiers hopped into the chase vehicle a second before Patricia's driver sped into traffic. The chase car was a larger sedan, big enough for four combat-ready infantrymen concealed inside, plus the driver and a front seat passenger—normally a combat controller.

If something happened, the big car would rush forward and deploy six trained Marlboro soldiers who would fight like demons to make sure she escaped.

And she would hate that, leaving them behind to face her assassins. But that was the immediate action drill they all practiced, and everyone knew their parts.

So much trouble just for me to get the runaround by the Legislature.

She agreed with the safety precautions, even if it took the fun out of day-to-day life. What she missed was flirting with her husband and watching her children's antics, both young and old. Life would be easier if the king would just revoke their house charter and start a real war.

By law, everyone in House Marlboro would be required to surrender material possessions and apply for a special type of parole until another house would sponsor them. In reality, her family—along with every other man, woman, and child of House Marlboro—would either fight back or become homeless and destitute. Some would be forced out into the wildlands or the villages along the coast of the White Ocean.

And would that be so bad?

Sometimes, that life appealed to her. She could imagine Ron being a village councilman and a craftsman, as he sometimes talked about. A man who did things with his hands and spent his leisure time with his family, unarmed and with no prospects of battle in his future.

Yet that idyllic image horrified her. Because she *could* see him in that role. And he could be happy living such a life, but at her core, she knew that was not who Duke Uron Marlboro was.

And how would I fare living such a pastoral life? I'd go stir-crazy. She'd make everyone's life a living hell.

"I've located your daughter, and she stated that she would be delighted to join you in whatever mischief you are about," Lieutenant Carmichael said cheerfully.

Patricia laughed. "I'm sure that's exactly what she said."

The officer held up one hand as though swearing to tell the truth, the whole truth, and nothing but the truth. "It is indeed, my duchess."

"Well then, let's pick her up and take her to see Abnercon." Patricia gazed out the window, watching the city pass by. They didn't go near the combined training grounds. After Ron's experience there, it was an area of the city to be approached with caution. Her driver also avoided the Cherry Blossom District, which upset her, because it was one of her favorite places in Lorne.

This place is already lost to us. We are outcasts but haven't yet admitted it.

Patricia's motorcade pulled into the stables, an excellent facility that Ron had recently improved to compete with Duke Bull's. When Fortune climbed in the car, she was groomed to the best of her ability given the short notice, but nothing could be done about her outfit—a pair of tight-fitting pants and jacket made for riding.

"You smell like a horse," Patricia sniffed.

"Thank you, Mother. I love you too." She leaned over and gave her mother a big hug and a kiss on the cheek, causing Patricia to squirm and laugh despite herself.

"We're en route to the harbor," Lieutenant Carmichael said. "The normal drive time is about two hours, unless you want us to push it. Lord Abnercon advises he will have transport to his yacht waiting."

"Very good, Lieutenant," Patricia said, then faced Fortune.

"What were you doing at the stables? I thought you'd be flying."

"There's more to life than flying," Fortune said, gazing out the window, avoiding eye contact with her mother.

Patricia leaned forward. "Fortune, what's going on?"

"Nothing. Maybe I like horseback riding," Fortune said. "Or the riders."

Patricia immediately relaxed. The explanation for her daughter's behavior seemed plausible enough. She was young, single, and interested in men her age. Completely understandable.

Still, Patricia wasn't completely convinced. She leaned back, but didn't consider the question resolved. *I'm watching you, young woman.*

They spent the drive talking about horses, airships, and gossip. When the harbor came into view, the conversation dwindled to nothing.

True to his word, Lord Abnercon had an excellent pontoon barge waiting for them, a craft that would carry them to the yacht in comfort. Patricia's husband, along with most of the other men in her life, would have thought a motorized launch sufficient. This was a nice change of pace.

Sometimes a lady wanted comfort and class... when she wasn't shooting the hell out of a Zezner assault force with mech guns.

She climbed the ladder, stepped onto the deck, and was politely given a moment to smooth her coat and trousers before Abnercon came forward to greet her.

"Duchess Marlboro, it is a delight to have you and your daughter on my humble craft," Abnercon said.

Patricia ran her eyes over the yacht, thirty meters from stem to stern. White pine decks had been scrubbed recently. Mahogany railing, towering masts, and tightly furled sails of the best fabric spoke of money and prestige. The crew stood confidently at their posts.

"Your *boat* is the best I've seen," she said.

Abnercon bowed his head to accept the compliment, then waved them toward the aft deck where refreshments awaited. "Her captain would prefer the term ship."

Patricia let the correction go.

Courtesies were exchanged. Food and wine were offered and sampled before they began the conversation in earnest.

"We have committed to the Blue Sun Project," Patricia said. "Someone has been blocking production and financing, especially of the smaller industries that are needed to make the mission a success."

"Such as?" Abnercon asked.

"We bid on three foundry ships, and only one responded to our offer."

Lord Abnercon held her gaze, his expression polite but blank.

"We still need two mobile shipyards and a void dock small enough to tow until we can find a better way to construct a modern fleet," she continued.

Naming those details shook something loose in the man, like he hadn't expected that level of sophistication. Many people assumed House Marlboro only cared for war. That they didn't know how to build at all, much less create anything entirely new.

She raised an eyebrow and crossed her arms.

Abnercon smiled. "But you already converted a mining ship to handle most everything a proper foundry can produce. What more do you need?"

Patricia restrained her initial response, struggling for a more reasonable tone. "We're talking about leaving the Gildain system in search of a planet that might not exist. We will never come back. One patched together foundry won't be sufficient for a nation in space."

He shook his head, laughing with genuine amusement. "Only a Marlboro would have the audacity to even consider towing a void dock. With three foundries, mobile shipyards, and a void dock, you could build entirely new ships."

"Yes, that is the point."

"True, and that is also what worries some of your rivals. They don't want you flying off to the next system, building an armada, and then coming back to conquer Gildain," Abnercon said.

"Who is spreading those slanderous accusations?"

Patricia felt Fortune's calming hand on her arm.

"Mother, we don't think Lord Abnercon would insinuate anything like that," Fortune said.

"No, of course not," Patricia huffed.

Abnercon waved away another tray of wine glasses. The attendant bowed and retreated out of earshot.

"I will look into the matter and remove barriers to the sale of the foundries and other materials you desire," Abnercon said. "I feel responsible, since I was the one who encouraged your husband to take on this venture."

"Yes, you were. Still, you have my thanks in regard to the supply issues."

"Is there anything else I might do to help?" he asked.

She thought about House Hawk and their expertise with experimental technology like anti-grav and starship drive design, but decided not to involve him. If he turned out to be false, or if he thought he might make more money by contracting Hawk's efforts for himself, Marlboro-Wilson would suffer.

"The foundries were my biggest concern," she said. "You've put my mind at ease. And you've been a delightful host."

"Feel free to stay the night, or the weekend. I have plenty of rooms, and my staff would be happy to serve you, even though I may need to leave in the morning."

Patricia stood. "Generous, but we must go. I promised Fortune we could drive along the coast and see more of her new favorite passion—all the wild horses that run on the white sands of the beaches near House Hawk's domain."

"House Hawk," Abnercon said. "Strange people. Nearly bankrupt, I fear, and too proud to accept loans."

"Too bad for them," Patricia said. "But surely they won't interfere with our sightseeing."

"Doubtful," Abnercon said. "They would probably be over-joyed to entertain you and your daughter, in their own simple way. I've heard they actually have several good pubs near their hold."

Patricia finished the pleasantries, Fortune acted like a lady, and they took the pontoon boat back to the shore.

"Wild horses?" Fortune asked.

"You've never seen the herds."

"Nope. And never really thought about driving the coast for that purpose," Fortune said.

Patricia let the topic drop as they walked to the car with Lieutenant Carmichael.

"So what is the real reason we're going there, Mother?"

"I want to talk to Duke Herman Hawk. It's about time the man sees the benefits of joining the BSA."

CHAPTER TWENTY-THREE

DUKE HERMAN HAWK met them at the edge of town in a flatbed lorry that had seen better days. Covered with dents, rusted through in places, and with mismatched wheels and tires, it was a strange vehicle for the leader of a house obsessed with technology and innovation.

"Welcome to Hawk Town!" Herman said, jumping down to shake their hands. "Not our town, actually, but the locals treat us like we own it. What brings you our way?"

"We came to watch the wild horses run on the beach," Fortune said, loudly and with total conviction.

Patricia jabbed her in the ribs with an elbow.

"Mother!"

"Don't get cute," Patricia said, even as she noticed that Hawk had seen the elbow jab.

Observant, that's good.

"Wild horses are majestic creatures," Hawk said. "I always plan to get out of the lab and watch them more than I do."

"Speaking of your labs, I'll cut straight to the point, Duke Hawk. House Marlboro is very interested in some of your recent tech designs."

Hawk's eyes lit up. "Well then, this will be a good visit for both of us. Shall we eat first or would you like to start with a tour?"

"Lord Abnercon fed us too much," Fortune said.

Hawk's expression darkened. "Good thing you didn't bring him. The locals have little love for that man." He pointed at the Marlboro car. "You can follow in your vehicle or ride in my truck, your choice."

"My lady," Carmichael said. "The limousine is armored. I would prefer we continue as we came."

"Of course, Lieutenant." Patricia then addressed Hawk. "We have been operating under very tight security as of late."

"Your choice. Not everyone appreciates this hunk of junk. It's a pure combustion engine. Don't see many of those anymore."

"I thought they'd been exiled to museums," Patricia said.

"We build a lot of obsolete things," Hawk said. "Old technology is often informative. Some secrets lie in the old ways."

The limousine followed the truck to the center of town where a blocky three-story building awaited. There were no guards. Citizens of Hawk Town walked right past the front door on a generic sidewalk.

"Your security could use some attention," Patricia said. She wanted to work with House Hawk, but not if they were going to be a liability. Lax protocol had become dangerous since the end of the Zezner War.

"We've got cameras and drones," Hawk said. "More than enough for us. Most of the other houses forget we're here."

"Cameras can't fight off assassins or thieves."

"True." Hawk's response was neither defensive nor informative. The man didn't seem compelled to explain himself, and Patricia liked that.

Entering the Hawk "manor" was like stepping into a large middle-class home. She'd expected a guard, or at least a doorman inside the entrance, but there was no one. The place was clean, the decorations dated but tasteful, and the lighting ample. Tapestries of Hawk lords lined the main hallway, which had a high ceiling and stairs running up one side to the next level. Everything was terra-cotta tile or polished wood.

"Our main laboratories are on the top level and in the basement. Everything in between is for day-to-day living," Hawk explained as he gave them the tour.

"Can you see the wild horses from the top level? Maybe there's a balcony or a roof veranda," Fortune said.

Patricia shot her daughter a look.

Fortune flashed a cheeky grin.

"I think you came to see what we have in the basement," Hawk said.

Patricia waited. The man looked uncertain.

"Your lieutenant will have to wait here. And I really shouldn't take you into our primary laboratory, but..." Hawk didn't complete his thought.

"But you are, aren't you?" Patricia said. "Why is that, Lord Hawk?"

He blushed. "I know a great deal about the Blue Sun project. Truth be told, I was glad when my sources informed me it was in the works. Your involvement is the worst-kept secret on Gildain. I assumed you would be coming to me when you realized the shortcomings of the current fleet."

Patricia smiled and canted her head. "You got it in one, Hawk. I think I'm going to like you."

"Yeah!" Fortune said. "You and your wild beach horses."

Patricia swatted her arm. "Pardon my daughter, Lord Hawk. My child thinks she's a comedian today."

Hawk blushed again, laughing awkwardly. "Well, sure. I only have sons, but they can be equally... fond of pulling my chain. Let me show you what we've been working on for the last ten years."

"I'll be honored to see your work," Patricia said.

Hawk led them to a stairwell, and they descended deep underground. There were no doorways for the first ten meters of the descent. Unlike the casual construction of the living area above, this section meant business. The metal staircase was starship-grade steel coated in a rubbery corrosion-resistant surface that enhanced traction.

Fortune's attitude changed, as well. She transformed from a lighthearted jokester to an attentive observer. Hawk grew nervous as they approached the first door, but also excited. He kept shooting them glances and explaining small details about the place.

"We put all of our wealth into these facilities. It may look humble to people on the outside, but House Hawk isn't as destitute as people assume." He paused, then looked them over like he was about to change his mind and deny them access. Then, some internal argument concluded, he nodded and returned his attention to the access panel.

Shielding the device, he punched in the code, and the door opened. Inside were two armed men in Hawk infantry uniforms, black with purple accents and silver stitching for the name tabs. Their helmets were mirrored from the outside, and the men who wore them didn't talk.

Herman didn't salute them, but merely passed by and approached a security booth. The man inside obviously recognized the duke but didn't open the next door—which looked like it could withstand a laser saw.

"These are my guests. I am not under duress," Herman said.

"Good to see you, Lord Duke. Please give the security code of the day," the guard inside the terminal said.

Herman spoke with extreme precision, each syllable exactly the same. "Sand horse x-ray seventeen bravo."

The door opened, but Patricia didn't enter. She crossed her arms and raised an eyebrow at the duke. "We came here talking of horses, and that's part of your secret password? Are you mocking us?"

"Uh, no." His voice faltered. "That's not it, at all."

Fortune stepped in, placing a calming hand on her mother

again. "It's voice recognition. He could probably say almost anything."

"Very observant," Herman said. "Although, in the spirit of our future cooperation, I can disclose that a portion of the voice code is preset."

"Of course," Patricia said. "Very clever. But what if the door were forced? Any of my troopers could cut it through in less than an hour."

"They would find nothing but smoking ruins. Personnel who were unable to escape via means I'll not discuss would have committed suicide to avoid interrogation."

"Are you certain your people have that kind of resolve?" Patricia asked. "I'm not questioning their character or bravery—"

"Or stupidity," Fortune muttered.

"—but what you ask is much harder than charging into battle. Harder than just about anything."

Hawk answered slowly. "Every man and woman beyond this point accepted an adjustment to their nanites. They made their decision already. There is no going back."

Patricia immediately thought of Doctor Stacks and his complaints about how hard it was to even study the nanites, much less modify them.

House Hawk has been seriously underestimated by everyone, including me.

"What do you have to show us, Duke?"

Patricia continued to size him up. Although a lord, the man had his sleeves rolled up. Three pairs of glasses in his front shirt pocket. A battered notebook in his left cargo pocket.

More than an intellectual. Applied science seems to be his thing. He's like Ron—happy in his work.

The man led the way inside with an energetic flourish. "We have working models on this floor. It might not seem like much, but it is one of my favorite projects."

Patricia watched and listened, gathering information to

make a judgment about this potential ally. Was he smart, or did he only think he was clever? Had his house wasted his family's fortunes, or invested them with more cunning in acumen than anyone realized? Hawk definitely lacked military strength—barely had a physical security element. Did technology make up for that clear weakness?

As for the man, he seemed athletic in an accidental kind of way, but she could be wrong. The old pickup truck had thrown her off, like it probably did many people. Images of her husband working in the shop, cursing and banging wrenches to get a mech to work, came easily to her imagination. Until visiting this place, she never would have thought a scientist might dig his hands and tools into a machine and come out filthy with grease and banged knuckles, like Ron.

At the end of this hallway, there was a regular door. Everything was clean and tidy, unadorned with anything not necessary to its basic functionality.

Fortune leaned close. "This place is a lot bigger underground than I thought. I think we are far beyond the outer walls of the building above."

"Agreed. Stay sharp. I knew I brought you for a reason." Patricia wasn't sure how she felt, but a tingle of hope and curiosity gave her a renewed energy.

Herman opened the door and waved them in with a grand gesture. "Behold, the model room. We've replicated what we know about the Blue Sun Project. I heard a rumor of a rumor that your husband once called it the Blue Sun Armada—a name that likely angers the king and other military lords, from what I understand. I only mention the armada because, when you look at it like this, it really does look like a grand fleet more than a collection of exploration vessels."

Ten feet into the room, Patricia found herself on a huge metal balcony overlooking a room five or six meters deep and nearly as high. She sucked in a breath and held it, her surprise matched by Fortune's reaction.

An unseen force suspended model ships in a formation only possible in space, in three dimensions. They moved slightly.

"How...?"

Duke Herman of House Hawk smiled, and this seemed to be a final revelation of his true character. He might be awkward, even now, but he was proud of his intelligence and what his house had accomplished. "Each of the ships are fully functional models. Down to the internal corridors and climate control systems. We are able to mimic the effect of orbital gravity with our anti-grav generators."

She spun to face him. "You know what you've done?"

He flinched at her sharp tone.

"Does the king know about this? Do any of his people have a clue what you've been able to do?"

"Make ship models? I doubt he'd care." He waved toward the ships, saying, "These are made out of extremely lightweight materials. Initially, it was a test of the anti-grav technology. We've been able to use it on heavier objects, but if you think this is going to change mechs or even industrial equipment, you're jumping a bit into the future."

"But does the king know you've done even this much?"

"House Hawk knows how to protect its breakthroughs." Herman furrowed his brow, squared his shoulders. Maybe he did have some fight in him. "Patents can be stolen, fortunes lost."

"But that's not the problem, Lord Duke. If the king learns you have this technology and didn't immediately apprise him of its potential, then you may find yourself in his prison," Patricia said. "Or executed."

Color drained from the man's face. "I never thought of that. I was worried that Danestar or Redwine would unfairly profit from our work without offering fair compensation."

"Let's just think this through," Patricia said. "My advice is free. I honestly never believed any house could be in more trouble than ours—never thought something like this would be an issue."

"But you recognized the problem immediately," Herman said. "Our policy has always been to maximize secrecy, because in the technological product and services industry, intellectual property is easily stolen by rivals."

"I'm not criticizing your actions. I'm sure I would've done the same thing. But now that you understand the danger, going forward without accounting for the king's wrath would be foolish."

Fortune's voice broke through the tension. "Mother, there's only one solution. House Hawk has to come with us on the expedition. They can't stay here."

Silence held the landing and the mocked-up space scene beyond it. Patricia thought she could hear the ships adjusting their formation—tiny engines warming, steering thrusters whispering with no obvious rhythm. Imagining consequences and weighing them against possible actions, she observed the Blue Sun Armada spread above and below her.

"I was already hoping to send representatives on the expedition," Herman said. "I... never considered... taking everyone. Will the king really be so angry?"

"How much time have you spent with the king?" Patricia asked, her voice stern.

"We met once."

Patricia nodded. "His family has remained in power for hundreds of years. That only happens when you know how to look for threats. Ruthlessly. The technology you've developed is a huge leap forward, and he will own it and you, if you survive the ordeal."

"Well, the technology isn't complete. Like I said, it only has limited applications. You won't see cars hovering around the city or mechs jumping into the clouds anytime soon," Herman said.

"Of course. And you probably understand better than I what

it took to achieve this level of technology," Patricia said. "You have my oath, and that of my daughter, not to reveal your secret. Until we think of something better, I recommend that you double down on your concealment of this breakthrough. And I do believe it would be prudent to bring your entire house, and everyone you care about, on our expedition."

The man slowly nodded. "Your house is at odds with the Crown. The advice you're giving me applies tenfold to your own family."

"You're more savvy than you act, Lord Hawk. Is that because you're clever and devious, or merely an extremely capable man without pretensions?"

He grinned. "I'm going to vote for the second option."

That warmed her heart. "Show me these ships, and tell me what we can do to make the mission a success."

A thrill ran through her. *This could change everything for us—and for generations to come.*

Duke Herman Hawk pointed into the formation of floating ships, selecting one that was three meters long, crafted down to the tiniest detail—every gun, launch bay, communications hub, and hatch. "That is a super carrier. See the launch bay down through its core—aft to stern?"

"Super carriers don't exist anymore. They haven't, not for centuries," Fortune said.

"Correct, but three Goliath-class freighters exist. They are easily large enough to be converted if you can convince the lien-holders to forgive a half dozen loans against them," he said.

"Your loans?" Patricia asked with a raised eyebrow.

"Only on one. We bought it at auction and found it more expensive to maintain than was advertised. The other two belong to merchants who also fell on hard financial times during the Zezner War. I am not asking for another loan, but merely sharing information I suspect might be useful to your cause," Herman said. "In case you wanted to purchase them at a discount."

Patricia let him squirm.

He tried a new sales pitch. "They serve their own purpose. For this model fleet, we assumed at least one would be converted to military use."

"None of the houses have anything like that. Not for three hundred years," Patricia said. "If Gerard learns of this..."

"He won't. After today's revelation, no one from my house will be given a chance to leak the information. I'll have my lead on this project document everything, then salvage the model—convert it back to a freighter."

"Smart. Show us everything," Patricia said.

The duke frowned.

"Show us everything you're comfortable sharing," she amended. "I think you and I both know that our fates are one. King Gerard does not tolerate challenges to his strength or his authority. He'll come for you next."

"Or first," Fortune said. "One of his special teams could storm this facility in an hour. Or they could turn it into a crater. Artillery accident."

Duke Herman Hawk gripped the railing until his knuckles turned white.

"Marlboro will stand with Hawk," Patricia said. "No one else is strong enough or has reason to take that risk."

The head of House Hawk nodded agreement.

CHAPTER TWENTY-FOUR

FORTUNE THOUGHT about her trip to the coast as she walked the flight line on the Nexus, a training field big enough to land a starship on or conduct mech formations with units from each of the great houses. It was a junction between all of the training grounds, with the Atana Training Ground (ATG) right next to the Marlboro Training Ground (MTG). Like many of the shared resources, the Nexus was a hive of activity and one of the main social hubs for Gildain's soldiers and pilots.

On the way back to Marlboro House, her mother had let her in on their plans. None of it allayed her worries and doubts. Everyone in the family understood, at least on a basic level, that Marlboro and House Bull—soon-to-be House Bull Danestar— were in the middle of an uneasy alliance. She worried about her brother and his obsession with Penelope Danestar. The news of her betrothal to Malcolm Sky Bull had changed him. Fortune no longer enjoyed spending time with her most fun and amusing sibling. Now he was always working too hard to prove himself, and looking for fault in House Bull.

Her own problems were even more complicated. She didn't deserve to be in the situation. Surrendering the ship that King Martin Gerard bought her to the BSA was probably going to start a war when someone discovered where it had been built and how she had acquired it. She lay awake at night plotting ways to get it back and destroy it instead.

Never accept gifts. That's my new policy.

Working on other airships calmed her. Like her father, she enjoyed turning wrenches and calibrating computers. The only difference was that her passion was directed at ships instead of mechs. She lay on a wheeled sled, checking the bearings of the landing gears for at least an hour. When she slid out, it was growing dark. Many of the mechanics were on their way home or loudly talking about where they were going after work.

She avoided them. From time to time, she could get away with socialization in places where her status wasn't important. But that was before the war ended and the assassination attempts began.

"Fortune Marlboro," a man said.

She stood and wiped her hands on a shop towel, staring down Lewis Fulton Cambridge, King Gerard's chief steward. He had an interesting look, a sophisticated outfit paired with a practical demeanor. It was like someone taught him about the highest fashions of Lorne but neglected explaining how he should act like an elitist jerk.

His name didn't come up often, but she heard her parents say he was efficient and unassuming—and that sometimes such a man could be dangerous. He was slightly taller than Fortune —slim, with dark hair turning gray. LFC, for Lewis Fulton Cambridge, was what her father called the royal functionary.

"That's me," she said. "What brings you here, steward?"

"You don't say that with an overabundance of respect," he remarked, "but I'm used to it. I have brought you a gift from the king."

Fortune stiffened, wishing she could jump in a cockpit and jet away.

"It's a small thing. Nothing to make you obligated." He handed her a bracelet made of white gold and diamonds.

Her gut clenched.

Never accept gifts…

She glanced around, despite her better judgment, looking for witnesses. Fortunately, nearly everyone was gone, and those who remained were arguing about sports teams and walking in the other direction, toward the main hangar exit.

Fortune raised an eyebrow. "He gives me a gift that could feed a family for a decade and calls it nothing. I don't want this."

"That is unfortunate. Sell it and feed a family if you wish," he said without humor. "That is not the reason for my visit, however. Please examine this document. It is the will of the king that you read it."

Now Fortune just wanted to punch this twit in his face. Instead, remembering what her mother had said and how Duke Hawk had reacted when he learned his entire family was in danger of Royal annihilation, she took the small digital document and began to read. Provoking the most dangerous man on the planet probably wasn't smart.

She wasn't sure what she expected to see. Poetry? Confessions of undying love? The promise of more gifts? Any of the above made sense, but not this.

At first, she skimmed the document, not really wanting to read it and instead trying to figure out how she could get rid of this annoying man and continue her day. But that wasn't going to happen. Before long, she was obsessing over every word. Once, twice, three times she read the document.

"Why would he send this to me?" Her self-control slipped. She wondered if this man knew how close he was to dying.

"His purpose should be obvious. The best medical advisors on the planet agree that a union between Marlboro and Gerard would not only result in healthy children, but *many* healthy children, all of whom would possess better genetics and nanite production than ever seen in our history," Lewis Fulton Cambridge explained, arms crossed. "It's counterintuitive that someone of your genetic weaknesses would parent a super race, but these are the facts."

"I don't think my father would approve of this courtship," she said.

"He must."

"But I won't. I don't want to marry anyone, and certainly not someone three times my age who has shown no great love for my father in recent months."

"That is unacceptably selfish. Think of the physical and mental proficiencies that would enter the human race. This isn't just a romantic or political proposal, but a step forward in human evolution."

"You really have a way with the ladies, don't you?"

"I only do one thing well, and that is enforce the will of our king," Lewis said. "Take the gift. Remember the document. Have all the time you need to decide, but be sure to make the right decision."

She watched him walk away, too stunned to curse.

———

FORTUNE SLIPPED AWAY from her security element, disappearing into the one-thousand-acre park that was central to all of the major houses. No trace of her brother's shenanigans remained. The damage that a company of Danestar mercenaries had caused was long since repaired—the walkway paving stones replaced and landscaping replanted and carefully nurtured.

She enjoyed the park, but not as much as Victor once had. As far as she knew, he didn't come here anymore. Fortune had preferred the Cherry Blossom District for her ramblings, or the Nexus training grounds. But that had been ruined for her as well, hadn't it?

A group of Zezner workers managed by their human foreman trimmed bushes and hauled away rubbish. The sight upset her, but she didn't know why. Wasn't her planet just at war with the Zezner? She didn't owe them a thing. Yet the sight of aliens doing menial labor made her angry.

She stopped by the work crew. "How goes your day, Zezner?"

"We are working hard. It is right," said the tallest one, an alien with dark blue skin and silver eyes.

She searched the collection of words Red Hot had taught her, then spoke in the alien's language. "Honor and respect to you. Always."

All five of the workers stared at her, then stood as one. They bowed and hugged themselves for several seconds. Then without another word, they resumed their work.

"What the hell was that?" the human foreman asked.

"I picked up a few words from a friend of mine," Fortune said, not bothering to identify herself. She rarely did. Who wanted to be known as the daughter of a duke all the time?

"Yeah? You like them?" the man asked.

"Do you?"

"I've got no problem with the Zezners, which surprised me when I took this job. Thought they'd push back, argue with me. They were right sons-of-bitches in the war. But now, they seem pretty regular. Don't complain like normal people do, which is nice."

"Did you serve?" Fortune knew he had, but it was the question you asked somebody in a situation like this.

"I did. Served House Atana, until they downsized their infantry. It helped me get this job, so I can't complain." He looked her over. "You're scrappy for a cute young thing. Did your family get involved?"

He almost asked her if she served but had veered off into a safer question, which irritated her. "Oh, yes. Very much."

Something clicked for the foreman and his eyes widened. "You're Fortune Marlboro!" He shook his head and moved his feet, almost like he wasn't sure if he should advance to shake her hand or retreat and duck a punch. "I asked her if her family was involved, and she said very much." He shook his head again, laughing under his breath. "Should have said *won the war*, more like."

That made Fortune smile. And it also caused the work crew to abandon their efforts and approach her. The dark blue leader stood as the others flanked him, hands respectfully at their sides. "Please give our honor and respect to Redion Axt of the Quest. We know you and your House. The Man of Marlboro destroyed many of our divisions."

Hearing that made Fortune nervous, but her gut told her this was not an insult or a prelude to an attack. "It was war. But now it's over."

"Well said, daughter of the Marlboro. There is no war for us. We plant bushes and flowers. But there will be nothing but war for you and the other near-humans."

"Sorry about that," the work foreman said. "They speak pretty good Gildain but can't get the word 'human' right. They always say near-human."

"Yeah, a friend of the family does the same thing. You get used to it," she said.

"You do." He thrust his chin at the landscaping project. "Come on, Blue. We better get this done or we'll be here all night."

"Yes." The Zezner leader and his companions returned to their duties as though nothing had happened.

Fortune watched them for several minutes, shivering against a cold that wasn't there. Something about the encounter disturbed her, but at least she wasn't thinking about gifts from the king or her father's rage when he found out the man wanted to court her.

Court me? That makes it sound like there would be some kind of romance involved. Dominate me, more like. That's what he wants. The hunger is in his eyes.

She continued through the park, crossing one of the wider bridges that spanned a pond full of year-round lily pads. She wasn't an expert in Lorne park botany, but the area was always verdant, regardless of season. In the winter, it was even more spectacular to see so many vibrant colors edged in ice and snow.

Walking distracted her pleasantly. On impulse, she flung the king's bracelet into the water. *Plink!* It slipped beneath a lily pad. Maybe she should've sold it and given the money to a charity, but that sin of omission was probably the least of her worries.

Looking up, she was surprised to see Penelope Danestar strolling toward her, a smile on her beautiful face. Her thick, blonde hair was braided on each side of her head with plenty left over falling in silky waves down her waist. The young woman was slightly taller than Fortune, which made them both very average in that regard.

"It sparkled all the way into the pond, whatever it was," Penelope said with an understanding smile.

Fortune should have been annoyed, maybe furious. This prima donna was the source of Victor's constant misery and bad decisions. But she had to recognize that they had a lot in common. Marital options were limited in Lorne.

"Good day," she said.

Penelope didn't seem to take offense at her cold demeanor. She was skilled at hiding her feelings, like every other young woman of the court. "Good day to you, Fortune Marlboro. How is your family?"

"Alive and kicking."

Penelope laughed merrily, brightening the day. "A good thing, that."

"And your family?"

"We still grieve my brother's death."

Fortune felt like a jerk. Her brother was heartsick. Penelope's brother had been blasted out of his mech and stomped to

221

paste. "My condolences, Penelope. None of us wanted our houses to be in conflict."

"They won't be for long," the Danestar woman said. "I am betrothed to Malcom Sky, now the adopted son of Duke Travis Bull. A situation that is both the cause of, and the solution to, the problems between our families."

"Never a dull moment in Lorne," Fortune said.

"Please... watch over Victor for me. Because I can't, for about a hundred reasons." Tears welled up in Penelope's eyes. She hurried away, hiding her face.

The more Fortune watched the woman who had so infatuated his brother, the angrier she became at King Martin Gerard and the customs that turned marriages into business contracts, destroying happiness for everyone associated with the process.

She was still thinking on this issue when she arrived home to find her mother and Peps examining clothing a Lorne fashion designer had brought to House Marlboro. Seven attendants assisted the seamstress, whom Fortune should know but didn't. Someone famous, a handsome woman taller than some of the male guards watching the door.

"These are excellent selections," Patricia said. "We will need time to consider which is best."

"Don't send them away!" Peps complained. "I want dresses."

"You never want dresses," Fortune interjected.

Peps clenched one fist, then shook it to express frustration. "I'm a girl. Girls wear dresses sometimes."

Fortune rolled her eyes. "Sometimes."

Patricia again thanked the designer and led Fortune and Peps to the inner courtyard of Marlboro House. "How was your walk?"

Fortune shrugged. "Saw some Zezner workers who sent their respects to Red Hot. And ran into Penelope Danestar."

"She is well, I suppose?"

Fortune told her the whole story, attempting to read her

mother's reaction but came back with no useful conclusions. Patricia Wilson-Marlboro might forgive the woman, or she might even now be fantasizing about driving a mech over House Danestar. Fortune couldn't tell.

She desperately wanted to explain her encounter with the king's steward, the documents speculating on progeny between a member of House Gerard and House Marlboro, and the king's demand that she allow him to court her.

Mate with me, more like.

The idea sent a shiver of dread through Fortune whenever she thought of her father's reaction, but facing her mother, she realized there was more than one way to start a house war that couldn't be won.

"Something's bothering you," her mother said.

"I'd rather be flying, is all. What's upsetting *you*, Mother?"

Peps bounced on her feet, clearly excited to contribute to the adult conversation. "A secret faction has been murmuring that House Marlboro is too powerful and must be destroyed while they're vulnerable. The spies' words, not mine."

Fortune raised a questioning eyebrow.

"Rumors, nothing more. And definitely not original. That one has been circulating in one form or another since I married your father."

"We should be okay, now that we have the Bull—or Danestar Bull, rather." Fortune saw her mother flinch this time.

"It's an alliance we don't speak of. Your father's decision to insulate us from the consequences…"

"Is annoying," Fortune finished.

"But smart," her mother said. "It pains him to keep secrets, even if they are transparent to a wife who pays attention and who wants nothing more than to be part of the fight."

"You want to fight House Gerard?" Fortune's heart pounded in her chest. What would her mother say? Could she tell her about the courtship proposal, and how the man had broken tradition by sending his steward directly to her instead of seeking her father and mother's permission first?

"I've always wanted to try the arrogant tyrant in combat," Patricia mused. Then added, "Never repeat that. Not even to family."

Fortune dropped her gaze and nodded vigorously. The moment her problem with the king came to light, Lorne and all of Gildain would burn with civil war.

"Why don't you wear dresses, Fortune?" Peps asked.

"Can't get in a cockpit wearing a dress."

"You're in a mood," her mother said. "Take Peps flying. It should improve your outlook and keep your little sister from making poor fashion choices."

"Threaten me with a good time," Fortune said. "Come on, Peps."

Her sister clapped her hands and bounced again. Maybe there was hope for the kid yet.

CHAPTER TWENTY-FIVE

STORM DROVE THE LONG WAY, leaving Marlboro House and accessing the public highway that provided glimpses of the thousand-acre central park. Ron watched tree lines, landscaped meadows, ponds, and walking paths flow by his window. He thought about Victor and his misadventure in courtship. Things might have gone differently if his son hadn't abandoned romance to rush through the park to warn the Marlboro House Guards.

Ron's fighters would've won the day, but at a much greater cost. And he might not have discovered the plot—though Travis Bull would've approached him, undoubtably.

The car also passed near the Cherry Blossom District where he had crushed Carter Danestar. He replayed that first encounter with Bull over and over. It kept him up at night, as did a dozen other worries about the future. He leaned closer to the window and peered toward the sky, searching for evidence of orbiting space stations and the Blue Sun fleet that grew at such a slow pace.

Building a thing was harder than seizing it on the battlefield. *Maybe that's what I'm doing wrong.*

Corporal Storm continued to Lord Abnercon's downtown

office where Ron was seen inside after a short wait. His driver wanted to stay with him—park the car and switch to his body-guard role—but Ron needed to do this alone.

He quickly climbed the sweeping staircase to the second level where every office had a balcony overlooking fountains and atrium gardens. There were a lot of workers, and a small army of plainclothes security officers who tried to appear incon-spicuous.

Abnercon's chief attendant showed Ron into the giant office where the financial expert came out from behind a large oak desk to greet Ron with a handshake. "It's good that you came. I feel I should move my office closer to House Marlboro for the sake of efficiency."

"Or you could just give me more money," Ron said.

"You have greater wealth than anyone but the king," Abnercon said. "Even after spending a generous portion on ship development. Though some say that might be better invested in ship building."

"I'm doing both, and you know it."

"Yes, but still—"

"You sound like the Bull, but of course you wouldn't be talking about confidential financial matters with another duke," Ron said.

"No, of course not. Though he is another client of mine, our conversations are very limited since he petitioned for Relief from the Crown and has no liquid assets to speak of." Abnercon motioned for Ron to have a seat, then returned to his place behind his desk. "What can I do for you today, Uron?"

"Grant about a dozen loans, bonded and insured, of course."

"That's going to be difficult, even for you. With your entire house leaving the planet, possibly for a very long time, how would one collect payments?"

"Abnercon, you're the one who started me down this path."

Lorne's greatest financier narrowed his eyes skeptically. "You've never gazed at the sky and wondered what's out there?

Someone like you, with such a thirst for adventure, has never thought of going to find new worlds... or old ones?"

Ron thought about distant worlds, including the Zezner home planet, Zeniis. "You know me too well."

"Of course," Abnercon said. "And I have a solution you may or may not have considered. What do you know about the *Exactas Meridias*?"

"It's a lost mining juggernaut, last seen in the far reaches of our system's asteroid belt. Or it's a fairytale," Ron said. He barely heard his own words, because the idea of finding the doomed vessel intrigued him powerfully. "Depending who you ask."

"I can tell by your reaction that you take my meaning," Abnercon said. "Researching the *Exactas Meridias* has been a hobby of mine since I was young, and that was a long time ago. You might consider me an expert hobbyist, at the very least. I'll send my files over. They may be helpful. If the legends of its unclaimed riches are even partially true, you can set up these foundry ships you have been developing near them and build whatever you need to complete the expedition."

"I'll look into it," Ron said.

They sat in silence for a moment, each pondering private thoughts. Ron looked around the room, noting the richness of the decorations—polished wood, expensive (probably accelerator round–proof) windows, and pictures of Lord Abnercon with every king and great lord throughout his extensive career in money management.

"Why have you been so interested in the Blue Sun Project?" Ron asked.

Abnercon folded his hands together and leaned his elbows on his desk, looking directly into Ron's eyes. "None of my children remain alive. I'm too old to go with you on this grand adventure. But I have a nephew."

"Raymond Abnercon," Ron said. "I've not heard much of

him since the end of the Zezner War, but I recall he served well, by all accounts."

"His parents would have been proud. Find a place for him on your mission."

"That's it?"

"I've been approached to broker a courtship involving a member of your household, but I can't say who," Abnercon said. "Confidentiality is of the utmost importance in these matters. I'm sure you understand."

"My family's coming with me, unless they request to stay behind and have sufficient resources to continue the Marlboro name. With recent events, that is impractical," Ron said.

Abnercon interlaced his fingers and put his elbows on his desk. "Understandable. What would be the conditions for you to consider leaving a family member with a good house?"

"I'd be wasting your time to lead you on," Ron said. "My answer was theoretical. None of my children, or my steward's children, are interested in remaining in what has become a very hostile political environment. And if they did try to stay, I'd bring them with me by force."

"You are committed to leaving forever?" Abnercon asked.

"There can be no other way. I'm placing all of my planetary assets, including real estate and financial trusts, into a master trust."

"Neither the king nor the legislature will allow so much prime real estate to go unused," Abnercon said.

"It could be leased in perpetuity, and you can advance me money based on that surety," Ron said, improvising some of this discussion.

"That's a good possibility. I'll have my people look into it."

And that is exactly what he has wanted all along, Ron thought. *Lord Abnercon might not be the villain in this scenario, but he definitely benefits from my decision to leave.*

CHAPTER TWENTY-SIX

RON WAS ready for some real training. He hoped that Travis Bull and Redion Axt were up for it. All three wore mech pilot suits, including helmets, integrated gauntlets, and armored boots.

Watching the exhibition at Ice Bay had been informative but left him eager to get into his own war machine and see what he could do. Victor had grudgingly accepted praise. His friends, Marsten and Kilo, looked ashamed that they had let their friend down. All of them were overreacting, except for Malcolm Sky, Duke Bull's adopted son who was being cross-trained with Marlboro units as a sign of good faith.

Malcom's grim expression had never changed during the entire exercise, as if he didn't give a damn what the crowd thought of their performance.

Ron strode across the Nexus. Minor houses, like Bull, had no permanent presence here and needed an invitation. Ron had invited Travis to bring a few squads under the pretense that he was evaluating their mechs for possible acquisition to resolve the post–house war lawsuit in which Marlboro was the clear victor.

"Are we going to train together in this scenario, or against each other?" Bull asked. "I'm not interested in an unfair contest if this is just a chance for you to vent your frustrations on me."

"You'd be a good match for me in training," Ron replied.

"Interesting you would say that." Bull twisted at the waist to pop his back, then continued walking toward the Marlboro training ground entrance. They were of a size, but Bull was heavier set with massive shoulders and a thick neck. Bald, but with a square beard, he intimidated most people.

Ron knew better than to underestimate the man, physically or intellectually. They continued toward the entrance. "Interesting how?"

Bull laughed. "Personally, I think I could kick your ass. But when you play it off so casually, I suspect I'm being set up."

"Maybe we should wager something," Ron said. "Winner takes a crate of premium cigars to distribute amongst his troops, and the loser has to recite Zezner poetry at the next royal banquet."

Bull roared a laugh and Ron found himself joining in. Redion bobbed his head and chuckled, the closest thing to a human laugh he'd been able to manage. The day immediately improved, despite all of the intrigue that had happened since the end of the war. Maybe this was just what he needed—to cut loose and enjoy some good, hard training.

When he turned, he spotted King Martin Gerard and Duke Adam Atana striding toward the ATG entrance. His laughter faltered.

Stars, he thought. *This'll look bad.* The consequences of this chance meeting could be dire.

Bull, for all his inadequacies, understood as well. "We better do something. Our pretense for being here looks better on paper than face-to-face."

"Follow my lead and make it look real," Ron muttered under his breath, then stood back, pointing in accusing finger at Bull. "Damn you and your parade horses!" He threw down his helmet.

"How dare you insult my house!" Bull shouted back, thrusting his helmet and his mech key forward menacingly, gripping each in clenched fists.

Redion moved between them, hands up, confused and alarmed at the sudden hostility.

"I'm tired of your stalling!" Ron bellowed. "I've had enough! You must pay your debts. I don't even need to see whether or not your pathetic piece-of-junk mechs work. The only place I'll get any money from them is in the salvage yard." Ron waved his arms at the Bull mechs fifty meters inside the gate, preparing for the training scenario.

"You must desist," Redion said.

"Stay out of this one, Red Hot." Ron hoped the Zezner didn't take offense.

"You know I am the one who is most correct," Redion said. "Calm yourselves, or there will be serious consequences." The long limbed, muscular, but lean alien seemed to get taller, like his joints were expanding, elevating his height to give him greater status in the argument.

Ron stared in fascination, almost losing his ability to act out this charade, when he heard the king's deep, mocking voice.

"What a pair of *gentlemen*."

It was all too much. Ron stepped into Bull's personal space, knowing the man would swing on him. The first punch nearly crushed the arm Ron raised to block, driving it back into Ron's body as it absorbed the impact. He countered a fraction of a second later with a straight thrust punch, then a haymaker with his bruised blocking arm.

Bull grabbed him, holding him in the clench position to avoid more abuse. Ron dug his left arm under Bull's right, seeking an underhook he could use to take the big man down. Bull twisted away.

Ron switched his feet, immediately driving his right knee upward, catching Bull in the side as he twisted to avoid the attack.

231

"Damn you, Marlbor—!"

Ron slammed his forehead into Bull's face, cutting off his words. Blood spattered the ground. Bull gouged him in the eye, then tripped him to the ground. Ron rolled to his feet, shot forward, and took Bull down as the man struggled to maintain his stance.

Both men gasped for breath but continued the aggressive pace of the fight. Ron didn't know if his adversary was as angry as he was, but suspected they were equally frustrated with the impossible reality of Gildain politics.

I served the king with every fiber of my being. We defeated the Zezner. And this is what I'm reduced to. The thought came and went faster than the punches and blocks.

Strong hands hauled him away from the fight, Redion on his left and King Gerard on his right. Atana pushed Bull back, not an easy task with Bull having a slight height and weight advantage.

"My good dukes, pardon me if I interrupt," Gerard said, stepping away from the struggle and smoothing his coat. "I hate to forestall a duel, but brawling, dueling, and engaging in other hostilities in the Nexus training ground, is a serious offense that cannot be ignored. Are you finished?"

Ron stepped back, glared at Bull, then smoothed his pilot suit and picked up the helmet that he'd dropped. "Of course, my king. It was a simple disagreement, no more."

Bull played his part by saying nothing but looking like he wanted to say everything. Blood trickled from his nose. Gravel was stuck to one side of his face where Ron had briefly pinned him to the ground.

"What say you, Duke Atana?" Gerard said. "Shall I bring them up on charges?"

"You would be within your rights," Atana said, sounding unsure. "Perhaps we should see what transpires from this point forward. Let their rivalry run its course. It could be entertaining."

Gerard laughed. "Very well. We were never here. Let's grab some cigars and a whiskey. We can inspect the ATG another day."

Atana bowed his head, made to follow Gerard, but stopped. "Thanks for rescuing my pilot at the ATG. That was an unfortunate incident."

"You would do the same for one of my pilots," Ron said, not believing for a second the statement was true.

"Perhaps. Not all of us are such strong swimmers, Duke Uron. Good day. And as the king said, I was never here. One piece of advice. Keep that Zezner savage in check." And with that, Duke Adam Atana set out after the king.

RON LED one squad of Marlboro training mechs, and Bull led his rough-looking but serviceable squad. They fought hard, with no quarter given, so long as it stayed within the rules of the exercise. At the end, they were tired and well pleased with the experience, each group giving the other a grudging respect.

On the field, Marlboro and Bull mechanics washed and serviced the machines. Ron and his ally sat on equipment crates, drinking water with electrolytes. Red stood by, content to watch the crews work without comment. He was an easy companion in that way, never needing to be entertained.

"What's on your mind, Marlboro?"

Ron grunted. "So far, you've always been the one to predict the next disaster."

"I've got nothing. But the incident in the Nexus was unfortunate. Don't you think it strange that they came to the training ground and didn't train?"

Ron had been thinking about that exact question during most of the exercise. He looked at his mech, standing slightly taller but narrower than Bull's mech. By his order, they were to be the last cleaned and shut down.

233

"You and I have one more mission today," he said. "Let's mount up and go for a run to the training grounds."

"I can do that. But what are you thinking?"

Ron reviewed figures in his head—the status of ships and the BSA in general. A track circled the complex, circumventing all of the house training grounds, so that anyone needing to test gear and pilots could run an endurance march. Ron knew there was a point with enough elevation that he could see the nearest spaceport and link up with his intelligence network.

"I think the king and his party came to make sure we were here, because they're going to do something they don't want us to know about," Ron said. He activated his bio-comm and called Gregory. "Can you read me?"

"Loud and clear," Gregory answered like he'd been waiting for the call. That's how he was, always dutiful.

"Select your best special operations personnel and send a pair of them to put eyes on each of the spaceports with BSA assets," Ron said. His heart raced. He wasn't sure how it had come to this, or how he had been outmaneuvered by Gerard, a man he'd never thought was particularly clever.

"All of the remaining BSA assets have been consolidated at the Gerard Launch Complex. The rest are already in orbit. I'll go myself. What am I looking for?" Gregory asked.

The bottom fell out of Ron's stomach. What was it about the king's response that had tipped him off to this crisis? Was it what the man had said or how he had delivered the words? Or was it just his mere presence?

"You already answered half of my question, unfortunately. But go and look anyway and watch yourself. Bring a security team. The king and his allies are going to seize the BSA assets," Ron said. "Then demand a concession I can't guess without more information."

Bull stared at him. "Tell me we're not too late."

"This isn't the king's final move," Ron said. "It's just an attempt to force my hand."

Bull clenched his teeth. "Explain."

"I reserved three ships in the Blue Sun Armada for unattached citizens of reasonable skill and experience."

Bull shook his head, anger clouding his expression. "Why would you do that? King Gerard will be furious. That challenges his reputation for being the one most concerned with the public welfare."

"How do you stop an avalanche, Duke Bull?"

"With dynamite," the man answered. "If you put it in the right place and use it at the right time. I knew aligning myself with your house would be dangerous, but this was unexpected."

Ron informed his crew of his intentions and was soon driving his battle mech off the staging line. Bull was learning to be quicker and more efficient, and soon joined him. They headed away from the others, stepped onto Endurance Road, and moved at a fast pace around the perimeter of the training grounds. None of the others were active; in fact, many of the designated training areas were almost empty of equipment.

His footfalls thundered louder the faster he moved. It felt good to drive forward, thinking about nothing but the present. He ran as though this were the only thing that mattered, striving for perfection. In the heat of battle, there would be no such thing. Only the foundation forged during training would remain.

I was built for war, just like this battle mech I'm driving.

Beside him, Travis Bull was made similarly, but also with the talent for ranching and animal husbandry. The more he thought about it, the more he realized most people had two or three main functions in society.

Ron struggled to identify what his secondary or tertiary purpose might be.

They reached the highest point of the track and assumed overwatch mode. Ron magnified his optics, aiming in the direction of the nearest spaceport where he'd last seen BSA assets still on-planet.

A company of House Gerard mechs, supported by police infantry, guarded the entrance to the facility.

"Well, it looks like you've done it, Marlboro," Bull said. "I warned you. Inviting independent citizens was a mistake."

"Most of the population is independent," Ron said. "Who do you think has been building my ships and keeping my secrets? Who among us are wired to defy the king? My decision was the right call. We need men and women outside of House politics."

"I wish I were outside of House politics," Bull grumbled.

Ron said nothing, choosing to move the pieces on the night boards in his head, looking for unseen opponents in the game and ways to counter their strategies.

"What are our options?" Bull asked.

"We have to take physical control of the BSA, by force or diplomacy. My nominal appointment by the Legislature isn't enough now," Ron said. He understood diplomacy was the best way, but… *I was built for war.*

And what else?

"I'm ready to be gone," Bull said.

"Same." Ron gazed across his home world's horizon and wondered if he would ever see another place so majestic.

CHAPTER TWENTY-SEVEN

"I'D RATHER you didn't come this time," Fortune said, immediately regretting the effect of her words.

Peps, looking smaller and younger than ever, stared up at her, eyes wide, hands hanging down at her sides. Tears welled.

Fortune waited, unsure if this was an act or real. So much it happened that the consequences of being wrong would be serious. She remembered that age, listening to the adults talk about people who'd died in battle, or the slim chances of success each time the Zezner launched a new assault.

"You're not faking it."

Peps shook her head as she stared at her feet. She sucked in a breath, and when she came up, she acted like a good Marlboro —emotions put aside for later when duty wasn't knocking on the door. But what was an eleven-year-olds' duty in a house war like this?

"Nah, I think you're having me on," Fortune said.

At first, it seemed that Fortune had miscalculated, but then her little sister flashed a mischievous smile. "I'd feel better if we went flying. Really fast. Or you could get them to build me a mech, like I ask for every single year for my birthday."

Fortune laughed. "I could probably get you a functional war

machine before that." She shook her head and waved her sister to follow her as they strode toward the auto port. "Airships are trouble, trust me."

"What?" Peps was practically running around her now in curiosity and mild confusion. "You practically *are* an airship, you like them so much."

"No one can *be* an airship."

"But you could."

"No, Peps. Because then I might fly away."

The brief improvement in the little girl's mood slipped dramatically, so Fortune ruffled her hair roughly enough to shove her sideways.

They went first to the carport and had the on-duty driver take them to a public air transport company where Fortune chartered a private flight to the Nanstrom Station.

On the way, they told jokes and laughed, and Peps showed Fortune all her favorite books—on the digital security device that she carried at all times since the Danestar attack, orders of Captain Echo.

Everyone in the family had bio trackers, of course, but there were other uses for the tablet—like reading—and it gave the youngest Marlboro a job she had to do every day, to be aware of and report back to Echo.

The transport was larger than they needed. The two girls had a nine-person cabin to themselves, with all the windows set to full transparency. That was one thing she liked about the slow air transports. Without the need for battle armor, they were mostly windows and provided an excellent view of Lorne and the surrounding countryside.

"I'm pretending I am a Zezner, maybe Redion's grandfather, seeing our planet for the first time," Peps said. "What do you think they thought, way back then?"

"Probably that this planet had everything their people could want. That they could start a life here and be happy."

Send them out to make the universe fit for expansion... The phrase sounded odd in her ears and she hadn't heard it for a long time. Just a random thought, like a half-remembered dream. Everyone had them, or that's what she told herself.

"Good afternoon, my ladies," the pilot said over the intercom. "We're about to land on Nanstrom Station. Please fasten your safety restraints and put away all nonessential devices. Thank you for flying Lorne Public Transport."

"This pilot is nice," Peps said as she complied. "She doesn't make so many jokes that I don't understand, like Father's pilots. They use worse language than Echo's soldiers."

"You're not wrong, little Peps."

"How long is everyone going to call me that?"

"Probably forever."

"Crap."

"Hey! Watch your language, young lady," Fortune said.

"Double crap. Goddamn sons-a-bitches!"

Fortune choked off her laughter, but it was too late. Her little sister had already gotten the reaction she was looking for.

"Why is it always so funny to grown-ups, when I say it like that?"

"It just sounds cute, I guess, when kids talk like salty infantry noncoms."

Peps sank deeper into her chair, crossing her arms. "That's not true. Because if that was true, then they would want kids to say that stuff all the time. But Captain Echo tells me not to say it in front of Mother and Father because it'll get him in trouble. And then he tries to talk nice all the time, until he forgets, and he says bad words and all of his sergeants and soldiers give him a hard time and say that he's ruining me and that he talks like a grunt."

"Mark is a good man. I doubt Mother or Father would ever be seriously angry with him, unless he let something happen to you, which he won't." She changed the subject. "Look at the station when we approach. Try to think where you would land if you were a pilot, and then try to remember all the call signs

239

and procedures you have to go through to contact flight control."

"Is that what you do?"

"Sure." It wasn't, because Fortune knew all of that like it was part of her.

Midshipmen Sage met them on the arrival platform. All smiles and energy, he strode straight up and shook both of their hands, which Peps thought was the best thing in the world—being treated like an adult.

"Welcome back to Nanstrom Station," he said. "We don't get many public transport shuttles these days. My people checked the manifest as soon as it was inbound and saw your names. Excellent to see you. Is everything okay?"

Fortune smiled at the young man. "We wanted a change of pace, and to be honest, I've been missing my airship and wanted to blow the dust out of its turbines for a little bit. Show little Peps what it can do." She liked the midshipman. His confidence and enthusiasm made the day a little brighter. He had that trustworthy aura of somebody who hadn't been born near House Marlboro but had become an enthusiastic supporter of her father and the BSA. Love at first sight, more or less.

"Let's at least have a look at her," Sage said.

They fell in beside him and he gave them yet another tour of the facilities, pointing out a huge leap forward in production results. Some of the ships were nearly completed. All they needed was to be moved into full orbit and assembled. Others were beyond the gravity well and receiving crew members and supplies for a long voyage.

On the next level, several squads of crewmen rushed to new stations. Sage held one hand to his ear, checking his bio-comm.

"What's wrong?" Fortune asked.

"Something happening on the surface. A shipment scheduled to arrive later today has been delayed." He looked unsure. "It's probably nothing."

"Do you need to go?" Fortune asked. "We don't want to hold you up if that alert is for you."

He shook his head. "No. Not yet, at least. But maybe we shouldn't dally." He smiled broadly. "The mission must always continue in the face of adversity. What would you like to see next?"

Fortune pointed at a military corvette with graceful, sweeping lines. "That was just a frame last time I was here."

"Our engineers and construction experts have been stream-lining the assembly process, getting better every day. I'm incredibly proud of them," Sage said. "Not like they're my subordinates or anything. I'm not trying to put on airs. But you know what I mean."

"I get it, and I'm proud of them too, even though they don't work for me at all," she said.

They took an equipment lift to a higher level, and when she stepped out, she saw her airship immediately. Her emotions went in every direction. It was a beautiful machine. She wanted to fly it hard and fast until its wings came off. But it was also a gift from King Martin Gerard, a trap, something to make her feel guilty and accept his advances.

"I really shouldn't let you fly it," Sage said. "Especially with the alerts."

Fortune's instincts flared. She needed to get rid of the ship now. "Just a little joyride. You don't even have to fill up the entire fuel tank. Just enough battery power to get us going, and maybe a half hour of circling the city would be good enough," Fortune said.

He laughed. "Oh no, I'll do much better than that. We don't like to do things halfway around here."

Fortune shrugged and gave him a wink. "That's what I figured. You walked right into my trap."

He laughed. "Got me good. I can't wait until the BSA is in space. We're going to explore the stars, can you believe it? I probably sound like a kid or something."

"Hey, kids are cool," Peps said.

Midshipmen Sage gave her a fist bump. "Here's to us cool kids."

This is going to work, Fortune thought. *And I'm glad I brought Peps. She needs to know how to handle a crash landing. Might as well learn today.*

———

THEY TOOK off as soon as the preflight inspections were done. Peps stayed silent. Fortune had taught her to pay attention during a launch or, in the case of an airship, a takeoff. She wouldn't let her little sister fly today, not at all, even if it was safe at certain altitudes. Such an indulgence might end with Peps feeling responsible for the destruction of this damn ship.

The controls felt good in her hands, like they were made for her. She doubted King Gerard knew her biometrics well enough to instruct his engineers for such specificity, and she doubly doubted that he was emotionally sophisticated enough to know she would like that. It normally took her several weeks to get a vehicle perfect, every setting adjusted to her flying style.

But for some reason, this thing was exactly right with no need to tweak anything. She left the station, waited for permission from the flight controller, then punched the afterburners, shooting away from the short runway. Soaring in low orbit, she could have just dropped out of the bottom of the station and began the last portion of a reentry sequence. Gravity and the increasing atmospheric resistance would soon exert its aerodynamic influence.

"Are you ready to go fast, Peps?" Fortune asked.

"I'm always ready! When you fly, that is. When Victor tries it, it scares me."

"That would scare me too." Fortune pushed the controls forward, then corrected her flight path, looking for an area to touch down. Faking the malfunction would be difficult, and getting people to believe she had handled it poorly would be nearly impossible, but it was going to happen, and this thing was going to sink in the White Ocean.

But she had to get there first, and that was just a little bit farther than she had promised Midshipmen Sage. Hopefully, he wouldn't get in trouble over this.

Guilt almost stopped her, but she didn't really have a choice. The king had put her in an impossible situation. This evidence had to be destroyed before her father found out, or worse, her mother.

"Royal Eighty-Two for Fortune One, how copy?" her radio said.

She checked the radar, and saw three of the king's elite combat fighters, pilots she'd never been allowed to duel in training. None of their flight logs were public record. They had an air of mystery about them like few other combat units in the king's service. She knew she was good, but she had to admit she was outclassed this time. Especially since there were three of them.

And the ships were probably armed to the wingtips.

"Fortune One copies," she said. "What can I do for you fine gentlemen?"

"It's not so much what you can do for us, it's what we were sent to do for you. Consider us your royal escort to the Gerard high-security airfield," Royal Eighty-Two said.

The guy really didn't have a sense of humor. Sometimes you could just tell by the sound of a person's voice.

"Is there a problem? This is my ship; you can check the record." She didn't want anyone doing that, but what was the alternative? The last thing in all of Gildain she wanted was a meeting with the king. And it would be ten times worse because Peps was with her.

"I triple-checked your ship registry before making contact," Royal Eighty-Two advised. "Please make your approach for the landing ordinance I've transmitted to your control panel."

243

Fortune began counting to ten in her head. When she reached three, she made a hard left, dropped a hundred meters in altitude, and gunned the afterburners. A thrill shot through her.

Peps squealed, a mixture of delight and fear. "I don't think we should be doing this! Those are the king's ships."

Controls that had felt so natural in Fortune's hands suddenly felt sluggish and stiff. She fought against them for several moments, then let go. Someone had taken control of the ship.

"I thought you'd try that," Royal Eighty-Two said. "To be honest, with your reputation, I would've been disappointed if you hadn't. But now you are going to land at the designated coordinates, even if I have to do it remotely."

Fortune thought about it, then keyed the mic. "No need for that, Eighty-Two. I'll land. You won't get any more trouble from me." She considered a second attempt and was bracing herself for the next escape maneuver, right up until the moment the controls were released back to her. She thought about Peps in the copilot's seat.

A barely audible click accompanied by haptic feedback from the yoke signaled the return of her controls. She reviewed the coordinates, then began her approach. "Fortune One for Royal Eighty-Two, do you have a name?"

"Lieutenant Colonel Charles Avery, at your service."

They both knew who the Royal pilot served. His response was a pleasantry and nothing more. She could tell by his voice he wasn't someone to be swayed from his duty. As a Marlboro, she could respect that.

The Gerard high-security airfield was meticulously kept and well-guarded. She landed, then climbed out of her aircraft with Peps close behind her. They stood and waited, but not for long. Colonel Avery and his wingman strode toward them moments later and snapped salutes.

"Colonel Charles Avery." He indicated the man on his left. "Captain Douglas Kirkpatrick."

Fortune gave them a nod. By both military tradition and House custom, she wasn't required to respond at all, but they were pilots, and that meant something. Beside her, Peps followed her lead, appearing several years older than she was due to her seriousness.

"Right this way," Avery said. "I'll hand you off to Cambridge and his security team."

The man was all business, which was for the best. They didn't have much to talk about unless she could convince them to toss a grenade or three into the ship that had become the bane of her existence.

The four of them strode briskly across the tarmac, Peps skipping every three or four steps to keep up. Along one side of the runway were twenty-five AT-VO fighters, just like the one that had been gifted to Fortune. The difference being that these were fully armed, rockets hanging under wings and specialized accelerator guns protruding from ports.

Twenty meters behind the flight line were concrete and steel hangars, permanent like everything else associated with House Gerard. It only made her long to leave the planet forever.

Let him have his ships and armies and bombproof buildings. We don't need that stuff anymore.

The thought was still heavy on her mind when Colonel Avery and his captain passed them off to Fulton Cambridge.

"I have a car," Cambridge said with a flourish and a bow. "It's best that we not hold the meeting in such crude surroundings."

"I'm not going anywhere until I understand why we've been kidnapped," Fortune said, crossing her arms.

Peps imitated her.

"No need to be uncivil," Cambridge said.

"You're talking to House Marlboro. You might want to reconsider your tone, and your presumptions," Fortune said.

Cambridge's gaze hardened. He wasn't a large man, nor robust, but that didn't hide the danger he presented. She had encountered him only a few times face-to-face, but his reputation was considerable and her father's opinion of him clear. A man of intellect, cunning, and absolute devotion to King Martin Gerard. "You stand surrounded by the might of the king's holding. Whatever you think House Marlboro can do against his Majesty..." He let the sentence die. "Unfortunately, the king will not be able to see you immediately. I am directed and required to escort you to a place of comfort until he is able to attend you."

"Unacceptable. We came here against our will and are being held for an undetermined time. That is the very definition of kidnapping."

Lewis Fulton Cambridge said nothing. After half a minute, he turned and waved for them to follow. "The car awaits." A squad of guards approached and flanked Fortune and Peps. Cambridge walked several strides ahead.

The car looked just like the official House Marlboro car, long, black, and armored beneath its posh exterior. A soldier stood by the back door, opening it when they approached. He stood respectfully with his right hand straight down at his side and his left on the handle. His uniform was parade dress perfect, his gold beret straight, except the right portion that canted downward.

"Get in, Peps," Fortune said softly.

Her sister did as she was told but looked absolutely terrified. Fortune's gut tightened. If there had ever been a time in her life when she wanted to cry, this was it. Why the hell had she allowed her sister to come on this fool's errand?

The door closed; the soldier went to the passenger seat and got in. The driver pulled away immediately, likely following instructions given long before they arrived.

Peps leaned forward, concealing the tablet Captain Echo had given her. Resting the device on her small knees, she typed furiously with both hands and hit the send button. The moment she was finished, she concealed the device again.

"What are you doing?" Fortune murmured.

"Captain Echo told me I have to tell him where I am, especially if I'm not at home," Peps said. "Did I do the right thing?"

Fortune studied the driver and his companion. Neither gave away any clues. She couldn't decide if they were just ultra-professional, fanatically loyal to their king, or were carrying out orders they didn't agree with. She hoped for the latter, but wasn't betting on it.

"I think so, little Peps." Fortune wasn't sure, but... that message her sister sent might have just kicked off a civil war.

CHAPTER TWENTY-EIGHT

VICTOR CROSSED his arms and stared at the Mechanized Elec-tro-Nuclear Combat Hulks being loaded onto flatbed trailers for transport. Better than looking at Malcom "Sky" Bull. Fourteen feet tall, Victor's red-and-gold mech folded neatly into a block a third of that size.

Kilo and Marsten's machines went on next, theirs had more red and less gold but were equally well cared for. Marlboro war machines were inspected twice weekly during the post–Zezner War peace. Cranes groaned, engines revving loudly despite the mufflers designed to quiet them.

Malcom's mech went on last. Repainted brown with white accents, the colors of House Bull, it looked shabby. Victor grudgingly admitted it was better taken care of where it counted than any non-Marlboro mech Victor had observed.

And the man ran it well—nothing fancy, just on target and on time every time, like a pro.

He was ten years older than Victor, still young by military standards. That didn't change the facts. The man was rough, crude, and uncultured—not deserving of a lady like Penelope Danestar.

Work crews strapped the load to the flatbed and stepped

back. Victor and his fellow pilots inspected their work. It was a silent, grim task. Normally Kilo and Marsten cracked jokes and gave the enlisted workers a hard time, earning laughs and good-natured ribbing in return.

Not today.

Because there was an outsider, and he was a threat. Everyone knew Malcom Bull was a dangerous, unknowable man. They also understood he was betrothed to the woman Victor Marlboro had been courting.

"You know what, Marlboro? It's time to be done with this," Malcom grumbled. "Say your piece and get over it."

Kilo and Marsten stepped to Victor's side, ready for a fight. Victor held his hand out, palm down, a signal to wait but remain alert.

"Penelope Danestar isn't for you. Let the Bull adopt you. Make some other marriage alliance," Victor said. He kept his voice level, his tone confident. Inwardly, a battle raged. Time distorted, sounds fell away from perception, and his vision was a tunnel focusing on Malcolm. "What does it matter to you? Have the Bull find a more powerful family. Danestar is nothing."

"But she's something to you, isn't she, Marlboro?" Malcom said.

"She is."

"Well, that's touching. But I really don't care. And you'd best be advised not to underestimate me."

"You're a mercenary. You can fight. I'll give you that," Victor said.

Malcom snorted. "Don't need your approval. Facts are in the doing."

Victor crossed his arms, locking his jaw to hold back words he'd regret.

"Never got respect before becoming a Bull. Don't imagine I ever will. And it wouldn't mean nothing to me, coming from a spoiled brat like you."

Marsten stepped forward, but Malcom aimed a finger at him. "That's far enough. I've got no problem with you, but you're going to have a big problem in about half a second."

"Who do you have a problem with?" Victor demanded, voice hard as ice.

Malcolm said nothing for several heartbeats. "Got no problems."

"I think you do," Victor said. "And you're right. It's time to settle our differences. Acron's Hill. Midnight."

"I'll be there unless you want to go right now. Have your army of servants put away your toys, and we can use fists behind the fuel depot. Out of sight from the locals."

"Be careful how you use the word 'servant.' Do not diminish honest work."

Bull bellowed a laugh. "That's rich, coming from a Marlboro brat."

"Why don't you shut your ugly face?" Kilo snarled.

Victor advanced chest to chest, nose to nose with Malcom, just to block his friends from getting in the middle of this mess, and to see if the mercenary would back down. "Tonight. Acron's Hill. ABA, hand-to-hand, and swords. If you don't have one, I'll loan you one of mine."

"I've got a lot of new toys since Lord Bull adopted me," Malcolm said. "Let's get our machines put away so I don't have to look at you until then."

Victor strode toward the convoy sergeant, twirling one hand in a tight circle, signaling it was time to move out. He didn't ride in the same vehicle as the intruder. Neither did he speak to his friends, though he could tell they desperately wanted to say something.

Because they were good friends, they probably wanted to talk him out of the duel. There were serious consequences that would almost certainly drop him to mercenary status if he wasn't killed. Laws were laws, and duels had been forbidden since his father was a young man.

———

VICTOR CHANGED into a fresh mech under-suit for the second time today. The locker room reeked of pine-scented floor cleaner, nearly overpowering the odor of his sweat. He'd showered the moment he returned from the training exercise, but his nerves activated his glands again with a vengeance.

Which wasn't normal. His body hadn't betrayed him like this before the final battle of the war. He ran his fingers through his damp hair, then selected gloves and a new helmet liner from his locker.

Mark Echo and one of his security squads entered, cracking loud jokes and giving each other a hard time. Victor's rare moment of solitude vanished. Now he couldn't hear himself think.

"Training again?" Echo asked as he passed near the end of the row where Victor had his locker. "I understand you put on quite a demonstration at Ice Bay."

"There's nothing better to do with the war over," Victor said.

Echo laughed grimly. "You're not the only one who misses the Zezner problem. It's getting harder and harder to keep my people out of trouble. Too much leisure time."

"Sure, I can see that. Idle hands and all that." Victor didn't want this conversation. Mark Echo wasn't just a soldier, he was a security specialist. The man observed every detail and asked questions about things other officers might overlook.

"We should spar some time," Echo said.

"Sure. Say when." Victor cursed inwardly. What if the man offered to run through some drills now? How could he refuse without exposing his intent to participate in an illegal dual at Acron's Hill?

Echo hesitated, looking him over, clearly in work mode now —his primary duty being to ensure the safety and welfare of each and every member of House Marlboro. "Good. It's been a while since you worked me over. Getting my ass kicked keeps me sharp. But I have a prior engagement."

"Of course," Victor said, relieved. "I might just go for an endurance march or something. Haven't really decided."

"Have fun with that." Echo made his retreat, but not before Kilo and Marsten came in wearing their own augmented battle armor. Echo gave him a second look, and why wouldn't he? Victor had just told him he intended to exercise by himself, and now his two companions showed up in full gear.

An awkward moment passed, but Echo returned to his own squad to continue some joke that probably made more sense if Victor had heard the first part of it.

"What was that about?" Kilo asked.

"Nothing." Victor closed his locker and spun the combination. It was far bigger than what a normal infantry soldier used, eight feet high and three feet wide so that the ABA could be parked inside with his other clothing and grooming supplies. "Let's take a ground car from the motor pool. I don't want to make excuses to the captain of the Marlboro House Guards twice in one hour."

"Sure thing," Marsten said.

He looked back toward the fading sound of the soldiers. "I'll keep a lookout. Let me know when the vehicle is ready, and you can pick me up outside."

"Good plan. Let's go," Victor said, leading the way toward the back door.

Acron's Hill was a small community that grew up around a falcon club. Ten kilometers outside of Lorne, it would've been bought and developed into vacation homes for its scenic beauty if it had not been protected by an order of King Gerard's grandfather.

About a hundred people lived and worked around a central square with dozens of quaint cafés and specialty shops people visited during the daytime. In the evenings, there was a low-key nightclub—the kind that played soft music and allowed no fighting. Just beyond the settlement was a field the locals pretended didn't exist.

They closed up shop when certain groups of people arrived.

The signs were obvious. Expensive, unmarked airships landed near the edge of the clearing. Spectators noisily gathered outside wearing masks and toasting each other for no reason. Sometimes there was music, dancers, and acrobats.

Victor felt exposed, even though he and his friends had gone to great lengths to conceal any identifying emblems from their training gear. "Don't get close enough to the spectators to talk. Why are so many people here?"

"No idea," Marsten said, looking around nervously.

Kilo thrust his chin at the crowd. A man wearing a jester's mask cavorted among the spectators, singing, dancing, and flinging confetti into the growing crowd. "They arrived after us. Look at those ground cars coming up the road. What I was told, by my uncle, was that someone in Acron's Hill sends out a message when duelists arrive. All of those people dropped what they were doing to be here."

"They must really want to see Malcolm get thrashed," Marsten said. "Identity cloaks be damned; everyone here knows who's who and what's what."

Victor knew the truth of it. That was the purpose of a duel after all—prove who was the better man or woman. Hard to do if the players were anonymous. The subterfuge was little more than a matter of form, good manners as it were. Who in their right mind would openly defy the law of the land?

All of that aside, he was thinking more of Marsten's statement and the sobering prospect of the fight, now that the time was upon him. "We haven't started yet. Don't forget how good he is."

"You can take him, Vic," Marsten said. Kilo nodded agreement.

Malcolm Sky Bull hadn't needed to do much to make his augmented battle armor plain and forgettable. He stood at one end of the field, armor powered up, gaze forward, completely ignoring the lords, ladies, and wealthy revelers.

Victor strode toward his adversary, sweating through his under-suit. Time felt out of whack. His arms and legs belonged to someone else. All he could think about was the plot against his father's house and how his actions could bring disgrace to the family, even if he won. Everyone, from the most common man to King Gerard, would condemn the illegal duel, despite being fascinated in private.

"There's nothing to be gained from this," Victor muttered.

"Too late for that," Kilo said. "But you are correct. Let me stand in for you. I'll make short work of the mercenary."

"I may be a fool, but I'm not about to let you pay for my stupidity." Victor faced Malcom. "You challenged me to a contest of arms. I accept. Shall we begin?"

"Whenever you're ready," Malcom said.

At least he had remembered not to use names.

Victor covered his left fist in his right hand and bowed his head, careful not to lose eye contact. Malcom did the same.

They dropped into fighting stances—no weapons other than the fists and feet of the strongest alloy available. The first part of a Gildain duel was the most primal.

Circling to his left, Victor lunged with a jab then immediately dropped low and dove for Malcom's knees. He was disappointed when he caught his adversary, slamming him to the ground on the first try. An easy win was worthless. Honor came through striving against impossible odds, overcoming adversity, and testing oneself.

Malcom let the force drive over him, rolling backward, pushing Victor into the air with his powerful legs—a perfectly timed and executed move.

Victor sailed five meters before crashing to the grassy field. His hands and feet cut the turf to shreds as he scrambled to his feet—and found Malcom already up and charging.

Striking like a runaway tank, Malcom carried Victor backward, driving him down, falling on him hard enough to rattle his teeth, even inside the impact-dampening armor and helmet. "At least try to fight back!"

Victor grunted something savage.

So much for an easy win.

Malcom pried at Victor's helmet latches. In seconds, he would pop it open, cast it aside, and leave Victor exposed to the onlookers. Humiliated and defenseless against a fully armored adversary, he'd be thoroughly defeated—not on the dueling field, but in life.

Victor grabbed Malcom's wrist with both hands and wrenched sideways and down. At the same time, he twisted his hips from under his opponent, sticking his butt out to one side. The awkward escape toppled Malcom onto his side and forced him to let go of the helmet clasp.

Victor punched Malcom's visor, rocking his head backward.

They pushed away from each other and stood. Malcom grabbed his own helmet and twisted it straight. "That was a good hit, Marl—"

Victor flew at him, swung wildly, then grabbed him around the waist. He lifted Malcom's ABA high, then suplexed him backward. No amount of armor could minimize the absolute suck of getting dumped on your head.

"Ahhg!" Malcom grunted, pain flowing out with a gurgling choke.

Victor kicked him in the face as he struggled to his feet. "You're no gentleman! Trying to use my name! Respect the customs of the duel or I'll make you pay double!"

Malcom partially deflected the blow and retreated at the same time. "Everyone knows who we are, fool. How many men with mechs have active feuds? How many fight like we do?"

Victor executed a perfectly timed spinning backkick that caught Malcom in the middle torso, lifting him onto his toes and buckling him in half.

"No one will say a thing. That's the way it works here," Victor argued.

Malcom fought for breath, circling to his left, his fists up. "I'm marrying Penelope Danestar. There's nothing either of us can do about that."

"I know," Victor said. "But I'll feel better after I pound your face in."

"Do you think she would like that?" Malcolm asked.

"No, but it's too late now."

Malcom nodded. "Then let's start fighting for real."

As one, they extended blades and shields.

CHAPTER TWENTY-NINE

SWORDS SANG with every block and parry. The crowd grew silent. Neither man hesitated to go for a fatal strike. Neither man spoke another word, and wouldn't until the outcome was decided by death.

An alert chimed insistently in Victor's helmet. He continued to fight, snatching glances at the message when he had time. His eyes finally sent the words to his brain, stunning him to near immobility.

He stepped back, oversized rapier ready, the tip hovering between his mech and that of Malcom Sky Bull. Victor's blood was up, and he longed to hear the steel ring again and again. Every clash was terrifyingly deadly. The weapon was more than twice as long as a normal sword and reinforced to pierce the ABA. Augmented battle armor couldn't stop the specialized dueling weapons. They would, however, immediately seal any wound and reduce the chance of operator death.

The ancient traditions of the blade normally inspired Victor, but now he wished he'd never come to this hill. It seemed foolish, and act of pride that probably cost the family everything. Why hadn't he been at House Marlboro to stop whatever had happened to Fortune and Peps?

"Why are you quitting, Marlboro?" The disdain in Malcom's voice was thick.

Victor hesitated, focusing on the alert flashing in the top left of his HUD.

Report whereabouts immediately. House crisis. Hostage situation. Prepare for war.

"Well?" Malcom pressed.

Victor took another step back, turned slightly, lowering his weapon by degrees. He scanned for further updates but couldn't find any details. The message had come from Captain Mark Echo. Technically, the head of the Marlboro House Guards could issue such an alert, but the parameters were strict and it was rarely done.

Victor read the code carefully. Captain Mark Echo had been unable to contact Victor's parents or Gregory.

Code 27 Omega: hostage situation: Fortune Marlboro: Peps Marlboro: Gerard Palace: more to follow: report location immediately: rally at Marlboro House.

"Vic, you there?" Captain Echo asked on a private comm.

"Talk to me, Mark," Victor said, aware this was outside normal protocol.

"Don't think I didn't know where you were going earlier. Give me the word, and I'll send a rapid transport for pickup," Echo said.

Victor knew the man was up to something. Rapid pickup wasn't something the head of the MHG asked about; it was something he just did in a situation like this. Another person might not appreciate the courtesy the man was giving him. More than Echo's career was at stake. He could be put out of the House and his reputation ruined.

"You know where I am and why," Victor said. "Forget the information. I can't come in, not right now."

"I need details, Vic."

"I may be in a position for a commando raid, but not one my

father or mother will sanction. Major Ruckus is more than capable of handling my unit until I get back."

"He may inherit it permanently," Echo said. "Godspeed, Vic. Get Fortune and Peps back if you can."

"They'll be the ones getting me out of the fire, but first I have to get Fortune into something that flies. Victor Marlboro, out. For honor and respect. You're a good man, Captain."

Victor saluted Malcom. "I yield."

"Bullshit."

Victor handed his weapon to Kilo.

The crowd gasped, then booed, then drank and made bawdy jokes without removing their masks.

"What the hell are you talking about, Marlboro? What are you, the first damn Marlboro in history to yield? What's this place coming to?" Malcom lowered his blade, but advanced, his roughed up ABA more intimidating than it should be, outdated as it was.

Victor whirled on the man, pointing. "I said I yield, and we're done here." He no longer cared about the use of names, or winning, or anything but fighting his way to Fortune and Peps.

"You understand our houses are more closely allied than most people suspect. Your father can't take all the heat for that, no matter how deep or complicated the farce," Malcom said. "If something's happened, if there's been an attack, I need to know right now."

Malcom Sky Bull was the absolute last person Victor wanted to talk to about this crisis, but he found the words spilling out before he could stop them. "Both of my sisters have been seized by the Crown."

Malcom handed his dueling rapier to his second—a scrappy fighter named Vance Traveler. "Take that to my father. Tell him our time has come. Nothing can stop the slaughter now." He returned to Victor and the others. "We will need real mechs. Not these rich-boy toys."

Victor stared back, surprised. A second passed. "Fine. Are you sure you're up for this? It's not your fight."

"Screw that. This entire planet is gonna burn. You know it," Malcom said. "Normally I wouldn't piss on you if you were on fire, but this isn't right. And I don't see much reason to hide our alliance now. Survive the rest of this night, and we can have a rematch. I don't accept your yielding. And if you think this is just about Penelope Danestar, you're an idiot."

"What else would it be about?" Kilo asked.

"Mind your own business, rich boy."

Victor contacted his personal squad, ordering them to divert the mechs that were still being transported from the training grounds back to House Marlboro. "Bring them to Acron's Hill at best possible speed. But don't draw attention to yourselves."

He drew farther away from the crowds, as distant as possible and searched for updates on his HUD. Kilo and Marsten waited somberly. Malcom paced back and forth like he wanted to fight the king's soldiers right now. Confused, the wealthy spectators grew bored and began to leave in small groups at first, then all at once.

Updates were sparse, only giving confirmation that Fortune and Peps had in fact been taken against their will. House Gerard was verified as the location. A new alert went out that several spaceports containing significant BSA assets had been seized by the king's soldiers.

"Attention, all Marlboro forces and our allies," Captain Mark Echo said. "Events have—"

Victor cut the channel and signaled for Kilo in Marsten to do the same. Both men looked pale but complied at once.

"I'll listen to the proclamation," Malcom said. "Won't obligate me to do a damn thing."

"Do what you want, but keep it to yourself. I've already disregarded the order to return to Marlboro House."

The flatbed trucks carrying their four Mechanized Electro-Nuclear Combat Hulks arrived. A few of the spectators saw this and began calling to their comrades who rushed back toward the hill, their excitement palpable.

"Mount up," Victor said. "Let's get moving. This is going to be a smash and grab. None of you have to go."

"We'll die before we let you have all the glory," Kilo said, face pale.

"There's definitely going to be some dying. I just hope it's not us until we liberate Fortune and little Peps." Victor climbed into his mech, checked everything twice, working quickly but thoroughly. As soon as his companions were ready, he took off at a fast run towards House Gerard in the distance.

"We work together, then none of us die," Malcom said.

Victor considered the man distastefully. "I can live with that."

————

THE FIRST TEN kilometers disappeared quickly. Victor monitored the power output of the compact nuclear power core in this unit and soon found himself staring at Gerard House at the top of the highest hill in Lorne. The place was on full alert, guards patrolling the perimeter and manning checkpoints.

Kilo, Marsten, and Malcom squatted next to him, keeping their profiles low and their stealth packages dialed to maximum. Unlike the units that Danestar had used to attack Victor's home, normal mechs could only hide when stationary, and not perfectly. Coming this close was a risk.

Getting to Fortune and Peps inside the king's stronghold was impossible. The defensive perimeter had two rings, one inside the other. The units appeared battle tested and alert.

"Do you have a plan, Marlboro?" Malcom asked.

"Not a good one." Victor continued his study of the perimeter, location and quality of the guards, and surveillance drones, looking for a weak spot that wasn't there.

Malcom laughed. "At least you're honest."

Kilo and Marsten shifted but said nothing. Victor's friends were nervous. He'd never seen either of them lack the discipline to remain motionless. It wasn't much, but Victor noticed the difference.

Mechanized Electro-Nuclear Combat Hulks had decent countermeasures for all of Gerard's security packages except for the unpredictable nature of the human element. He knew from experience that quantity had a power all its own—a lesson the king knew well.

One wrong move could get people killed.

"I'm opening our mechs to the primary Marlboro combat channel," Victor said, words barely audible on their squad comms.

"I thought you were afraid of disobeying an order to run home," Malcom said.

"Our chief of security put out the initial alert. Standard procedure. By now, my father has learned what happened. All hell is about to break loose."

"Great. How does that help us?" Malcom looked behind them, then scanned three hundred and sixty degrees, a good habit for any soldier in a static position for more than a few minutes. He might have been a mercenary until recently, but he'd been a good one.

"When the House Marlboro shock-and-awe cuts loose, we'll use it as a distraction. Go in fast. Get Fortune to a ship. She'll do the rest. No one can outfly my little sister."

"Maybe she can steal something big enough to take all of us, mechs included," Kilo said.

"We'll have to scuttle the mechs once we reach the ship," Victor said, then reviewed floor plans of House Gerard—something only a few houses dared possess and only in secret. "You never saw any of these maps, Bull."

"Don't call me that. Makes me think of my adoptive father. But I take your point. Hate me if you want, but we're in this together now."

"And why is that?" Marsten asked.

"I like to fight," Malcom answered. "And no one has a better reason to hate Martin Gerard than me."

———

RON CALLED his commanders to the Marlboro armory, arriving before some but not all of them. Officers from the rank of captain and up gathered in Hangar 1. Their platoon leaders and top sergeants assembled outside, already drawing up possible operational plans.

When the orders came, few adjustments would be necessary.

How many of them realize we're going against the king? Ron pushed the question out of his mind.

Patricia gathered her commanders and briefed them before joining him in the center of Hangar 1. Rows of mechs stood ready, just like in Hangars 2, 3, and 4. Tanks and other armored vehicles populated 5 through 10. Airships were primed on the flight line and some were already in the air.

It was like the final days of the Zezner War—always ready, never hesitating to take action.

Each mech squad was comprised of five mechs, each with a pilot, relief pilot, and a three-person support crew—twenty-five soldiers. Unlike Gildain most Gildain infantry units, each squad was led by a sergeant or higher, sometimes a warrant officer or other specialist. Each mech platoon comprised four squads, plus an officer who had additional personnel to handle communications, transport, and supply issues.

Twenty-one mechs per platoon, over a hundred people, sometimes as many as a hundred and thirty—the table of organization was much different from that of infantry or even armor. They trained, fought, and lived together most of the time. Each unit, down to the individual mech team, was designed to be self-sufficient for up to a week—longer if the mission called for it and supply chains were maintained.

"We're as ready as we can be, husband," Patricia said.

He nodded. "I'm ordering all other assets into AT-VO transports. Bull and the rest of our allies are doing the same. Our fallback point is the fleet. Take a good look, because it may be the last time we see Marlboro House. The BSA might be half finished, but we'll make it work."

"You should give that speech to the troops," she said.

"Won't you miss what we're leaving behind?"

"Of course. But we didn't choose the time, terrain, or circumstances of this fight," she said. "What is the Marlboro way?"

"Family. Duty. Honor," Ron said. "We did our duty. The king is the one who failed."

Patricia kissed him, then stepped back. "I will see you at Gerard House. We will get our daughters back. And maybe kick a little ass on the way."

Ron saluted. She returned it.

"You're not going to forbid me from fighting?" she asked loud enough for her commanders to hear.

"Would it do any good?"

Everyone laughed.

He strode to his mech and climbed the ladder. Worry fell away as his focus shifted to what he knew best. War. Exhilaration pumped through his veins. Lingering behind the familiar emotion was sadness. This was too abrupt, not at all the way he had envisioned their departure.

Something was bound to go wrong. A mass exodus was hard enough to execute with careful planning. This would be analogous to an improvised retreat, but permanent in ways no one from Gildain had ever imagined.

———

FORTUNE COUNTED the guards—three in the room, two outside each of three doors, and one on the balcony. *That might be the best way out if the drop wasn't five meters onto paving stones.*

Little Peps, tearstains on her cheeks, glared at the guards. They fixed their gazes over her head, standing like statues. Maybe they were good men with families and lives of their own. But all she could see in them was King Gerard and his persistent malice against her House.

These weren't soldiers who could be tricked or appealed to. No doubt they had been selected for their diligence and extreme loyalty. A chill went up her spine. Would they commit murder for the king?

She hugged herself and thought they would.

"Stop antagonizing the soldiers, Peps."

"I hate them!"

"Save it for the battlefield."

"Like anyone will let me fight."

"When you're older, Peps," Fortune said. "I guarantee we'll still be fighting this war when you're old enough."

There was one officer among these guards, their leader—someone with authority to make decisions in a crisis. His eyes flicked toward Fortune at her words. Maybe he found the idea of perpetual war against House Marlboro daunting.

She stared at him until he resumed his study of the far wall. One by one, she studied her jailers, and the luxurious cell King Gerard had put them in. Couches, lounge chairs, and a bed large enough for three people spoke of extravagance. Which of his mistresses had been evicted to accommodate her and her sister?

"Let's have a look outside, Peps."

"Okay."

The balcony guard held up one hand. "That's close enough."

"Wouldn't the king want us to see the sunset? I thought he was a romantic." Fortune had no idea if Martin Gerard was any such thing and doubted that was his reputation with his men.

But the words seeded doubt. The guard looked to the supervisor for guidance.

Fortune moved quickly past him, ready to jump—and throw Peps if she faltered. It couldn't be that far and they had good nanites.

The balcony guard lunged to grab her. "Hey, I said stop!"

Fortune blocked his grab, striking the inside of his forearm with a knife hand, immediately following up with a palm strike using her other hand.

Peps ran to the edge... and froze.

"We have to jump!" Fortune ran to her side, looked down, and sucked in a breath.

"It looks high," Peps said, voice weak.

Fortune grabbed her by her upper arm, holding her back. "It is, Peps. We'd get a lot worse than broken bones from that drop."

The balcony guards plus two others from the room and the supervisor grabbed Fortune and her sister, dragging them roughly into the suite.

"That was foolish, Fortune Marlboro," the officer said. "Try us again, and I'll lock you both in a closet."

CHAPTER THIRTY

RON FELT the familiar thump of his mech's power coming on line, booster cells activating nuclear fission in the mech's core. The heart of the machine was nearly indestructible, otherwise battlefields would be soaked with radiation and Gildain would have been doomed centuries before. Instead, there had often been battles against the Zezner that left nothing but the fission capsules—safe enough to eat off, even if the driver and the rest of the machine had been blown to smithereens.

"My Company, my Two Hundred, and my Wings are fully deployed. We're moving to our position twenty-five klicks south of Gerard House," Patricia said over the battle comm.

"On time and ready to fight as always," Ron said. "Marlboro Force 1 is ready to advance from the east. Gregory, report."

"Marlboro Force 2 is standing in reserve but expecting an early call to the party," Gregory said.

"Marlboro Force 3 is standing by, guarding the spaceport," Major David Ruckus said in Victor's place. Victor's men respected him and held radio silence per regulation. That didn't change Ron's anger and disappointment. Victor knew his place and had chosen to go rogue when discipline and unity were the only things that would save the family.

Ron suspected most of them knew where Victor was and looked forward to having him at the head of their column as soon as possible. They would do their duty until then, as always.

Reports came in. Ron viewed screen after screen in his HUD even as he started to move. Mechs, tanks, infantry transports, and AT-VO ships spread out from Marlboro House.

Smaller forces deployed from House Bull, Danestar, Redwine, Longreach, and Thunder. Ron sent most of them to guard the spaceport and begin the evacuation. So far, none had abandoned their alliance as they had every legal right to. Right or wrong, Marlboro was now in open rebellion against the Crown. No prior obligation to Ron or his House was legally binding.

Beyond his direct view, House Spirit and Atana deployed and raced toward the spaceports. House Bronc, the final member of Gerard's coalition, deployed but remained near their own territory, stomping about in their mega mechs as expected. Lord Bronc took a long time to warm to a fight but was unstoppable once he did.

Ron relied on satellite tracking and reports from his scouts. This wasn't a scrimmage like the Bull Danestar attack. Air raid sirens blared from every corner of Lorne. Civilians fled to their shelters. The stomping mechs shook the ground. Contrails crisscrossed the sky, and ships began to move out of their orbital patterns into pre-combat positions.

———

RON MOVED TO THE FRONT. His officers raced at the head of their own units. "Marlboro Force 1 has spotted the enemy," he announced.

"Marlboro Force 2 copies," Gregory said.

"Wilson Force 1 moving toward contact with the left flank,

south to north at fifty kilometers per hour," Patricia said over the battle comm.

"That's fast, Wilson Force 1," Ron said.

"They're pulling back even faster," she responded. "Probably shifting their strength to meet your advance. Watch yourself."

"Always," Ron said, then addressed his officers. "I will attempt to parley. Overwatch, how do we look?"

"Outstanding, Duke," General Silo responded from the aerial command craft. "No need to dress battle lines at the moment. That will change, of course."

Ron reviewed what he had in the field. Four mech elements, Marlboro Force 1, 2, 3, and Patricia's Wilson assets. Also waiting in reserve were three tank companies and an equal number of mobile infantry—men and women in heavy infantry ABAs riding in armored cars. Tanks bolstered his center when needed and could be a threat no enemy could safely ignore. The infantry was best used to hold objectives once taken, but could also be deployed for a variety of other assignments.

Unlike other lords of Gildain, he didn't send them against mechs or tanks unless they could attack from a fortified position, or ambush other foot soldiers.

Icons multiplied in his HUD as Gerard, Spirit, and Atana units lost their stealth fields. The enemy moved from static positions to meet the Marlboro advance, no longer concerned with concealment.

"Gregory, advance and support," Ron said, voice grim. "Ruckus, you may need to divide your force, leaving two-thirds at the spaceport and sending the rest here as reinforcements. But wait for the call."

"Yes, Duke," Major Ruckus answered.

Ron strode ahead of his troops, then stopped with his mech hands held at waist level, palms to the sky in the traditional request for parley. "Duke Uron Marlboro requests parley with

King Martin Gerard, ruler of Gildain." He threw the last part in hoping there was a slim chance to resolve this peacefully.

"I see you, Ron," Gerard said, then advanced.

Ron gritted his teeth at the casualness of Gerard's response. Didn't the man see he was about to destroy Gildain?

Patricia's voice came through their private comm. "He's attempting to bait you, husband."

"You're not wrong."

"Remember why we're here. Get the girls and withdraw," Patricia said.

He knew she was right but didn't want to talk about it. The closer the gold-plated mech came, the more he wanted to charge with guns blazing and power-sword growling.

Gerard stopped three meters short, the exact distance prescribed by tradition. "Are you in there, Ron? Why so quiet?"

"I was thinking what to say," Ron said, restraining himself from committing murder.

"I'm listening."

"Why did you kidnap my daughters?"

"Why have you been conspiring against me?"

Ron said nothing. An admission at this point was worse than a confession, and there was no way to win the argument.

"I have adequate proof," Gerard continued. "More than enough to convince the Assembly of Lords and the Legislature that your charter should be revoked and assets distributed evenly amongst the other houses. They would back me for that reward alone, even without proof. You know it."

"No one in the Legislature, Assembly of Lords, or the Decision House will condone kidnapping, not even by you, King," Ron said.

Gerard interrupted. "*Your* king. Don't forget that."

"Return my children and I will renew my pledge of fealty," Ron said, tasting bile.

"Or what?"

Ron expected the worst from the tyrant but was stunned by

the blunt hostility in the man's tone. What happened next was even more disconcerting.

King Gerard hailed him on a private comm channel, not something that was done during a public parley. "My doctors believe a union between our houses would yield a genetic leap forward that would change history. They predict that there will be a synergistic effect between my nanites and those of your daughter."

"And kidnapping is how you propose a marriage alliance? Have you lost your mind?"

Gerard took another step forward. When he spoke, his voice was low and harsh. "I am not interested in marriage. Leave her to me and I will send the little brat Peps home. She's useless. Fortune is my only interest. Take your house in search of the Ancient People of Earth and never return. I will build a dynasty with the children your daughter will bear me. I'll protect her far better than you have, even with your troops and your reputation. She'll be deified, like me. Leave Fortune to her destiny. I command it."

"Death first," Ron snarled. In the back of his mind, thoughts he hated grew, resolved, and died. Fortune, who had been so sickly as a child, was now the pinnacle of genetic advancement. How could that happen?

"Your death, Marlboro, or that of everyone you care for? Retreat immediately and I'll consider allowing your shuttles to take off without shooting too many of them down."

"Return my daughters at once," Ron said.

Gerard turned his back toward Ron, strode toward his own line, and opened the main battle comm. "House Marlboro is in open rebellion, despite all I've done for him. Destroy them. Take prisoners if they surrender—and treat them well. There is honor in fealty, but none in remaining under the command of an outlaw duke."

"You can't make a declaration like that without a review by

the Legislature, the Assembly of Lords, and the Decision House," Gregory blurted across the challenge comm.

A high-pitched wail of feedback cut through the channel, marking the start of official battle. Parley sessions normally followed traditional forms, but in the early days of Gildain, a more primitive time, hostilities began with deliberate insults such as this and attempts to scramble communications.

Gerard's battle line surged forward.

"Marlboro Force 1, advance," Ron said. "Our object remains to take the palace and liberate Fortune and Peps Marlboro from this unlawful tyrant."

Ron rushed forward. His mech pilots knew his habits and burst forward at his side.

Mechs clashed. Thunder echoed across the field. The ground shook beneath them.

"Weapons free, Marlboros!" Ron said.

Accelerator guns opened fire. Supersonic projectiles seared the air, erupting on enemy mechs. Ron surged forward, taking his place at the front without recklessly breaking rank—as he had done a few times in his youth.

"Permission to engage," Gregory asked.

"Hold, MF 2," Ron answered. His mech vibrated from the power plant pumping bursts of energy to the accelerator weapons. He longed to clash with his power-sword. Gerard's bodyguards surrounded him. Two out of three mechs carried oversized shields no human could lift without assistance. In the mechs, they were easily handled.

The royal defenses slowed down the entire formation. Ron signaled his squad leaders who pivoted, adjusting a few meters each. The effect was to maximize their attack.

He couldn't resist. Rushing ahead of the others, he slammed into the shield bearers, scattering them like pins. He shoved his fists forward, accentuating the effect while also keeping his balance. They went down, but he remained on his feet.

A fresh pair of shield bearers jumped to block him, using

booster packs long out of style for the extra weight the turbines and full packs created. Ron had to admire their skill and dedication to a man who didn't deserve it. Too bad a penny-pinching fool who worried only about his own life had outfitted their mechs. The royal guards would have been better served by superior weaponry and improved mobility. As things stood, the mech soldiers, the finest in House Gerard, were little more than accelerator round magnets.

He fired a burst from his largest accelerator weapon, sending rounds directly into the bodyguard on the left. Pieces of armor flew away, but none of the hits were lethal. Ron knew how many layers had to come off before damage was taken by the pilot.

No concern for the stunned adversary on his left, he whipped up the power-sword and rushed the man directly ahead of him.

Behind the rows of bodyguards, growing even now as more arrived to protect their sovereign, King Gerard stood, weapons up but not firing.

Does he not know what to do? Is he playing some other game?

Ron's squad engaged, creating a double phalanx with him as the centerpiece. They drove King Gerard and his bodyguards backward step by step. Explosions sprayed dirt into the air. Smoke filled the battlefield. There was so much noise that the battle comms was nearly useless even inside the sound-canceling helmets.

"The king is falling back now!" Gregory shouted. "We are hitting them hard on the right flank."

"Good work," Ron said, although the enemy's retreat didn't reassure him. There were reasons a numerically superior force pulled back like that, none of them good.

"Spread out," Ron ordered. "Prepare for artillery barrage."

He looked beyond Gerard House, searching for the big guns. He didn't believe that the king had a howitzer battery on his grounds. Artillery guns were so large they were normally kept at separate locations. Which of the king's vassals would provide artillery support? Where would it come from, nearby or from kilometers outside the city?

His answer came in the form of meteors plummeting from orbit.

"Orbital bombardment inbound! Execute immediate countermeasures. Triple the distance between units. All units not engaged, proceed with the evacuation, full emergency protocols!" Ron shouted, striding amongst the ranks, not quitting the battlefield until he saw that his people were doing the best they could to survive what was coming.

The first void rock hit what had been a manicured field, fountaining earth and landscape stones a kilometer into the air. The mushroom cloud reached up and up. Several mechs disappeared in a flash of energy. Ron was hurled backward, mech and all, landing on his back and tumbling despite the weight and agile countermeasures built into Marlboro mechs to prevent them from losing their footing.

He killed the comms before he screamed in rage and fought to regain control of his armor. His men and women didn't need to hear him in distress. Every man and woman had their own problems. Survival first, rally second, then vengeance—that was the Gildain way.

The consequences of what had just happened defied imagination. The king had ordered an orbital assault on his own planet to eliminate a rival so he could kidnap Fortune.

Madness.

CHAPTER THIRTY-ONE

VICTOR CHANGED COURSE, veering around the meteor impact. A hundred square meters of bluegrass and turf geysered skyward like a reverse waterfall. Impact and noise dampeners groaned in his mech, his view screen flickering from the power diverted to protect his hearing and internal organs.

"We're too damn close, Marlboro," Malcom grunted, battered from the same shockwave.

"He's right, Vic," Kilo seconded.

Victor adjusted course. "Keep moving. Follow me. There won't be another chance."

Static washed through the comms, garbled commands to rally at the spaceport breaking through the noise. But in the next moment, Victor heard his mother giving the enemy hell.

"Stand and fight, you Gerard lackeys! Feel the wrath of Patricia's Company!"

"Check your tactical maps," Victor said with a smile. "Watch out for Marlboro and Wilson units taking the fight to the enemy."

"I've got MF 1 and 2 six hundred meters off our left flank. And Wilson deep into Gerard lines. Move to support, or bypass?" Marsten asked.

"We continue the mission," Victor said.

Malcom gave him a nod, a peculiar thing in a fourteen-foot-tall mech, and they took the lead, blasting enemies right, left, and center. Gerard forces had pulled back, consolidated their lines, and should have been hard to beat.

But they didn't expect an attack, not after the ruthless bombardment.

Victor poured on the speed to strike first, then barked his wrath over the challenge comm. "Missed me, Gerard scum!"

He fired both accelerator barrels, nearly a hundred rounds a second, blowing apart the flat footed mech that barely started to raise his useless shield. Others retreated in good order, gathering around a large gold-plated mech.

"Fools. They should have counter-attacked," Malcom said, sending a stream of rounds to encourage their retreat. "And you should conserve some of that ammunition."

"Noted." Victor steadied his breathing, trying to slow his madly beating heart. He knew the man was right and this wasn't a place for prideful arguing.

"Assassins! Protect the king!"

Two squads of mechs charged through the smoke and flying debris. The ground pitched and heaved even though the orbital strikes were punishing Marlboro forces and their allies. A tank rolled around the corner, large enough for Gerard and two of his bodyguards to crouch behind. The blocky war machine locked its treads to the ground, aimed, and fired in the direction of the primary Marlboro assault.

Gerard and his closest men raised fists to the air and shouted as though they'd already won the battle. But they didn't step out from behind the tank's heavy armor.

"That coward," Malcom grunted. "I'm going after him."

"Later," Victor snapped. "We're here to save my sisters."

"Good luck with that." Malcom altered course, stomping paving stones to dust.

Victor suppressed a curse. "You'll die in five seconds."

Malcom never looked back. "What do you care, duke-ling?"

"I need your help. And you still owe me the rest of a duel," Victor said, striding toward the palace, unable to wait for the unlikely—and unreliable, it seemed—ally.

Marsten and Kilo flanked him. Accelerator rounds cut holes in the smoke that ricocheted off Marsten's cockpit. He was nearest the Gerard regular troops, the men and women who were doing the actual fighting.

Malcom stopped, retaliated against the mech shooting at Marsten, chopping the thing down at the knees with precision shots. It fell forward, guns blowing holes in the ground as it face-planted.

"I'm coming, Marlboro," he said, racing to catch up. "But if he hunts us down because I didn't take him out, I'm gonna say I told you so."

"Good enough." Victor bolted up a series of wide stairs and splashed through a fountain, shouldering aside a statue of Martin Gerard's grandfather on a horse. The rest of his unorthodox squad blasted through a maze of tall bushes, then found more stairs to destroy.

Kilo stepped through a poorly constructed staircase, his mechanized foot thrusting deep into a hole because there was no foundation beneath the marble stairs. Someone had cheated the king, most likely charging double and doing shoddy work with lots of polish on the outside.

"Do you need help, Kilo?" Victor asked.

"Not at all. Did that on purpose. One moment while I catch up." Kilo crawled on his hands and knees until he reached the top of the section, the struggled to his feet. Neither crawling nor standing up was easy for a mech pilot, but he managed the task quickly.

Victor scanned the area for comms, hoping against hope Fortune had taken control of an ABA and reconfigured the comms to a Marlboro channel. What he got instead was a chipper little voice.

"Victor, is that you? This is Peps. I'm with Fortune. We're locked in one of the royal apartments!"

"Peps? How do you have comms?" Victor asked, signaling his squad to turn toward one of the auxiliary buildings near the artificial river snaking into the gardens.

"Mark told me to never, ever go anywhere without comms, then he hid a booster unit in my school tablet, the one with butterflies painted all over it," Peps said. "Everyone thinks it's a cute toy."

"It is cute," Victor said. "Like you, little Peps."

"Don't make me mad, brother. I'm glad to see you for once. I mean, I don't see you yet, but I sure do want to. So don't spoil the moment."

A voice interrupted her. "Hey, what are you doing with that?"

"It's mine, you asshole!"

"That's it—into the closet!"

"Leave us alone, you stupid cocksucker!" Peps screamed. "Don't touch my sister!"

"Kid talks like a soldier," Malcom noted.

Victor realized belatedly that he'd been using an open channel. "She spends too much time with the house guards." He sped away from the action but toward his objective. The royal apartments stood apart from the palace and nowhere near the battle. Rumor had it King Gerard kept half a dozen mistresses there.

Victor clenched his teeth, kept his mouth shut, and refused to let Malcom hear what he thought of this development. Was the king after Fortune? What would a man with everything want with a tomboy fighter pilot better at avoiding relationships than maintaining them? Surely, he wasn't wanting to marry her, even for the alliance—and peace—it could bring. Fortune had terrible genetics and worse nanites. It was one of the reasons none of the other houses had proposed marriage alliances.

Malcom, Marsten, and Kilo fanned out behind him, shooting at the lighter Gerard resistance here. Most of the royal forces were defending the king, but some had stayed at their posts and did their duty. King Gerard had so many mechs, tanks, and ABA squads around him now, they were tripping over each other.

Marsten screamed, then went silent as his mech careened sideways, fell, and plowed into the dirt. The afterimage of a heavy accelerator round punching through his cockpit burned Victor's vision. He'd seen it happen but hadn't been quick enough to process the image. For an instant, it felt like he was looking backward in time.

"Kilo, recover him," Victor said.

"On it." Kilo reversed course, darting back to Marsten's downed mech.

Malcom strode silently at Victor's side, shooting when he had a target and pulsing his energy shield only when absolutely necessary.

Strong work, Victor thought. Few mech pilots outside of House Marlboro ever got it right. With shield power constantly in short supply, and their relatively light stopping power in the best of circumstances, a good pilot used them but rarely, at the precise moment when they would yield the best result.

It was like playing catch-and-deflect with supersonic accelerator rounds—guesswork and luck as often as not. And yet, it was more than that. Victor anticipated a shot, pulsing a small section of his shield the moment he saw a fixed gun aim and fire from a balcony. Lucky for him, he'd guessed correctly. The gunner aimed for the top of the cockpit because he had the height advantage.

Had Victor's adversary been straight on or lower, he would have gone for the centerline or legs. Either attack could disable a mech without injuring the pilot much.

Not that they care about that.

The round deflected, smashing into another of the king's buildings.

"Which balcony?" Malcom asked.

"Not sure. But I didn't hear one of those crew-served guns being fired in the background when Peps called. Follow me." Victor charged into the foyer of the posh building, destroying the door arches and crushing floor tiles.

Malcom came in through the wall, spraying masonry everywhere. "I'm going to like this part!"

They rampaged through the twenty-room apartment, destroying spas, music rooms, and dining tables.

"Peps, can you hear us coming?" Victor asked.

"Hear you?" Peps blurted. "I can feel you! We're in a closet, but Fortune says we're going to make a break for it and meet you in the main hallway."

Guards in gold-plated ABA infantry units filled the hallway. Victor blasted them back without hesitation, but he aimed at their feet. It was a common Marlboro tactic in lower intensity conflicts, because much of the force was directed into the ground. The effect was to hurl them violently backward. Some would die, others would be maimed, but it was the least amount of force he could use in such a scenario.

Like his father, Victor hated slaughtering infantry in ABA units, no matter who they were.

Seconds later, another guard, this one not wearing an ABA, staggered into view holding his throat where someone had punched him, forcing him to drop his rifle. Fortune rushed after him, jumped, and kicked him in the chest, hurling him into another room.

She snatched up the rifle, then faced Victor to wave him forward.

"These aren't MHB mechs," Victor warned. "We don't have room for passengers."

"We'll ride on top!" Fortune shouted.

"No good. We draw a lot of fire. Follow us to the airfield. We'll go slow. You've gotta keep up."

"Fortune says she understands," Peps said, her voice modulating through the comms as she ran. "She says it's too hard to yell at you in that thing."

"I'll lead the way, Marlboro," Malcom said. "You look after your sisters."

"Thanks." Victor didn't know what else to say.

"But keep up. It'll take both of us to fight across the flight line, even if they leave it mostly unattended."

They burst out of the building and were quickly joined by Kilo. His stalwart friend dropped the escape pod containing Marsten, who climbed out, shoved Peps inside, and ran beside Fortune the rest of the way. Kilo reattached the armored escape pod with Peps inside to his back and brought up the rear of their strange formation.

"We're going to make it!" Peps shouted.

"Of course, little Peps. There was never any doubt." Victor didn't have the heart to curse her for jinxing them.

CHAPTER THIRTY-TWO

"GIVE ME GOOD NEWS, VICTOR," Ron demanded as he strode up and down the battle line, trying to anticipate where Gerard, Atana, Spirit, and Bronc would push next. Martin Gerard's allies had finally deployed their full strength and there was no resisting them now.

Marlboro was in retreat.

"Fortune is flying us to the spaceport. Peps is with us. Marsten and Kilo are both seriously injured, and Malcom Sky Bull is with us as well. I'm sorry, Father," Victor said.

"We'll talk later," Ron said on the private channel. "You brought back your sisters, so maybe I don't disown you when this is over."

"For honor and respect," Victor said.

"Always," Ron answered.

Three rockets arched toward him, perfectly timed to catch him between shield pulses.

In his own mech, Redion stepped in front of him, the tech still unfamiliar to him. He staggered like a drunk as he took the brunt of the damage. If he'd looked uncoordinated before, now he was a hopeless mess, falling flat on his back. "I require a mech with four legs, Duke Marlboro, if you wish me to be of any value on the field of battle."

"You will have the best imitation Zezner mech we can build, Red!" Ron heaved him up, not something he encouraged his pilots to waste time on because it nearly always resulted in two mechs down instead of one. "I'm in your debt, Redion Axst."

"Impossible, but I take your meaning," Redion said. "How much longer must we stall the Gerard dogs?"

Despite all the exhaustion and loss of the last six hours of civil war, Ron laughed. "You swear like a grammar schoolboy."

"Am I not doing it correctly?" Redion aimed at an approaching mech and fired one perfectly placed accelerator burst.

"Peps can teach you the finer points of profanity, just don't tell her mother."

He checked his units. MF 1, 2, and what was deployed of 3 were badly hurt. Nearly every mech had taken damage, and too many were lost during the orbital bombardment. But once his troops weathered that treacherous attack, casualties had been light.

"If I had numbers, I could roll Gerard House back and demand Martin's surrender," Ron said.

Gregory answered. "I've thought the same thing. But we're committed. It's not so easy to pull our soldiers and civilians back from the BSA deployment."

Ron signaled Gregory to fall back to the spaceport and board the remaining MF 2 units. Patricia moved into Gregory's place on Ron's flank.

"Had enough?" Ron asked.

"I could do this all day, husband. But it seems the tide has turned against us." Her voice hummed with vitality. Anyone else would be exhausted.

Ron certainly was, but mostly because he wondered about Fortune and her nanites and why the king had attempted to steal her. And thinking of nanites brought headaches, confusion, and blinding fatigue.

One glance at Redion was enough to evoke other questions. *Am I nearly human? What does that mean? Is it a bad thing or a blessing?*

If all the people of Gildain are somehow artificial, for what purpose were our ancestors created? Will we find the Ancient People of Earth in the Blue Sun system?

Combined with the physical and emotional demands of battle, the mental torture was almost too much. He had to retreat, and not just because the king of Gildain and his strongest allies were pushing forward with a vengeance.

"Sadly, wife, it is time to quit the field. Would you be so kind as to attend our recalcitrant children at the spaceport and ensure they have boarded?" Ron asked on the Marlboro main battle channel. The banter would lift the spirits of their people.

"Gladly," Patricia said. "I will see you on the BSA *Indomitable*."

Ron fired his left accelerator gun at a House Spirit squad of mechs probing too far forward. It was probably a distraction, but he couldn't allow them to be so bold. On cue, his long-range marksmen followed his lead, punishing the scouts.

Sure enough, Atana tanks rolled forward from another quarter, and on the far right flank, Bronc behemoth mechs raced for an advantageous position. The ugly, brutish war machines traveled surprisingly fast, patterns of gray on their armor further blurring their images at this distance.

Bronc pilots also had the unnerving habit of zero communication during battle. Either they had the best combat comm security on Gildain, or their pilots didn't need to talk to carry out their missions. Not hearing cross chatter was like listening to the void—something Ron and his people were going to do a lot for the rest of their lives.

"It is time to fall back, Duke," Redion said, then pointed to

Marlboro and Bull Danestar AT-VO fighters racing overhead to provide them cover.

Ron gave the order, then stood with his personal squad until all of Marlboro and her allies were boarding launch shuttles.

"Your turn, Duke," Master Sergeant Neen said. "I'll stand with the squad until you have driven your mech onto the shuttle."

"Master Sergeant, you have earned every honor, and I have no right to deny you a single privilege," Ron said.

"None of that, Duke. This is procedure. By the numbers," Neen argued.

"Nevertheless, I will stand last on Gildain. Take the squad onboard. Arguing will only cause delay. In this, I will not be denied," Ron said. None of the bluster of battle colored his tone. He could have been having a whiskey and a cigar with his top noncommissioned officer. The moment was unique, thoughtful and sad, but strangely exhilarating.

Everything after this would be new.

"As you wish, Duke." Neen hustled the last Marlboro mechs through the spaceport and onto their shuttles. "Move your asses, you worthless slackers! The longer you mess around, the longer the duke is standing out there with his manhood in the wind!"

Ron smiled. *Noncoms. Thank God Peps hadn't spent much time around Neen; she'd really have a vocabulary problem. The house guards are bad enough.*

A breeze cleared smoke from the field of battle. Beyond the conflict, Lorne's glittering skyscrapers towered over landscaped parks, the pristine industrial district powered by solar panels, thermal heat syncs, and nuclear plants that never failed. He could glimpse green fields beyond Lorne, harvesters working in well-synchronized rows despite the chaos kilometers away.

Gildain.

If I were preparing a world for true humans, this would be utopia —except for the murderous intrigues of House Gerard.

If I'm only a near-human, then a true member of that mythical race would do better, surely. They wouldn't spoil the planet with lies, treachery, and greed.

A tear ran down his cheek and he didn't know why. He didn't feel like a failure, but he knew something wasn't right, and the cause of it was, to some degree, his fault.

Never mind that now, he thought. *Our destiny lies in the stars and near a blue star lifetimes away. If I meet the Ancient People of Earth, perhaps they will forgive my weakness.*

PLEASE LEAVE A REVIEW!

I hope you enjoyed *Blue Sun Armada*. Please, help an author out; tell a friend about the book and leave a review.

Thanks!

WHAT'S NEXT

Stay tuned for **Crisis: Blue Sun Armada, 2!**
(Coming summer 2021.)

ALSO BY SCOTT MOON

THEY CAME FOR BLOOD

Invasion Day

Resistance Day

Victory Day

Departure Day

A MECH WARRIOR'S TALE

(SHORTYVERSE)

Shorty

Kill Me Now

Ground Pounder

Shorty and the Brits

Fight for Doomsday (A Novel)… coming soon.

CHRONICLES OF KIN ROLAND

Enemy of Man

Son of Orlan

Weapons of Earth

DARKLANDING

Assignment Darklanding

Ike Shot the Sheriff

Outlaws

Runaway

An Unglok Murder

SAGCON

Race to the Finish

Boom Town

A Warrior's Home

Hunter

Diver Down

Empire

FALL OF PROMISEDALE

Death by Werewolf

GRENDEL UPRISING

Proof of Death

Blood Royal

Grendel

SMC MARAUDERS

Bayonet Dawn

Burning Sun

The Forever Siren

SON OF A DRAGONSLAYER

Dragon Badge

Dragon Attack

Dragon Land

TERRAN STRIKE MARINES

The Dotari Salvation

Rage of Winter

Valdar's Hammer

The Beast of Eridu

THE LAST REAPER

The Last Reaper

Fear the Reaper

Blade of the Reaper

Wings of the Reaper

Flight of the Reaper

Wrath of the Reaper

Will of the Reaper

Descent of the Reaper

Hunt of the Reaper

Bastion of the Reaper

ORPHAN WARS

Orphan Wars

Song of War

BLUE SUN ARMADA

Blue Sun Armada

Crisis…coming soon.

SHORT STORIES

Boss

Fire Prince

Ice Field

Sgt. Orlan: Hero of Man

The Darklady

ASSASSIN PRIME

The Hand of Empyrean

Spiderfall

ABOUT THE AUTHOR

Scott Moon has been writing fantasy, science fiction, and urban fantasy since he was a kid. When not reading, writing, or spending time with his awesome family, he enjoys playing the guitar or learning Brazilian Jiu-Jitsu. He loves dogs and plans to have a ranch full of them when he makes it big. One will be a Rottweiler named Frodo. He is also a co-host of the popular Keystroke Medium show.

COOL STUFF FROM THE MOON

Want to know when the next story or book is published? Sign up for my newsletter:

https://www.subscribepage.com/Fromthemoon

Thanks,
    Scott Moon

———

Printed in Great Britain
by Amazon